Snowflakes
and
Secrets
in the
Scottish
Highlands

BOOKS BY DONNA ASHCROFT

Christmas in the Scottish Highlands
If Every Day Was Christmas
The Christmas Countdown
The Little Christmas Teashop of Second Chances

The Little Cornish House
Summer in the Scottish Highlands
The Little Village of New Starts
The Little Guesthouse of New Beginnings
Summer at the Castle Cafe

Donna Ashcroft

Snowflakes and Secrets in the Scottish Highlands

Bookouture

Published by Bookouture in 2022

An imprint of Storyfire Ltd.
Carmelite House
50 Victoria Embankment
London EC4Y 0DZ

www.bookouture.com

ISBN: 978-1-80314-523-5
eBook ISBN: 978-1-80314-522-8

Natasha Harding
For believing in me

1

As soon as they turned into the end of the long driveway, Merry McKenzie recognised her Aunt Ava's cottage from the photos the older woman had posted to her. Over the last few weeks she'd memorised the picturesque blue-grey double-fronted building with its curved thatched roof and sky-blue front door, framed by meandering Scottish hills.

The taxi driver edged cautiously along the snow-laden track and Merry pressed her nose against the icy passenger window, feeling bubbles of apprehension as she spotted the various animal enclosures, a large greenhouse and what was probably a complex allotment area blanketed in pretty pillows of sparkly white. There were large animal tracks all over the garden and Merry wondered if a creature had hidden itself away behind a random tree or snowdrift and was even now waiting to pounce. She was sure they had bears in Scotland – and hadn't one of her older brothers once told her bears ate people if they were starving? She gulped as the taxi driver pulled up outside the cottage. Then Merry surveyed the façade with its gorgeous leaded windows and streamers of ivy dappled with snow that hugged the bricks like a huge green scarf – and felt something inside her click. She spotted a cherry-red Jeep parked up to the right of the building, underneath a makeshift lean-to smothered in the remnants of the recent blizzard. A white Ford Ranger had been squeezed in beside it and there was a fresh set of tyre tracks leading from the main road. Lights were on in the cottage and Merry guessed her aunt had left them on ready for her arrival.

'Well, we made it eventually – only five hours late,' the driver announced in a gruff Scottish lilt as he opened his door and hopped out. Merry clutched her laptop bag to her side and swallowed. She hadn't travelled as far as Scotland from her home in leafy Hertfordshire – never mind setting foot on an aeroplane – for over two years. Her heart thudded loudly as adrenaline surged through her and she stepped out of the car too, ignoring the ice that immediately enveloped her ankle boots, soaking her socks. The driver hefted her three suitcases onto the doorstep and looked about. 'So the aunt you've not seen since you were a child, whose house you're staying in for a month so you can take care of her animals, has already left for India?'

'Yes.' Merry sighed, wishing she hadn't confided quite so much to this stranger during the long journey here from the airport – but they'd been stuck in traffic after inclement weather had closed the motorway, her phone had run out of charge and she'd wanted to take her mind off her impending adventures. What if the driver was an axe murderer – what if he decided to return after dark? Her stomach hollowed, then the front door swung open to reveal a woman wearing a bright blue jumper with 'Careful, or you could end up "trapped" in my freezer' emblazoned in jaunty gold lettering across the front.

'Merry?' she asked, inclining her head at the taxi driver as he said his goodbyes, then waved out of the car window as he sped off. 'I'm Rowan Taylor, I run the cafe in Christmas Village and live about half a mile down there.' The older woman pointed somewhere over Merry's shoulder but didn't give her a chance to look. 'Your Aunt Ava guessed you'd been delayed and asked me to wait here to let you into the house. She had to leave a few hours ago, unfortunately; she was so sorry she couldn't stay and greet you herself. But her flight to India's about to take off.' She patted her watch as if that explained everything.

'I thought she might have gone,' Merry said, feeling guilty. She hadn't been able to travel here until today because of a commitment to her dog-walking job. One of her regular clients had been in hospital until late last night and Merry had been the only person available to care for his elderly poodle. 'My mobile died on the way up so I wasn't able to call Aunt Ava myself.' Merry didn't add that the taxi driver had hogged the car's charger for the whole of the trip.

'Never mind.' Rowan stepped back into the warmth of the hallway. 'Come in lass, it's cold.' Merry grabbed one of her suitcases and Rowan picked up the other two and led her down a narrow corridor, past closed thick doors positioned to her left and right, until she entered a large farmhouse-style kitchen. The room was rectangular and ran across the whole back of the house. Despite its size, it was cosy and surprisingly warm. There was a rustic oak table to the left of the space with four high-back chairs; surrounding it was a small kitchen area with dark grey wooden cabinets, white counters and a deep butler sink. A voluptuous velvet green sofa draped in blankets had been positioned on the opposite side of the room in front of a fireplace topped by a thick wooden mantelpiece. Someone had loaded it with ivy and Christmas ornaments and there was a large fir tree bulging with multi-coloured baubles positioned to its right.

'This is your aunt's favourite room,' Rowan said, putting Merry's suitcases onto the floor beside a doorway that opened to a set of stairs. Merry placed the one she was carrying next to it. 'She decorated the whole place for you yesterday afternoon because today is the first of December. When it gets dark you'll see lights dotted around the garden, too. There's a Christmas tree in the sitting room at the front of the house – although if you're anything like your Aunt Ava you'll spend most of your time in here.'

A silver-grey tabby cat wandered into the kitchen from the hallway and surveyed them both with curious green eyes.

'That's Simba,' Rowan explained as the cat's tail twitched and it wandered closer to the roaring fire. 'Chewy, your aunt's house rabbit, is around here somewhere...' She searched the space before shrugging. 'He's probably hiding. The two of them are great friends so don't worry about leaving them alone. The rest of the animals reside in the garden, either in pens or roaming free. Ava's already taken care of them all for today so you don't need to worry about going back outside.' She looked out of the large window over the sink and frowned. 'It's starting to snow again: I probably need to make a move before my car gets stuck.'

Merry dipped her head even as her stomach clenched at the thought of being left alone. She'd known this was going to happen when she'd agreed to house-and-animal-sit for her aunt's eclectic menagerie of animals for the whole of December, but that didn't make the reality any less scary. It was getting dark and she was in the middle of nowhere. A thousand worst-case scenarios filled her head and she placed her laptop bag onto the table and swiped her sweaty palms on her bright yellow jumper. 'Did my aunt leave any instructions on what I should do?' Ava had promised to leave schedules for the animals as well as tips on everything Merry needed to know – from where to buy food in Christmas Village to how to set the fire.

'Aye.' Rowan pointed to a rectangular folder on the top of a fridge-freezer before drawing Merry's attention to a series of pink, blue and green Post-it notes that had been stuck to various pieces of furniture. 'Most of what you need to know is in that folder.'

Rowan marched up to the fridge and tapped a fingertip onto a blue Post-it which had been taped to the front. 'The rest you'll find on these. This is the vet's number – Jared Dunbar has lived in the village for years and he'll be able to help with any animal questions or emergencies. My number's underneath if you need anything, or just fancy a chat. Ava told me she's left instructions about some important family business she needs you to take care of. She wanted to explain it to you herself but...' Rowan opened her palms wide before jabbing a finger at the fridge again. 'I brought you some stew from the cafe and a loaf of fresh bread. There's some vegetables and a few other meals I made myself. Make sure you visit the cafe soon, I can promise you home-cooked food and a village of people who are dying to meet you.' She grinned, her dark eyes warm and Merry's stomach clenched despite the woman's friendly demeanour.

'I'm not very good with new people.' Her cheeks went hot. At least, she wasn't these days.

'Ach, that's not a problem, lass, you'll be fine after a few weeks of living here,' Rowan said kindly. 'I'll pop back later in the week to see how you're getting on. Oh.' She paused as she headed back towards the hall and pointed to a set of keys hanging on hooks at the edge of the kitchen. 'Those will get you in and out of the house; there are locks on some of the animal enclosures, but you won't need to worry about those. Ignore any gossip you hear about a wandering Yeti.' She rolled her eyes. 'That's just a lot of nonsense, nothing to worry about.'

'Yeti?' Merry squeaked. Perhaps her older brothers had been right. They'd been horrified at the idea of her coming to Scotland alone, citing all kinds of dangers – from wild stags to treacherous blizzards – but she'd ignored them, determined to restart her dormant life.

'The keys to Ava's Jeep are hanging there too,' Rowan continued. 'Apparently you're insured!' She beamed.

Merry didn't have the heart to tell the older woman that

while she had her license she hadn't actually driven in over two years. 'I prefer walking. I'm not too far from the main high street, am I?'

Rowan frowned. 'There's a shortcut behind the hen house at the back of the garden. Ava will have included a map with the notes. But don't go hiking around here after dark on your own,' she warned.

Merry swallowed. 'Because of the Yeti?' she croaked, her legs suddenly liquifying.

Rowan let out a sharp snort of laughter. 'No, lass, because of the snow. You don't want to go getting yourself lost when it's so cold.' She shook her head, still chortling, and headed back towards the front door again. 'Don't forget to read those notes!' With that, the older woman winked and shut the door.

Merry took a few moments to absorb the silence before she followed the path Rowan had taken into the hallway and double-locked the front door, driving a large black bolt over it and then dragging a heavy chair from the kitchen and setting it in front. She pulled her mobile from her pocket and grimaced when she remembered the battery was flat and imagined how many texts she'd probably received from her over-protective brothers by now. At least they'd know she'd landed – no doubt they'd spent the day keeping an eye on their shared tracking app, at least until her phone's battery had died. Merry dug into her handbag and pulled out her charger before plugging it in. Ignoring the knot of anxiety in the pit of her stomach, she marched back into the kitchen and grabbed the folder from the top of the fridge, before settling down on the sofa to read.

Scratch, tap, scratch, tap. A few minutes later Merry dropped the notes and leapt to her feet, her heart thundering as a round bundle of fur scampered out from behind the back of the sofa, its tiny paws clicking against the shiny red tiles. 'Chewy...' Merry blew out a breath as she bent down to scratch the creature behind its ears. 'I'm going to have to get used to

these noises or I'm not going to last – and I'm not going home!'
Clenching her hands into fists, she sat back on the sofa and
pulled the rest of the A4 pages out of the cardboard folder so
she could flick through her aunt's instructions. There were
more contact numbers, a map of the homestead which detailed
exactly where each of her aunt's animals were located, and
included feeding times and dietary requirements, as well as
details of their personality quirks. She'd memorise it later and
take the notes with her when she ventured outside in the
morning.

Merry settled deeper into the sofa and yawned. It had been
a long trip from Hertfordshire and the stress of the five-hour
delay had made it even more tiring. She flicked through the
documents, her eyes drooping, until she reached a page headed
'TOP SECRET' which had been scrawled dramatically in red
capitals in her aunt's untidy handwriting. Merry had never met
her Aunt Ava in the flesh, but they'd talked dozens of times on
the phone over the last couple of months. Ava was her mother's
sister – she'd fallen out with Merry's dad soon after her mother
had unexpectedly died twenty-five years before, leaving the two
sides of the family estranged. But Merry had found an old letter
from Ava in her father's office and had written to her recently
on a whim and her aunt had replied, triggering a back and forth
of notes and cards and a couple of long phone calls. So being in
Chestnut Cottage, reading Ava's letter, was like suddenly
having her in the room.

Darling Merry, what I'm about to tell you is of the upmost
importance and for your eyes only...

Merry took an unsteady breath as the thump of her heart
accelerated – what exactly was her aunt about to reveal and
why did it involve her?

I'm so sorry I wasn't at Chestnut Cottage to greet you before I left for my flight to the animal rescue centre in India, but I truly appreciate you stepping in to take care of my pets while I'm gone. I'm looking forward to finally meeting you face to face when I return in the new year. I can only imagine how brave you've needed to be to travel all the way to Scotland alone, but I'm so glad you've found the courage to come to Christmas Village and to move forward with your life.

As you are aware, I won't be contactable throughout my trip to India because where I am is so remote.

Not that Merry's Aunt Ava had embraced much in the way of new technology in Scotland. She hadn't got a computer and barely charged her brick of a mobile phone which Merry noticed had been left behind on the kitchen windowsill. Her attention flicked to the canary-yellow rectangular handset attached to the wall beside the fridge and she shook her head... She probably ought to use it to call her brothers, but she wasn't ready to deal with their fussing and demands that she come back home.

Which is why everything you need to know is in these notes. I'm adding this letter now, so apologies for the untidy hand-writing, but the taxi is due in less than ten minutes and I've a lot to explain. If you have questions, they'll have to wait until I return to Scotland because NOBODY aside from you, me and one other person in the village knows. I cannot stress how important it is that you keep this to yourself...

Intrigued and a little excited, Merry sat up straighter on the sofa. This was why she'd come to Scotland: to break away from her boring world, to do something with her life...

For the last forty years I have had the privilege of being Secret Santa for the adults in Christmas Village. My mother was Secret Santa before me, and my grandmother before her – so this is an important family tradition which is paid for by a trust fund set up by your great-grandmother over a century ago.

If your mum was still with us she'd almost certainly have been involved with Secret Santa. She'd probably be here now, doing it with you. I had planned to organise all of the villagers' gifts before leaving for the rescue centre so I didn't have to bother you – but unfortunately the inclement weather has delayed the arrival of my purchases. Which is where, dear Merry, you come in.

'Wow,' Merry choked out. It sounded like a huge responsibility. Could she really take it on? She nibbled her lip. Then again, wasn't this the whole reason she'd come to Christmas Village? To finally achieve something and restart her life. She nodded: this adventure was made for her. She was called Merry after all, a Christmas name fit for a Secret Santa. Perhaps it was a sign? She sighed, looking around the room, wondering what kind of gifts she'd have to wrap, how her Aunt Ava had decided what to buy. Perhaps she'd work it out once everything arrived?

When the presents finally turn up, I need you to wrap and tag them. I've included a full list of recipients – there are twenty in all – and what I've bought them on the following page. In the next few days your mystery helper will deliver a sack. Please pop the wrapped and labelled presents into it and leave the package outside the back door of Chestnut Cottage on the morning of the twenty-fourth of December. It will be collected and the gifts will be distributed at the village carol concert on Christmas morning, around the Christmas tree on the high street. You should attend to represent our family, of course.

Please remember, under no circumstances can you share any of this information with anyone. This secret has been in our family for generations. Thank you so much, Merry, for helping us to keep it.

With love

Aunt Ava xxx

'Okay, wow.' Merry put the letter on the rest of the pile and took a deep breath. She could keep a family secret and wrapping and labelling gifts wouldn't be too difficult. It would probably be easier than taking care of her Aunt Ava's pets. She glanced at her laptop bag, which she'd left on the kitchen table before getting up to stretch her legs, then she opened the fridge so she could make herself some food.

An hour later Merry pulled her laptop out of the bag. Chewy was hovering at the corner of the fire, so she picked the rabbit up and settled him onto a cushion beside her on the sofa so she could stroke him behind the ears. According to the first paragraph of her aunt's notes, which she'd skimmed through earlier, the rabbit enjoyed company in the evenings and was partial to a cuddle. She settled back in the seat and lifted her legs underneath her, moving the letter and pages of notes out of the way to the other side of the rabbit before settling down to work. She was here to finish her novel, to stop making excuses and to finally send it off to a publisher. For the first time in two years, Merry wasn't going to let fears or insecurities get in the way. As she read through the first paragraph of her book, her eyes began to droop.

It was absolutely freezing. Merry yawned and tried to get comfortable as she opened one eye, adjusting to the light, which had dimmed to an inky black. Her laptop was still open and resting on her lap but the battery had died, suggesting she'd slept for so long it had gone flat. She yawned again and took a deep breath, gradually waking, before checking her watch. It was nine o'clock. Almost time for bed. She had to ring her brothers before turning in. She scraped a hand across her forehead, still groggy, and wriggled her legs out from under her, groaning as they complained. Then she put her laptop safely onto the closest coffee table. As she stood, paper shavings tumbled onto the floor like snowflakes and she bent to pick up a handful as her attention drifted back to the sofa and the half-chewed remains of her aunt's letter and notes. Her eyes shot to the rabbit lying beside them – its eyes were glazed and all four of its paws were pointing up. Then Merry let out a piercing scream.

2

_____

Theo Ellis-Lee pulled another one of the hideous doors off the front of a cabinet in his kitchen and carefully balanced it against the others, wondering why anybody in their right mind would choose to buy shocking pink units. Had the previous owners been colour-blind, seduced by a rock-bottom deal or related to Barbie? He grimaced. He'd lived in this house for over two months now after buying it on a whim and escaping from the disaster that had become his life in London, but he hadn't got used to the colour. Tonight, while he crammed down a hastily assembled sandwich, he'd finally had enough. So he'd booked a visit from a local kitchen designer before unscrewing the offending doors from their hinges. His mind wandered to his ex-fiancée Miranda Middleton and her penchant for bright colours before he shut the thought down, wishing he could somehow eliminate her from his history.

'Dot!' Theo held up a finger as his Dalmatian suddenly charged into the kitchen and collided with the bag of tools he'd left in the middle of the floor. The dog only had three legs and sometimes gravity got the better of her so he took a step forwards in case he had to prop her up – but the minx merely shook herself and sprinted into the hallway after an imaginary predator. Theo grinned; she'd always been independent and brave despite her affliction. Next time he had a relationship, *if* there was a next time, he'd be looking for someone just like that. He was done rescuing women – all the way over being taken for a fool. He sighed as he wandered to the large picture window at the end of the kitchen, which overlooked Holly Loch. The sun had set hours before but ambient light from the full moon and a billion stars illuminated the water and trees that fanned the edges of the shingly beach. He'd never tire of that view – or stop congratulating himself on his escape into the wilderness.

His mobile began to ring and for a moment he considering ignoring it before he relented and picked up.

'Theo, lad?' His new partner, who had brought him into the Furry Friends veterinary surgery – Jared Dunbar – asked, not waiting for a response. 'I've been called out to two emergencies and despite my advanced age I've not figured out how to clone myself yet. I know you're not strictly on call but let's chalk it up to the unpredictable life of a country vet. Can you take one of them, please? One of the houses is fairly close to you.'

'No problem,' Theo said, opening the door to his utility room and grabbing his medical bag, stopping momentarily to scribble down the address Jared recited. 'What's the emergency?'

'A rabbit's eaten something he shouldn't. I didn't get many details because the woman who rang was very upset. The owner's a good friend and one of our regular clients so I'm hoping it's not as serious as it sounds...'

The roads were slippery with compressed snow and it took Theo longer to get to the address Jared had given him than he would have liked, considering he was responding to an emergency. He was further delayed because he had to park and open the heavy wooden gate at the far end of the drive before pulling his battered Range Rover up in front of the building his satnav had assured him was Chestnut Cottage. It was a pretty house and someone had gone to the trouble of decorating the garden with multi-coloured fairy lights which illuminated the deep mounds of snow, lines of animal pens and small hen house. He hopped out of his car and made his way towards the front door. He paused momentarily when he heard a rustling sound in the garden but it was so dark he couldn't identify what had made the noise.

The cheeks stained with trails of black mascara did nothing to detract from the beauty of the woman who opened the door – and as light hit her face it took Theo a few seconds to move his lips.

'Sorry.' Shaken, he moved through the door.

'Who? What? No! I haven't got much money but you can take whatever I have,' the woman squeaked, stumbling backwards out of his way as he heaved the heavy door shut behind him to stop the frigid air from leaking inside.

'I'm not here to rob you!' he grumbled and guilt stabbed at him when he noticed her eyes had widened with fear. 'I'm sorry.' He lifted his bag and held up a palm. 'I'm Theo Ellis-Lee, the vet. You called about an emergency?'

'Oh… I thought you'd be much older.' The woman paled and slumped against one of the walls, looking unsteady. 'Sorry, I'm a bit jumpy. It's all been such a shock.'

Theo moved forwards when she looked like she might pass out. 'You were probably expecting my partner. Are you okay?' He cleared his throat as he took in her fluffy pink socks, luminous yellow sweater and the jeans that hugged a tiny figure, all of it perfectly complementing her pretty face. 'Do you need to sit?'

'No, I'm…' She swallowed, gathering herself. 'I'm sorry but I think I might have got you here under false pretences.' She heaved her shoulders before spinning around and striding down the hallway. Theo followed the woman into an open-plan room with a large kitchen area and seating in front of an open fire. There were curls of ripped paper scattered all over the tiled floor. The cat lounging in front of the roaring flames didn't look up as he drew closer.

'Is the cat sick?' Theo pointed his bag towards the hearth, wondering if Jared had got the wrong end of the stick, but the woman shook her head.

'It's my aunt's rabbit.' Her eyes lurched around the room. 'I'm not sure where he is. He was dead, then...' She shook her head. 'I called the vet – you – and when I turned around he'd just... disappeared. I don't understand, it's like someone *took him*.' The last words were blurted in a horrified whisper and Theo wondered if the woman had been drinking. A half-full bottle of brandy sat on the kitchen table with an empty glass beside it.

'You mean a body-snatcher?' he asked dryly. *Dear God*, he was dealing with a crazy person. 'Are you... I mean...' His eyes shot back to the table and she flushed, her lips instantly thinning.

'I've *not* drunk that much – one shot and it was medicinal. He was right there.' She jabbed a finger at the sofa before picking up a half-chewed whorl of paper from the floor. 'I fell asleep and he shredded all my notes. There's hardly anything left – only a few pages.' She waved it at him, sounding hysterical. 'He wasn't breathing; his legs were stuck in the air!' The woman held her arms upwards, miming what she'd seen, and her eyes flooded with tears. Theo had a sudden urge to comfort her so he took a step away. He was done with rescuing beautiful women. He had to keep all his annoying natural instincts in check.

'Well, he can't have gone far,' he soothed, putting his bag on the floor and pacing towards the kitchen cabinets, looking in the corners, before heading over to the sofa. 'Did you check behind here?'

'Of course I did!' she snapped, watching as he walked behind the furniture.

That's when he saw the bundle of fluff trying to bury itself in the far corner of the room and bent to scoop it up. 'Your dead rabbit, I presume?' he asked, trying to keep his voice clear of sarcasm. He must have failed because she shot him a look of pure loathing.

'He wasn't there earlier,' she grumbled. 'I checked the whole room. He was *dead*...' The woman frowned as she took the rabbit from his hands and cuddled him to her chest. 'Thank you for finding him,' she added, sounding like she meant it. 'I still don't understand...'

'Some rabbits play dead,' he said, taking pity on her. 'Usually when they're scared or unsettled – it's like a defence mechanism.'

She nodded, stroking her small hands over the creature's ears. She wore pink nail varnish with sparkles. The frivolous colour reminded him of Miranda, but despite that, he had to drag his eyes back up to her face.

'Perhaps he's missing my aunt Ava?' she suggested.

He shrugged. 'Or he heard a loud noise; it's difficult to be sure. You said he's eaten some of your paperwork?'

She nodded again, her eyes scanning the tiles, and frowned before leaning down and putting the rabbit on the floor. 'I suppose I should have expected it; his name's Chewy.' She looked up and gave a lopsided smile which hit him somewhere in the solar plexus, stirring hormones that he'd long ago hidden away.

'It's best to keep paperwork away from pets,' he snapped, irritated by his reaction to her. The answering flush on her cheeks made him instantly regret his bad temper. 'Um.' He softened his tone. 'Sometimes that type of thing can get stuck in their throats, choke them.'

Her eyes widened and she hugged the rabbit closer. 'Then I suppose we had a lucky escape.' She let out a long sigh as she picked up the remnants of the paperwork and swallowed. Theo could see a hand-drawn map and what was probably a letter, but most of the other pages were little more than scraps.

'Were the documents important?' he asked, unable to stop the words. He should be leaving now and working out her bill. The rabbit was fine and the emergency over, but his feet refused to co-operate.

The woman let out a soft moan as she flicked through what was left. 'He's shredded all the instructions about how to look after the animals. My aunt Ava's away until January and I can't contact her at all. I'm supposed to be looking after her pets.' She sucked in a breath. 'I don't even know what animals she owns.' Her voice pitched up. 'Let alone how to feed them, what they need, their individual quirks...' Her eyes dropped to the rabbit.

'Well, you know Chewy shouldn't be left alone to... well, chew,' he muttered, letting out a long sigh. 'As for the rest, the cat will need feeding twice a day – aside from that he'll probably do his own thing.' He blew out a breath. He'd regret this, he knew he'd regret this, but he was a vet; he couldn't leave a load of help-less animals to fend for themselves. It had nothing to do with the fear he could see in the woman's eyes. 'I'm sure all of your aunt's pets will be registered with our practice. I'll check the records first thing, then I'll come straight over so I can talk you through who's who, feeding regimes, and anything else you need to know.'

Her small shoulders sagged in relief. 'Thank you,' she said softly. 'I don't know what I'd do—'

'I'm a vet: keeping animals safe, making sure they're taken care of, is my job. I'd do it for anyone,' he grumbled, annoyed at the way his body continued to respond to her.

She frowned and one eyebrow shifted at his tone. 'Then my name's Merry McKenzie,' she said calmly even as her shoulders stiffened.

'So?' he asked, knowing he was being rude and wishing he could leave before he made any more of a fool of himself.

'For your invoice – I don't want my aunt to pay for any of this,' she said, her cheeks turning so red they'd probably stop traffic. 'I understand you're not doing me any favours.'

'Right.' He jerked his chin, feeling like an ass, before picking up his bag and heading towards the exit. 'I'll see you tomorrow,' he said as he reached the front door.

Merry stood at the end of the corridor watching him intently. 'Look out for the Yeti...' he heard her whisper, but when he turned to see if she was joking, Merry had already shut the door.

Theo tramped through the snow to the car then sat, staring at the house, wondering what had just happened. Why had all his good intentions flown out of his mind at the first glimpse of a woman who needed rescuing? Shaking his head, he slowly reversed, promising himself that the next time he saw Merry McKenzie he'd be keeping his wayward instincts firmly in check.

3

The canary-yellow phone in Ava's kitchen had shrilled for the first time at five a.m. and then proceeded to stop and restart at least seven times before Merry finally heaved her exhausted body out of bed to answer it. It was her own fault: she'd been too strung-out to call her brothers the evening before so she'd texted that she'd arrived safely and then switched off her mobile. She should have expected them to try the landline. She'd barely slept, listening out instead for sounds of mythical creatures or people trying to break in, almost jumping out of her skin each time a neighbouring owl hooted. She swiped a hand through her hair, attempting to ignore the guilt and worry being heaped on her shoulders with shovels the size of building skips.

'You have to come home. We all know how easy it is to get a life-threatening injury,' Liam McKenzie – pathologist – declared before she'd even said hello.

'Honestly Merry, how are we going to feel if you injure yourself again? Especially when there's no one close by who can help,' Noah McKenzie – her eldest brother and a policeman – added gruffly on their four-way family call.

'I've got a few days off, I can drive up and stay with you,'

Ollie McKenzie – fireman –offered. 'I know you think we're being over-protective but—'

'We don't want you to get hurt again,' Liam added softly in his oh-so-reasonable voice. 'Ever since Dad died of pneumonia and asked us to look out for you—'

'You have, I know,' Merry said, wearily looking around her aunt's kitchen and pressing a fingertip to the long silver scar that lined the edge of her face. She hadn't started the fire yet because Chewy had eaten those instructions too and so it was freezing. Perhaps her brothers were right: could she really survive up here alone? She glanced at her laptop, remembering the reasons why she'd come, and shook her head. 'I appreciate everything you're saying and everything you've done, but you can't protect me forever. I know my car accident scared you.'

'You being in a coma for three months scared us even more,' Noah said gruffly.

Merry swallowed. 'That was over two years ago – and I'm fed up of being wrapped in cotton wool. I need to get on with my life. I used to manage a clothes shop before the accident; I had my own friends.' All of whom she'd lost touch with because it had been easier to stay in her bedroom protected by its four walls rather than socialise. 'I haven't had a boyfriend in years. I barely go out.' She sighed. 'I'm twenty-five, I still live with you, Liam; I have to branch out on my own.' Her chest heaved with the pressure of admitting the truth. Hiding away – maintaining the status quo – would be so much easier but if she didn't break free now, she never would.

'And do what? Be a writer? You know how many people fail at that. You've not sent a book off for anyone to read since you uploaded it to that stupid website...' Noah paused, perhaps unwilling to reopen that particular wound, managing to pry the scab loose despite his good intentions. 'What if someone else tells you it's no good? It *eviscerated* you.'

'And I got over it.' Merry swallowed. *Sort of.* 'Besides, the timing was all wrong.' She'd uploaded some of her book a couple of months after coming out of the coma in an effort to reconnect with the world. But the nasty response from a stranger had sent her scurrying back to the safety of her bedroom. 'I'm going to finish my novel and send it to a publisher. It's time...'

'But you have a perfectly good job,' Liam said.

'Walking your friends' dogs. It's not enough,' Merry said desperately. 'Mum was a writer...'

Her mother had passed away after a short illness when Merry was five. She'd learned about her mum's love of writing when she was nine and found a pile of manuscripts in a filing cabinet in her father's office. She'd read them all and discovered her mother had been talented, with a love of romance. Merry had started her own novel when she was fifteen in an effort to bond with the woman she'd barely known – and her hobby had expanded from there. But she'd always wanted it to be more.

'Yep, but she wrote for herself, she didn't put her work into the world to be ridiculed and torn down. I don't understand why you have to,' Ollie snapped, getting increasingly wound up.

Tempted to just give in, Merry shook her head then straightened her shoulders. 'I'm staying in Christmas Village until January,' she said calmly, feeling like Captain Scott in the Antarctic declaring his intentions. 'So you'd better get used to it. I need to do this, I need to stop being so...' *Afraid, timid, useless.* 'I have to find a life of my own. I'm just existing...'

'This is because of that teacher – Mrs Adams – isn't it?' Liam asked in a rare moment of insight, mentioning Merry's A level English teacher from years before. 'Is it because she died?'

Merry swallowed the lump in her throat. It had been just one stupid moment, seeing the obituary in her local paper. Her head had suddenly filled with all the older woman's kind words and encouragement, the times she'd read Merry's stories and told her she was talented, that she could be anything she set her mind to.

Such a seemingly small event, but it had made her look around the kitchen she shared with Liam and see the reality of her life for the first time in years. A couple of days later, determined to escape from her stalled life, she'd written a letter to the eccentric aunt she'd never met and... well, that had been that.

Theo the vet arrived twenty minutes after Merry's shower so her hair was still wet when she opened the door. Last night she'd been so overwhelmed by Chewy's supposed death and disappearance she'd barely given the man a second glance – but the breath caught in the top of her throat when she took him in properly for the first time. He was huge – bigger than all of her brothers and they were tall – with broad, muscular arms and shoulders that suggested he worked out. Probably bench-pressing sheep, horses or the odd tractor in the afternoons. He wore a black jacket, jeans that hugged his thighs and green wellies that were so large she'd probably fit both her feet into a single one. He had one of those angular jaws she'd written about in her novel, but hadn't been sure existed in real life. A full mouth that was probably more kissable than hers – which sucked because she'd been told it was her best feature. In summary, he was hot with a capital H, O and T.

The breath whooshed out of Merry's throat and she stepped aside silently so he could enter the hallway and she wouldn't embarrass herself by trying to talk. Theo had brought a Dalmatian today – it had three legs, an adorable heart-shaped spot on its nose and it came hopping in first.

'This is Dot, she's good with house pets. Is it okay if she comes in too?' he asked as the dog continued down the hall.

'Of course. As long as she's not going to eat what's left of my notes.' Merry managed to gather herself and make a joke, which was obviously bad because Theo didn't so much as smirk.

'Our receptionist told me where to find your aunt's files so I have a list of all the animals,' he said instead, barely looking at her. 'I thought we could walk around the garden and you can make notes.' He stared at Merry, clearly expecting her to do something.

'Oh, a pad,' she muttered before heading into the kitchen. She'd seen a pack of Post-its and a pen in a kitchen drawer; they'd do for now. He followed her into the kitchen and stood with his legs spread wide, looking around.

'Want a coffee, or something sweet? Rowan Taylor, from the cafe in the high street, left me the ingredients for ginger-bread lattes, they're really very good,' she offered, determined to be friendly. 'I won't expect you to dock money off the invoice in lieu of refreshments.' She tried joking again but got the same dull stare. Was the man really this humourless, or did he have a problem with her?

'It's cold in here. Shouldn't you get the fire going?' His eyebrows met and she gazed into irises the colour of a tropical lagoon.

Merry puffed out an irritated breath. Those were the perils of being a romance writer, glamorizing even the grumpiest of men. But she already knew she'd be hopping onto her laptop after he'd left so she could perform eye-colour surgery on her hero, in the form of 'find and replace'. She dragged her attention to the hearth. 'I haven't worked out how to light it. I don't have one at home.' Merry swallowed, feeling inadequate. 'Chewy shredded those notes too.'

Theo looked at her for a beat, his mouth performing a series of odd contortions. 'Cats prefer being warm,' he said as if he were convincing himself. He put his bag on the floor and walked to the fireplace, bending his knees and stretching his jeans around his bum, showing off yet more Adonis-worthy muscles.

'I could probably Google it.' Merry sighed. She wandered up to join him and leaned down. He smelled of mountain air and apples, and the scent was sexier than something so wholesome had a right to be. She watched as he expertly piled wood and kindling into the hearth before lighting it and adding the fireguard.

'Think you'll be able to do that yourself next time?' He quirked an eyebrow and she nodded, standing and stepping back.

'Consider me taught,' she said, mentally filing away everything Theo had just done. Knowing she wouldn't ask for a repeat lesson in a million years.

'So.' He looked meaningfully at the Post-its. 'I don't have all day. Shall we start out front?'

'Okay.' Merry went to gather one of her aunt's huge coats, a hat and some boots from the small cloakroom under the staircase. She tugged them on, then followed Theo as he marched to the front door with Dot at his heels and opened it. Merry stepped tentatively behind him and left the door on the latch. As she stepped outside into the snow, she took a moment to look at her surroundings properly. They really were in the middle of nowhere, surrounded by mountains topped with white – and a cloudless blue sky that looked like it should exist somewhere hot, like Greece.

Theo spun around unexpectedly as Merry got as far as his car, then he strode back to the doorstep before grabbing something sticking out of the small metal mailbox fastened to the wall. He drew out a bright red velvet sack and an envelope and handed them to her. 'I spotted these when I arrived, wasn't sure you'd notice them,' he said gruffly.

Merry quickly stuffed the card and bag into an enormous pocket in the lining of her coat. She'd check through it all later.

Her aunt had mentioned her Secret Santa accomplice would drop something off soon, and she knew she couldn't say anything about it to Theo. Not that he seemed remotely curious. Instead, he walked back to the battered black Range Rover.

'Sorry Dot, you'll have to wait in the car or you might scare the animals,' he said, opening the boot and popping the dog inside with obvious regret. Then he walked towards the right of the driveway into a clear opening where Merry saw a series of small and large animal pens. There were also tracks in the snow: far more than yesterday and some looked huge. She trotted faster, ignoring the sudden rush of blood in her ears, almost bumping into Theo's back as he stopped in front of a wire pen. In the centre sat a small wooden house with a bridge leading to the ground. A honey-brown chicken suddenly poked its beak from out of the oval door.

'*Buk, buk, buk.*' The creature pecked at the ladder, looking annoyed, and Theo pulled some notes from his pocket.

'So this is where the chickens are kept, obviously.' He scanned the paper and let out a snort of laughter Merry hadn't been expecting. It was an odd sound coming from such a serious man and she smiled. 'Cluck, Eggitha and Hennifer. Your aunt's a comedian.' He shook his head, still grinning, his handsome face lighting up. The man was so gorgeous Merry half expected sunbeams to shoot from his eyes. She averted hers before she did something embarrassing, like drool.

'These girls will eat almost anything: compost, weeds, leftovers from the garden, but at the moment you'll mainly use shop-bought feed.' He pointed towards a dark green metal shed at the rear end of the garden. 'I'm guessing the food will all be kept in there. Chickens like their surroundings clean so you're going to want to muck out the pen and house regularly.' He turned and skimmed Merry from head to toe, setting off an impressive firework display low in her belly. 'You might want to put on some old clothes before you do it,' he said dryly. 'I assume you have something suitable?'

Merry dipped her chin – she probably had something that would do in her suitcase, otherwise she'd wear her pyjamas. No one aside from her ever got to see those... She heard an odd rustling sound and looked around nervously before hugging herself.

'Collect the eggs twice a day. It's not good to leave them sitting,' Theo continued, opening the gate so he could wander into the enclosure. All three chickens appeared and trotted to the ground complaining loudly, obviously expecting their breakfast. Theo peered into the coop and put his hand inside, drawing out a couple of eggs before handing them to Merry. They were still warm.

'They're perfect,' she said, her voice husky. She'd only ever seen eggs in the supermarket before today. 'I almost don't want to eat them.'

She looked up into Theo's face – he was looking at her, his eyes filled with confusion. Then he shook himself and the sour expression returned. 'Seems a waste after all their hard work,' he said roughly. 'Do you know how to make an omelette?' he asked seriously, making her wonder where the question had come from.

'Of course,' Merry answered, irritated. What kind of an idiot did Theo take her for? It was exactly the type of question one of her brothers might ask, exactly the way they'd underestimate her before trying to take over, making her feel helpless, making her question her ability to manage alone. This was *not* what she needed. 'Shall we get on? I'm sure you don't have all day,' she snapped. He looked surprised, like he'd been bitten by a kitten or something. His lips pursed and he strode out of the coop, shutting the door, ignoring the irate chickens as they began to cluck.

'I'll help you find the right foodstuff and we'll come back

and feed these guys before we do anything else or they might start to riot,' he said, still avoiding her eyes. He marched towards the back of the garden and Merry trotted in his wake feeling like a naughty schoolgirl. That's when she heard the rustling again and when she looked to her left, a huge bird with green and brown plumage and a furious-looking red face came charging from behind a tree, yelping and cackling, waving its wings, its beady gaze fixed firmly on Theo.

'That's a turkey. What in hell?' he gasped.

Merry could hear Theo's dog barking wildly in the car as the vet took one look at the bird and tried to step in front of her. Merry saw a small spade lying in the snow a few metres away and something made her run over, pick it up and wave it frantically in the air.

'Go, away, shoo!' Theo shouted, stepping in front of Merry again and waving his arms as the creature continued to run at them, cackling and clucking, its wild eyes making it look like something out of a bad horror movie.

'I did not come to Scotland to be eaten by a bird!' Merry screamed at the creature, and her voice seemed to stop it in its tracks. It glared at Theo again, made a few spluttering sounds then waddled from side to side like a Sumo wrestler limbering up for a new attack. Merry waved the spade one more time and Theo took another step forwards, trying to shield her even more.

'Stay back, it might peck you,' he ordered as the creature started to wriggle, suggesting it was getting ready to charge. Merry had a sudden image of the hero in her romance novel stepping in front of her heroine as they faced an angry lion, preparing to attack. Only in her book, the heroine drew out a pistol and shot it in the air, frightening the lion and saving them both. Merry took a deep breath and tried to move ahead. Theo put an arm out to stop her – but she stubbornly continued to step forwards. Then she caught her foot on a piece of bramble and plummeted head first into the freezing snow. She hissed and looked up, expecting to be accosted and pecked. Instead, the turkey seemed to frown, its little eyes switching back and forth between her and Theo. Then it sagged and cackled once more, before turning and slowly lumbering off towards the back of the house.

As it disappeared, Theo let out a long breath then leaned down and pulled Merry up without comment. She stood, shivering as snow dripped from her coat, feeling impotent and humiliated as he shuffled through his notes again, seemingly oblivious to her embarrassment. 'It says here your aunt has a turkey called Henry who roams free.' His mouth pinched. 'It needs locking up or I don't know how you're going to look after the rest of this menagerie.'

'I'll be fine,' Merry said, as her stupid voice trembled. 'I got the feeling Henry's problem was with you,' she whispered. 'Perhaps you could try smiling once in a while?'

Theo raised an eyebrow, taking in the snow covering her coat, and something inside her snapped.

'I'll be okay,' she growled, ignoring his look of scepticism. 'I have a weapon.' She pointed to the spade which she'd dropped when she'd fallen. Some ass-kicking heroine she was turning out to be. 'And at least it's not a Yeti,' she added quietly as her stomach rolled.

Theo of the gorgeous face and permanent frown didn't laugh, but he did pick up the spade as they made their way carefully towards the metal shed at the back of the garden. All the while Merry wondered once more if she'd bitten off more than she could chew – but she knew the last thing she would do was call on her brothers, or Theo, for help. If she had any chance of making the changes to herself and her life that she'd promised, she was going to have to get through this adventure alone.

4

Merry pulled off her coat and threw it over the sofa as soon as Theo had gone. It had taken another forty minutes for him to talk her through how to take care of the rest of her aunt's pets and she had hundreds of Post-it notes crammed into her coat pocket which she'd transcribe onto her laptop later. Theo had kept hold of the spade the whole time but Henry hadn't put in another appearance. Merry had been able to sense the turkey watching though – had felt the trickles of dread creeping up her spine, draining any residue of courage. She bent to feed another log onto the fire before slumping next to her coat, immediately spotting the bright red sack poking from one of the pockets and drawing it out – along with the letter Theo had handed to her. She leaned her head back on the sofa and opened the square envelope.

Dear Merry,

Thank you so much for stepping in while your aunt is out of the country. As Ava will have mentioned, my family is responsible for collecting and delivering the Secret Santa sack every *year ready for distribution. Please ensure you have wrapped and labelled the presents your aunt has provided carefully as each gift has been selected with the perfect person in mind. On the morning of the 24th of December please leave the filled sack outside of the back door of Chestnut Cottage before 7 a.m. and do not look out for me.*

Thank you for being our Christmas Village Secret Santa this year xx

The letter wasn't signed, which Merry had half expected. It would have been nice to be able to talk to someone about the tradition, but she'd have to wait for her aunt. She drew herself up and went to gather the remainder of Ava's instructions, flicking to the letter at the back. She read the letter again and searched for the sheet that listed the villagers' gifts alongside each name. But as she browsed through the few pages her insides turned to ice. It had to be here somewhere. She leafed through them again. She'd been so upset last night, she'd only taken a cursory glance at the notes before realising the animal instructions had been shredded. When she'd seen her aunt's letter about Secret Santa had survived, she'd assumed the list would be intact too... Gulping, Merry flipped through the remnants twice more before pulling up a chair and putting her head in her hands. She'd screwed up completely. The presents were going to arrive and she had no idea who they were meant for. She'd only met Rowan and Theo so far, had no idea what her aunt would have chosen for either of them – unless she'd bought the vet happy pills or a personality transplant. A tear snaked down her cheek and she swiped it away, irritated. This was supposed to be a new start, a chance to prove to herself that she could be anything she wanted and she just kept messing up. Merry got up and found her mobile. Realising it had no signal, she wandered to the yellow phone, wondering if she should just give in and call one of her brothers when she heard a sharp rap on the front door.

When Merry opened it she half expected to find Theo on the other side, still frowning – instead there was a young woman holding a cake tin. She was pretty, about five foot five with dark, chestnut-brown hair that poked from underneath a white bobble hat and tumbled past her shoulders. A red bicycle with a large basket on the front had been propped against the porch.

'Hi, I'm Belle Albany.' The woman beamed, handing Merry the tin. 'I baked you chocolate brownies and thought I'd pop over to welcome you to Christmas Village. There's no rush to give me back the tin.' She cocked her head. 'Everything okay?'

'Um, yes.' Merry swiped at her face, conscious it was probably still tear-stained. 'I was chopping onions,' she lied. 'Do you fancy a hot drink to go with those?'

'Please.' Belle smiled, following her into the kitchen and removing her coat. 'I also wanted to check you're still okay to visit my class on Wednesday. I teach at the Christmas Village primary school,' she explained when Merry looked at her blankly.

Merry put the tin on the table and went to put the kettle on. Had this been in Aunt Ava's notes too? 'I didn't manage to catch up with my aunt; my visit was delayed and while we talked on the phone a few times before yesterday she didn't mention anything about a school...' She grabbed mugs and plates from one of the cupboards and opened the tin which instantly flooded the room with tantalizing fragrances.

'Ava told me you're an author?' Belle asked as she pulled up a chair at the table and sat.

'Well, yes – no, I'm not published.' Merry's cheeks flushed. She never called herself that, didn't deserve the label.

'But you write novels?' Belle leaned down to stroke Simba as the cat wandered up to sniff her legs.

'I've been working on one for years.' Merry finished making

the coffee and took a cup to Belle, grabbing a kitchen chair so they could sit face to face. 'It's a romance.'

'Then you're exactly who I need. My class are about to write their annual Christmas stories and the children so enjoy meeting interesting visitors. It would be lovely if you could help me to motivate them – talk to them about what inspires you, how you come up with your characters and plots. Ava said you'd be available to visit once a week until the end of term?' Belle's forehead creased when Merry widened her eyes.

Merry shook her head. 'I'm really not a teacher.'

'Good, because I don't need one of those,' Belle said brightly, tapping the top of Merry's hand. 'I need a writer, someone new. I'd love it if you could come. The children are adorable and the classes will be lots of fun. It'll give you a chance to meet some new people too. Your Aunt Ava was worried you might get lonely out here on your own.'

'I don't know...' Merry said, looking around the room. Then again, a new adventure could reignite her confidence? She took a deep breath. One lesson wouldn't hurt, would it? She swallowed the lump of anxiety in her throat. 'Okay, I'll come on Wednesday and we can see how it goes...'

'Great!' Belle said. Then they chatted a little more and finished their coffees before the teacher jumped to her feet. 'Come at eleven o'clock.'

But as Belle cycled away, Merry felt a tidal wave of nerves as she imagined speaking to the class. She closed her eyes, pushing the feelings away. She had to force herself to go; perhaps she'd enjoy it, and if she was lucky, even make a new friend in Belle?

'Class, I'd like you all to say good morning to Ms McKenzie.'

Merry stood beside Belle at the front of her Primary Three class, gripping her hands into tight fists, trying not to look scared. She'd been fighting her nerves since the moment Belle had left Chestnut Cottage two days earlier and a little voice had told her not to go out today at all and to feign illness, but then this morning Rowan had pulled up in her white Ford Ranger and offered to drive her and Merry hadn't had the heart to refuse. Instead, she'd bundled up her laptop and a few pages of her novel. She was supposed to be being braver, after all. Besides, if she was lucky the children might provide some Secret Santa clues.

Merry let her eyes explore the classroom. It had a small carpeted area at the front and a series of desks faced her. The ceilings were high and the space was airy and light. Belle had hung glittery stars and colourful streamers and pictures of Father Christmas across the walls and the overall effect was festive and delightful. There were carefully handwritten projects pinned onto a huge noticeboard at the back of the room with tinsel intertwined between them and Merry wondered if that was where the children's stories were going to be displayed.

'Good morning!' The eleven children boomed, their fresh faces eager.

Every cell in Merry's body tensed. She had little experience of kids and no idea what to expect. Would they laugh at her, cry, throw pens – or something worse?

'Hello.' Her voice came out as a high-pitched squeak and one of the boys in the front row of chairs giggled into his hand.

'Magnus Thomson, we don't laugh at our visitors!' Belle scolded, frowning. The boy's cheeks flushed. 'Ms McKenzie is a very busy writer and she's given up her precious time to come here to inspire you. She'll be talking about her book and helping to motivate you before you write your Christmas stories. In the last lesson you'll each get to read your story to her and she'll give you feedback. Then we'll put them all on display at the back of the classroom and your parents will be able to read them when they come to watch the school nativity play. Who knows what kind of talent Ms McKenzie might uncover? We don't want to scare her off.'

A pretty girl with long blonde hair shot a hand into the air, bouncing with excitement. 'Nessa McLeod.' Belle nodded and the child directed her attention to Merry.

'I like your jumper,' she said, gazing at the chunky knitted sweater Merry had thrown together with a pair of black trousers. 'Yellow's my favourite colour.'

'It's mine too.' Merry smiled.

'It makes me feel happy,' the child added.

Merry grinned because that was exactly the way she felt. It was why her wardrobe featured a lot of bright colours. If she wasn't loud and exciting, at least her clothes were.

Belle cleared her throat. 'Did you have any questions about Ms McKenzie's writing, Nessa?'

The child nodded, her cheeks flushing. 'What sorts of books do you write? I like stories about angels and bears, with pictures.'

'Um, they don't have any of those in them,' Merry said, feeling guilty when the little girl's face dropped. 'They're about...' She grimaced, anticipating the reaction, wishing again that she hadn't come. 'People falling in love.'

'Does that mean you write about girls?' a boy with jet-black hair complained, screwing up his nose as the two boys sitting beside him groaned.

'Angus, Adam and Lennie, why don't you all stay behind at the end of this lesson so we can talk about being polite,' Belle interrupted before Merry could respond. 'There's nothing wrong with stories about girls.' She narrowed her hazel eyes. 'I'm fairly sure your mams would agree with me about that – perhaps when they come to pick you up after school we can discuss it?'

The three boys slunk lower in their seats and a girl sitting at the back of the room sniggered. 'I like stories about girls *and* boys.' She flushed to her blonde roots. 'And donkeys.'

'Thank you Mazey, so do I.' Belle folded her arms and tracked across the carpet so she could pull up one of the small chairs beside the front row of children and sit. She looked a little ridiculous with her knees bent so they were almost the same level as her waist. 'I don't know about you, but I've always wanted to write a book,' she said, softly stroking a hand over her blue trousers. 'Do any of you have questions for Ms McKenzie? You're going to plan a story in our lesson next week, so think carefully about what you'd like to know before asking.'

A small boy with curly honey-brown hair and ruddy cheeks plunged his hand up, fidgeting in his seat.

'Yes, Ace.' Belle turned to face him.

'Do you have any car chases in your book?' he asked seriously.

'Um.' Merry's cheeks tingled. She'd never considered it, but perhaps it would be a good idea to include one? 'Not at the moment, but I haven't finished it yet.'

'How long have you been writing your story?' Lennie asked, cocking his head.

'I've started a few, but I've been writing this one for about five years,' she said faintly. How had she managed to waste so much time? What had she been doing? Hiding away, pretending the big wide world didn't exist? It was the type of question Merry usually avoided, but the eleven small faces now gaping in shock gave her a jolt.

'It must be a *very* long book,' Ace murmured and Merry didn't have the heart to tell him it wasn't. 'I think chases are a good idea – cars, horses, even people,' he added. 'Most people enjoy them.'

'I'll bear that in mind,' Merry said as an image of Theo behind the wheel of his old Range Rover chasing Henry the crazed turkey filled her head and she quickly blanked it. What was it about the grumpy vet that meant she couldn't stop thinking about him?

Belle clapped her hands when some of the children started to talk amongst themselves, proving Merry wasn't holding their attention. 'Can you tell us how you come up with your characters please, Ms McKenzie?'

'Oh, okay.' Merry perched on the side of Belle's desk because her knees felt wobbly. She wasn't used to being the centre of attention and having all these faces gawking at her was a little overwhelming. 'I make them up, but I start by thinking about all the qualities I admire in a person. I think it's important that I like the people I write about.'

'Unless they're baddies,' Adam said solemnly.

'That's true.' Belle studied the children, who'd stopped talking now and were fully entranced. 'It's good to be able to distinguish between characters with good qualities and those with bad. Class, what kinds of things do you like about people, characteristics or traits you might like them to have?' The teacher stood and stretched her legs, padding over to where Merry was standing so she could pick up a black marker. 'I'll start. I like people to be kind and helpful, and friends who encourage and give you space to change and grow.' She wrote 'space, change, grow' on the whiteboard.

Ace put his hand in the air again and Belle tipped her chin.

'I like people who smell of chocolate,' he said seriously.

'Interesting.' Belle wrote *smells nice* on the board too.

'Smell is important,' Merry agreed. 'My hero smells of mountain air and apples.' She'd added the description to her novel yesterday afternoon.

A small girl waved and this time Merry pointed to her, feeling a little more confident. She could do this: it wasn't so bad being in company and talking about her book.

'I'm Lara Smith,' the girl said in a whispery voice. 'I want my heroine to have brown hair like mine.' She stroked a hand over it then shrank into her chair when the rest of the class stared.

Merry straightened her shoulders. 'What a brilliant idea.' She spoke louder, feeling protective, and smiled kindly when Lara flushed. 'You can do anything you want, because it's your story,' Merry added warmly. 'That's what's so wonderful about making things up. Your characters can have brown, blonde or even blue hair. They can be frightened, courageous, outgoing or shy. They can love animals, fly planes, even rescue their friends.' *They can be all the things you're not, all the things you wish you were...*

'Could your heroine rescue the hero?' Mazey asked, her eyes fixed on Merry. 'I like books where that happens. I think girls can do anything boys can.'

Merry looked at the young child and nodded. 'So do I,' she said softly. She'd had no idea children could be so wise. 'My heroine's called Carmel Martin and she rescues the hero Dan Curtis all the time.'

'Can you tell us more about your story?' Belle asked.

'Of course,' Merry said. 'Dan and Carmel have been hired by a museum curator.'

'Is he a goodie?' Adam asked, putting his hand in the air again.

'Yes.' Merry chuckled. 'He's very good. He's asked them to transport a large diamond across the South American jungle because he doesn't trust the post.'

'My mam doesn't either,' Adam said seriously.

'Where are Dan and Carmel going?' Belle asked, clearly intending to quickly divert the class's attention away from the merits of the postal system.

'Tinsel Mountain,' Merry explained. 'That's where the museum's located. They need to get the diamond there by Christmas Eve, just in time for a big exhibition. But someone's following my hero and heroine and he plans to steal the jewel.'

Mazey's mouth stretched into a wide smile. 'I like the sound of your book,' she murmured. 'I'd definitely read it – and so would my mam.'

Merry found herself grinning back as something in her stomach opened and flowered. 'Thank you,' she said softly. It was the first time she'd been bold enough to talk about her story in public since she'd been told it was rubbish online and suddenly she was glad she had. A wave of enthusiasm engulfed her. She'd get the laptop out as soon as she got back to Chestnut Cottage.

'I wondered if it would be a good idea if you spent the rest of the lesson coming up with ideas for your characters?' Belle suggested to the class. 'Then when Ms McKenzie comes next week she could look through what you've done and we can talk about the elements of a good story?'

Merry nodded.

'Can you read some of your book out when you come back?' Ace shouted from the back and the rest of the kids bobbed their heads. 'Maybe you'll have put in a car chase by then?'

Merry chuckled. 'Okay,' she said. Maybe it wouldn't be so bad to return. It hadn't been as awful as she'd expected and it had been good to get out of the house – she was surprised at how exciting it had felt to talk about her book too. She smiled at Belle who nodded. 'If you'd like. I'll have a look at my story and see what I can come up with...'

5

When Merry left Christmas Village primary school the snow was falling again – small wispy slivers of ice that made everything look magical – and she felt lighter as she stomped along the pavement in a pair of her Aunt Ava's snow boots. Belle had offered to lend Merry her bike and Rowan had told her to call if she needed a lift, but Merry had resolved to walk. Boosted by the lesson and positive reactions from the children, she didn't want to let the feelings go. Besides, being outdoors was good for inspiration, perhaps she'd even come up with an idea for a car chase?

Using the map Aunt Ava had drawn – which, miraculously, Chewy hadn't gobbled up – Merry made her way along the pavement. She walked in the opposite direction to Christmas Village high street, carefully searching the hedgerow looking for signs of a cut-through which would lead to a path that would take her to Chestnut Cottage's back garden. It was a twenty-minute walk and she'd need to feed the animals when she arrived. Merry knew she'd have to keep a lookout for Henry the whole time – he'd stared at her for the last couple of days, looming in the corner of the garden behind a tree, looking menacing, but he hadn't actually attacked. She'd kept the spade handy and waved it a few times. Perhaps his problem really had been with Theo? As she continued to walk along the pavement searching for the opening, Merry kept checking over her shoulder, sensing something was watching her. Finally spotting a gap further down on the other side of the road she stepped off the pavement, passing a small row of snow-laden fir trees on her left. Then she heard a loud howling sound from behind.

Startled, Merry jumped and twisted, her heart hammering as her imagination conjured a creature with huge teeth and bulging eyes. She tried to channel her heroine Carmel, but instead of feeing brave, she felt her hands start to shake and her heartbeat pounded in her ears. She couldn't see much more than outlines through the snowflakes which had grown heavier and thicker as she'd been walking but could just make out a large figure in the distance. Was something stalking her? She began to run, but her foot suddenly slipped out from under her as it made contact with a patch of ice and she landed heavily on her bum, catching her laptop just before it hit the ground.

'*Heerrruuuuhhhhhh.*' The sound moved closer and Merry rotated and squinted, searching for the origin of the weird noise. She tried to scramble up when she realised the figure in the distance was a grey donkey. It flared its nostrils and let out another loud braying sound.

'Shoo! Go away!' Merry yelled, waving her arms above her head as the creature drew closer. Why hadn't she brought the spade? The donkey opened its mouth, exposing a set of shiny white teeth. Did they eat plants, or laptops, or were they carnivorous? The donkey ignored her warnings, its huge blue eyes taking her in as it wandered even closer until it was nuzzling Merry's bag. She tried to get up again, but her leg slipped out from under her once more and she hit the ground with another hard bump. 'Dammit,' she moaned as a car slowed and drew up beside her. She squinted up and immediately recognised the battered driver's door of the black Range Rover, gritting her teeth as the window slowly wound down.

'What are you doing?' Theo asked as his eyes dropped to Merry's legs before popping up to peruse the donkey. 'Were you trying to walk one of your aunt's pets?' His tone was incredulous. 'That wasn't mentioned in the surgery notes.'

The donkey let out a *hee-haw*, before sniffing the air, then turning and wandering off.

'We need to catch it before it disappears,' Theo said quickly, opening the car door.

'It's not my aunt's,' Merry said sharply, putting a hand onto the road and carefully levering herself up. 'At least, I don't think it is.' She pulled a face when she tried to put pressure on her knee and pain shot through the muscle and bone.

'Are you okay?' Theo asked, climbing out. He placed a hand under Merry's arm, making her skin shimmer with pleasure.

'Yes,' she hissed, tugging her laptop closer to her chest – although she wasn't sure if it was in an effort to protect it or herself.

'I'll give you a lift.' He guided her gently around the car without waiting for a response. Merry didn't want to go, but her knee ached and she knew she'd be an idiot to refuse. Before Theo climbed into the driver's side he walked a few metres down the road. 'The donkey's disappeared.' He shook his head. 'I'll see if I can track it down once I've dropped you off.'

It was a quiet drive to the house. The Dalmatian called Dot barked a couple of times and Theo put the heater up, perhaps in an effort to make Merry more comfortable – or maybe because it made a lot of noise and he didn't want to talk? She waited as he pulled up outside Chestnut Cottage and heaved the gate open, driving in and stopping so he could close it again. She started to offer her help but was silenced by an impatient glare. As Theo parked, Merry's mobile buzzed in her pocket as it caught a signal and she pulled it out.

Where are you? Liam had texted, underneath an alert that told her she'd missed seven calls. *CALL ME!* he'd added minutes later.

Liam tried to get in touch, are you all right? Remember I can drive up and get you anytime you want. Ollie had messaged moments later and Merry guessed her brothers had had one of their 'Merry's in trouble' conflabs. *Don't forget to put the fire out before you go to bed – baking soda works, make sure you use enough. In fact don't put the fire on at all, fluffy socks and blankets are better.*

'Dear God,' Merry muttered.

Are you eating properly? Noah's text delivered the nagging hat trick. She shut down her phone and put it back in her pocket as the contented feeling from earlier – the lift the lesson with the children had given her – dissolved. When Theo opened the passenger door and tried to help Merry out she glowered so hard he held up both palms.

'I'm just trying to help, don't bite.' He looked over his shoulder as something rustled in the garden. 'Henry.' His lips thinned but it did nothing to detract from the beauty of his mouth. Merry had a sudden urge to reach out and ruffle his hair, to do something to make him less appealing. Instead she carefully climbed down too, holding onto the laptop as Theo went to release Dot from the boot.

'You don't need to stay,' she grumbled as she hobbled slowly towards the front door, keeping an eye on the garden, wishing she'd left the spade closer to the driveway. What if the bird charged: would any of them come out in one piece?

Merry exhaled deeply as she made it to the safety of the doorstep. Then she spotted five large cardboard boxes piled up in the far corner of the porch. They'd mostly been sheltered from the bad weather but the top of each box was still covered in a smattering of fresh snow. Dot scampered onto the porch as the rustling in the garden grew louder.

'Do you think you could open the door?' Theo cleared his throat, coming up behind her, sounding more worried than annoyed. He had his veterinary bag in one hand and was holding it up as if he intended to swing it to protect himself, if need be.

Merry quickly tugged the key from her pocket and opened the door. Perhaps sensing Henry was getting close, Dot zipped inside and Merry walked in behind her before putting the laptop on a side table and carefully turning again, intending to pick up one of the boxes.

'I'll do it,' Theo said, jabbing a finger towards the kitchen. 'Go and sit so I can take a look at that knee.'

She was going to argue but her leg hurt and the boxes were too big for her to carry anyway. Still, it rankled – she didn't need another bossy man in her life taking over; she already had three.

Merry walked slowly into the kitchen and pulled off her coat. She'd left the Christmas tree lights on and if Ollie were here she knew she'd be in for a long lecture. She wandered to the fireplace, then chucked on a few logs, carefully sticking her leg out straight so she could bend to light it. Then she limped to put the kettle on as she heard the front door close. She turned to see the vet slowly heave the five boxes out of the hallway and place them onto the kitchen table. 'That's a lot of shopping.'

Merry hobbled to one of the kitchen drawers and pulled out a pair of scissors before carefully opening the top box. It was filled with bubble wrap and she drew out the first item, partially unwrapping it to reveal a sapphire tiara. She shut her eyes as she heard an odd, choking sound coming from Theo's throat.

'Well, I'm sure the chickens will appreciate the sparkly jewellery.' He waved a hand at the Christmas tree. 'Speaking of sparkles, it's not a good idea to leave the lights on when you go out.'

'I'll bear that in mind,' Merry said, gritting her teeth.

'Do you want to sit and I'll check your knee before you

check out the rest of your stuff?' His voice was oddly disappointed.

'They aren't for me,' Merry snapped. 'They're...' She flinched suddenly and slammed her lips together, annoyed with herself. She'd almost told Theo about Secret Santa. Also, he'd seen the gift. She'd been so excited about seeing her aunt's purchases that she'd forgotten she should probably keep them hidden. Then again, chances were, when it came to Christmas morning, Theo would be alone glaring at his dog rather than carol-singing or taking part in the Secret Santa event so he was unlikely to make the connection.

The vet knelt, before opening his veterinary bag and waving at the chair until Merry slumped into it. Her knee still hurt and she was suddenly filled with an overwhelming sense of foreboding. All the boxes looked full. How many gifts was she supposed to match with their intended recipients working alone? Could she work it out or, for the first time in generations, was her family going to let the village down? Would Secret Santa be able to visit? And if he did, would the presents all be wrong? Merry dropped her face into her palms.

'Is it painful?' Theo asked kindly, patting a tentative hand on Merry's arm. 'I'm sorry, I had no idea.'

She swallowed. 'It's not that. My knee hurts but...' She lifted her eyes to the boxes, wishing she could confide in him. Ask for assistance.

'Is there something wrong with the delivery?' Theo guessed.

Merry sighed. 'I'm sorry but I can't tell you.'

He looked surprised. He drew away from her and his expression blanked. 'Of course,' he said curtly, gently cupping his hands around her knee and prodding, checking for breaks or swelling. 'My guess is you've sprained or pulled something. Put some ice on it, and I'll come back tomorrow to check.'

'Are you qualified to treat humans?' she asked.

He shrugged. 'It's either me or a thirty-minute drive to the local doctor's surgery.' Theo lifted an eyebrow and she shook her head.

'It's not that bad,' she said hopefully.

'I'll keep an eye on it and if it gets worse I can drive you.' He turned towards the front door. 'I'll feed the animals now if you can watch Dot.' His eyes drifted to the dog who had curled in front of the fire which was crackling and spitting. 'She'll be happier here in the warm – probably safer, too.'

'I can feed them myself, later,' Merry murmured, groaning as she tried to move her leg. 'Okay, maybe it would be better if you did it,' she added when Theo didn't comment. 'But please don't forget to add it to my invoice.'

'I...' Theo looked taken aback. 'Sure, no problem,' he agreed, stepping away from her. His eyes rested on the boxes again and he opened his mouth before closing it. Then he frowned and headed towards the front door. Merry let out a long sigh, wishing she could call him back. But she had no business expecting this man to help her even more than he already was. If she was going to take back control of her life, she was going to have to figure out who all the Secret Santa recipients were herself.

6

'So what's new on the far edge of nowhere?' Jake Ellis-Lee's voice sounded tinny through Theo's mobile and his brother had definitely picked up a slight Australian drawl.

'Says the man who's been bumming around the other side of the world,' Theo said dryly. He paced his consultation room in the veterinary surgery, taking in the black counters, shiny white cabinets, computer and weighing scales. Despite the cork noticeboard displaying multiple colourful leaflets, he hadn't made a mark on the space and after two months still didn't feel like he belonged.

'What are you up to?' Jake asked.

'I was going to make myself a coffee before I saw my first client.' Now he'd have to forgo the hot drink. But Theo always answered the phone when Jake called just in case his brother needed him. 'How's the surf?' He could picture Jake now riding the waves, his lean body nut-brown and glowing. He could imagine the man-eating sharks his brother had joked about, too.

'Amazing.' Jake sighed. 'You should fly out and visit.'

Theo perched on the edge of his desk and gazed out of a large window above the round, clinical sink. It was a clear day and the sky was blue. Cows stood contentedly in a field layered with snow in the farm next door to the surgery. 'Soon,' he promised.

'Yeah, would that be before or after hell freezes over?' his brother asked sadly. 'You missing Miranda?'

'Nope.' Theo shook his head. 'From what I hear, she's still loved up with my old business partner and they've both moved into our old house.' He swallowed the feelings of bitterness before they consumed him. She'd hurt him badly, used him up before spitting him out, but he wasn't going to let it destroy him. It was why he'd come to Scotland, after all. A new start – for a transformed, far less accommodating him.

'But she paid you for your half of the house, right?'

Theo didn't respond. There was no point. She would eventually but he knew she'd ensure it was painful and drawn out. Her own particular brand of punishment because he'd finally seen through her, finally had enough.

'Right,' Jake said softly, his voice gravelly. 'On a more positive note, it's probably the last chance she'll get to screw you over.'

'Let's hope so,' Theo said lightly. His ex had taken him to the cleaners – wrung out most of his bank account and told him she'd needed the money because she was in terrible debt. Miranda had always needed something and for four years he'd been determined to fix every one of her problems, to make her life perfect – until he'd finally seen through all the drama. Realised she was more than capable of rescuing herself. That was about the time she'd set her sights on his partner...

'So, have you met anyone new – I'm guessing you know the saying about getting back on the horse? As a vet it ought to be part of the curriculum,' his brother joked.

Theo could hear the hush of the sea hitting the beach in the background and wondered where Jake was now. Probably waiting for a bigger set of waves so he could hop back on his board. For a second he wished he could be content with a life that was just as carefree.

'I'm looking,' Theo admitted as his mind strayed to Merry McKenzie and he tugged it away. What was it about her he was so drawn to? His innate need to rescue someone – the parts of his DNA he seemed incapable of shaking? 'I registered with an app someone recommended but no one interesting has come up.'

'Except there's something in your voice. What aren't you telling me?' Jake asked slyly. 'Who is she?'

'No one important.' Theo grunted. 'She wears yellow. Yellow's not a sensible colour.'

'Too happy?' Theo could hear the grin in Jake's tone.

'Happy can be needy,' Theo said. 'I don't trust it.' Miranda had worn bright, joyful colours which had served as a mask, a distraction from her true agenda. He knew if he waited long enough Merry would probably have one too. But Theo wasn't going to let himself get close enough to find out.

'So you're looking for someone miserable?' His brother sounded amused.

'I'm looking for someone who can take care of themselves.' Theo closed his eyelids as the image of his perfect woman popped into his mind. She was small with dark hair that swept down past her shoulders and almond-shaped brown eyes. *Hang on…* His popped open. 'Purple is the colour of a practical woman,' he said, thinking about the yellow jumper Merry had been wearing yesterday, how pretty she'd looked as she'd limped to the chair in her aunt's kitchen. Then he thought about those boxes filled with who knew what. Miranda had a fondness for shopping. She'd maxed out his credit cards then left him to pay them off. Yes, Merry had told him the boxes weren't hers, but she could have been lying. 'Purple screams power and ambition. I'm looking for someone who can keep *me* for a change,' Theo said seriously.

His brother snorted. '*Mate*, you're dreaming! You'd hate that... You raised me when Mum and Dad died and still can't stop yourself from watching over me. You adopted a three-legged dog, fell for a witch of a woman who used you. I mean, it's definitely your turn to be taken care of but...' Jake sighed. 'It won't make you happy. You enjoy caring for people, protecting and saving them – animals too. It's in your nature. You're basically a German Shepherd in human form.'

'Things change. I will too – watch me prove it,' Theo said, suspecting he needed to prove it to himself too. But he had to try. He wasn't prepared to open himself up to any more hurt. Someone knocked on the door of his consulting room. 'I've got to go,' he said with a surge of regret.

'Yep. There's a wave here with my name on it anyway. Laters.' Jake hung up.

When Theo opened the door, Kirsteen Findlay was waiting on the other side looking unhappy. 'Something wrong?' Theo asked, knowing the receptionist, who sometimes doubled as their veterinary nurse, wasn't a dramatic woman. If anything, she could be too calm. He paced into the large bright waiting room, expecting to see nothing short of Armageddon, but it was empty.

'We've got another ten minutes before our first appointment.' Kirsteen read his mind. 'The problem is with Jared.' She shook the multiple bracelets on her wrist as she pointed to his partner's consulting room, which was on the opposite side of the surgery building, but the door was shut. 'He limped in three minutes ago.'

'He's hurt?' Theo asked, quickly tracking past the reception desk where the older woman usually sat to greet and register their clients.

Kirsteen nodded, keeping pace. 'He took an emergency call first thing and something must have happened to his leg when he was there because I swear I saw blood on his shirt.' She looked annoyed. 'The eejit told me he was fine and asked if we had any camomile tea.'

'Another injury.' Theo thought about Merry. He'd have to visit her later – his conscience wouldn't allow him to leave her without checking in. Perhaps this time he really would invoice her for the time? Even if it was just to prove to himself that Jake was wrong and he could be selfish. Theo knocked on his partner's door and opened it without waiting. The older vet was perched on the chair behind his desk with a leg raised up on a stool. Theo couldn't see any signs of an injury because the limb was concealed by brown corduroy trousers. He could see blood on the cuffs of Jared's white shirt, though.

'What happened?' he asked, striding forwards and peering around the office. The older man had a series of cow paintings decorating the walls – presents from doting clients because they knew of his fondness for the animals. The remainder of the room resembled Theo's office, although there were piles of clutter and books scattered all around.

'Nothing, lad, I'm okay.' Jared winced when he tried to ease his leg to the floor. 'A daft injury, just a bruise. I slipped on some ice after helping one of the Browns' cows give birth. Slippery sucker.' He chuckled. 'All my own fault.'

'What about the blood?' Kirsteen wandered up behind Theo and slammed a mug of camomile tea onto the vet's desk.

'Don't fuss, lass. The blood was from Bessie the cow; she sliced a chunk out of her nose while she was in labour and wiped it on me. My leg is fine.' Jared picked a packet up from his desk and popped two paracetamol onto his tongue before slurping some of the hot drink. Then he waved the empty foil wrapper. 'Now I've had these, the pain will go off in a while.'

Kirsteen let out a loud huff which was out of character. Her whole demeanour was odd. Less her usual zen, more stressed out. 'Can you take on all the emergency calls and house visits until we work out if this is serious?' She spun around to talk to

Theo, taking no prisoners as she swivelled back to glare at the older vet. 'I'll watch Dot,' she added. His dog was sleeping at the end of his consulting room but she wouldn't be happy about being left.

'It's not necessary,' Jared complained. 'I'm not injured.'

'If that's true, you'll be able to take over all the out-of-surgery visits again this afternoon, won't you?' Kirsteen brushed strands of her elegant blonde bob out of her face. She was a pretty woman, somewhere in her mid-fifties. She'd told Theo as much on his first day in the surgery over a coffee in their staff kitchen. She'd also confided that she was divorced with two grown children – and then she'd given him the name of the dating app she used. Apparently she had plenty of years left in her for romance which meant he did too. *Her words*. As Theo had mentioned to Jake, he'd only got around to signing up to the app the week before but hadn't been very enthusiastic when he'd started to look. Perhaps he wasn't cut out for another relationship at all.

'I really don't think—' Jared started.

'I'd appreciate the fresh air,' Theo said, reading their receptionist's expression. 'Will you be able to look after my appointments while I'm gone?'

'Of course. I'll rejiggle them.' Kirsteen patted Theo on the shoulder without giving Jared time to respond. 'Everyone who can walk unaided please follow me to the front desk.' She ploughed ahead, her long skirt swishing under her white medical coat, and grabbed a folder out of a tall grey filing cabinet. 'I need you to visit Evergreen Castle first. Edina Lachlan called yesterday and asked if someone could give her donkey his vaccinations.'

'I can go myself once these painkillers kick in,' Jared shouted from his office.

The receptionist rolled her eyes. 'He's a dunderhead,' she said to Theo softly. 'A good man, but a dunderhead. Please leave before he tries to make it to his car. I don't want to rugby tackle him in front of you.' Kirsteen shoved a folder into Theo's hands and waved him out of the door as his partner hobbled into reception.

Evergreen Castle was an impressive building that stood at the end of a long, wide drive flanked by shaggy fir trees. Surrounding it were acres of land covered in lush layers of thick snow dotted with shrubbery. The castle had many windows across its right side and an impressive turret in the far corner of the structure. Even from here Theo could see someone had strung Christmas lights across the façade of the building and he wondered how it would look when it got dark. He slowly drove his Range Rover down the driveway, following the instructions on his satnav, double-checking the information in Kirsteen's file to make sure he was in the right place. As he approached the castle, he spotted a small woman standing in front of the large arched front door crafted from oak. She wore a thick tartan coat and— *was she wearing a tiara?* Theo thought about the one Merry had unwrapped the day before and stopped the car as he drew closer and saw the woman wave.

'Morning, lad. I've been expecting you,' she said in a thick Scottish accent as Theo parked and hopped out. 'I'm Edina Lachlan. Are you the new vet?' She scanned his face and smiled widely when Theo nodded, making the wrinkles on her face deepen. 'Kirsteen called to say you were on your way. Ach, lad, you're almost as handsome as my grandson – it's enough to make a person wish they were thirty years younger.' She wriggled her eyebrows which was a little disconcerting. Theo grabbed his bag from the back seat of his car before offering her his hand.

'Theo Ellis-Lee. I'm here to see a donkey?'

'Aye, that'll be Bob.' Edina lifted her chin. 'He's got his own barn to the left of the castle. My gardener, Logan Forbes, swept it out earlier and he's just been fed. I'm hoping that means Bob will still be around – he regularly goes off on walkabouts.' She headed in the direction she'd pointed out, moving at a remarkably spritely pace, and Theo had to trot to keep up. As they turned the corner of the castle he spotted a grey donkey in a clearing, sniffing the air. It had blue eyes and looked exactly like the one that had been in the road, standing over Merry, the day before.

'I think I might have seen Bob in the village yesterday afternoon,' Theo said.

'Aye, he went missing for a few hours. Popped up at dinner time though,' Edina said lightly. 'The lad does enjoy his outings into town.'

'You probably ought to secure the barn or he might get into an accident.' Theo tramped over to look inside the wooden building, frowning when he noticed a series of hand-drawn pictures pinned to the walls. Was everyone in this village crazy? 'Doesn't he eat those?' he asked incredulously.

'Nae, lad. Those were drawn by the school children at our local primary school. Bob loves them,' Edina explained, reading his face. 'My grandson is dating their teacher, Belle. She's a lovely lass.' A gust of wind blew around them and she shivered. 'The weather's turning. Do you fancy a hot toddy while you're here?'

'Not when I'm working,' Theo murmured, wandering over to the donkey who immediately nuzzled his veterinary bag. He stroked a hand over Bob's ears. 'I read in this guy's notes that he doesn't mind getting injections?'

Edina pulled two carrots from the pocket of her coat. 'He'll be happy enough if we feed him these. Shall I distract him for you?' She leaned forwards and her tiara began to fall so she pushed it back into her hair. Theo stared, fascinated, and she grinned. 'You're wondering about the headgear?'

'Well, no… yes, actually,' he admitted, pulling a face. 'It's none of my business.'

'Ach, lad, I'm nae crazy. My husband.' She leaned closer and he could see her dainty bone structure, the intelligent blue of her eyes. 'He brought me all sorts of bonnie jewellery when we were younger but didn't like me wearing it in case it got broken or lost.' She shrugged. 'He's passed now but it taught me an important lesson. Our time on this earth is short, so we might as well make the most of every second – and that includes wearing our best jewellery every day if we want.' She smoothed a hand across the tiara. 'So I wear a different one of these every day to celebrate that I'm still alive. Also…' She flushed. 'My beau who runs The Corner Shop in the high street likes them. Not that he'd admit it.' Her eyes glittered. 'Do you have a lass?' She turned away to offer Bob a carrot.

'There's no one in my life at the moment,' Theo answered. 'I'm taking some time out.' The donkey nibbled the top of the vegetable as Theo drew a syringe from his bag and prepared it, sterilising Bob's flank as he stroked it before carefully sliding the needle in while the animal continued to munch.

'You're good at that, very patient. I'll warrant you'd have a lot to offer someone.' Theo looked up to find the older woman watching him, her gaze intent. 'And there are a lot of pretty lasses in Christmas Village. You just say the word when you change your mind.' She winked.

The high street was busy as Theo drove his Range Rover along the main road, past a beauty salon called The Workshop where a woman wearing a short red dress was hanging tinsel across the wide, shiny window. He passed Rowan's Cafe which Kirsteen had assured him made the best lunches in Scotland – he really had to make a point of visiting it soon. The post office next door was closed and a few shops further on sat The Corner Shop which Theo knew sold newspapers and an assortment of eclectic but useful goods. As he passed a snow-covered bench at the far end of the thoroughfare, a black and white cat darted from underneath it and suddenly froze in front of his car. Theo skidded to a stop and sat studying the scrawny creature which had long shaggy hair and one open eye. The other was puffy and almost completely shut and he suspected it was the result of a recent injury, although he couldn't tell if it was healing well. He put on his hazard lights, ignored the traffic which had started to build up behind him and jumped out of his car, crouching in front of the bumper so he could get a better look at the cat's face. The scruffy imp took one look at him and let out a woeful howl before scurrying back towards the pavement. As Theo rose to follow, a car edged out and overtook, so he stepped out of its way and hurried to safety.

'Everything okay with the car?' A man with salt-and-pepper hair, wearing a thick Aran jumper and navy trousers, marched from the doorway of one of the shops. He was followed closely by a small black Scottie dog.

'There was a cat in the road.' Theo scratched his head. 'I think it might be injured.' He squinted in the direction the animal had run but it had disappeared into a large clearing, past a huge fir tree decorated with red and silver baubles. 'There was something wrong with its eye.'

'Aye.' The man's spine was almost unnaturally rigid and Theo suspected he might have served in the military once. 'I've seen the creature a few times. I think it's a stray. Good boy, Iver.' He leaned down to scratch his dog behind the ears.

'I'd like to take a look at the cat.' Theo scanned the under-growth. 'The injured eye might be susceptible to infection. Any chance you could let me know if you see it again?'

'Are you in the habit of picking up strays?' the man asked. 'Ach.' He grunted. 'You're the new vet.'

'Yep.' Theo shook the hand he was offered.

'I'm Tavish Doherty. That's my place. I've been running it for years.' He pointed in the direction of The Corner Shop. 'I haven't seen you in the village before?'

Theo shrugged. 'I've been settling in.' In truth, he hadn't felt much like socialising. Miranda had knocked the stuffing out of him and it was taking him a while to find his mojo again.

'After two months, you should have found your feet unless you're a complete eejit. There's a quiz at the local pub tonight and my team's short.' Tavish stared at him. 'I'm assuming you'd like to join us, lad?'

'Um.' Theo took a step back. 'I can't leave my dog for a whole evening – I'm sorry, I'll have to pass.'

The older man grinned, but the curve of his mouth was more wicked than welcoming. 'No problem, pets are welcome in Christmas Pud Inn.' He looked in the direction the one-eyed cat had scampered in. 'In return, I'll look out for your stray and let you know if it turns up. You can give me your contact details when we meet in the pub.' He flashed his teeth. 'A little insurance to make sure you come.'

'Fine.' Theo sighed. If he was going to make a life in Christmas Village he'd have to make an effort with the locals at some point. Besides, with any luck he'd meet a nice uncomplicated woman while he was out...

7

Christmas Pud Inn was busy even though it was only early on a Thursday evening. Theo wandered into the pub and spotted Tavish sitting at a large table next to a hearth with a crackling fire. He was surprised to see Kirsteen sitting across from Tavish and beside him Edina, who was now wearing an emerald tiara, but he didn't recognise any of the other faces. Kirsteen spotted him first and he waved then made a quick detour to the bar so he could buy himself a pint. Dot followed closely at his heels – his dog could be skittish at times so he took his time making sure she kept up and wasn't startled by any loud noises or the crowd. Christmas music started to play softly in the background and, while he waited for his drink, Theo perused the fairy lights that had been strung across the ceiling and the large blue spruce to the right of the bar. The tree had been decorated with silver, gold and red baubles and there was a large fairy spying on him from the top.

'Glad you made it,' Tavish said as he joined their table, pointing to a chair next to a young man Theo hadn't met. 'This is my son, Sam Doherty. He's just left the army after a ten-year stint. He's been helping me in my shop – good thing too because

I'm getting a bit old now to do all the shifts myself.' His eyes sparkled. 'My boy could do with meeting some people his own age.'

Sam offered Theo a hand. He had blue eyes, a dark beard and hair the same shade which had been clipped to his scalp.

'Hi,' Sam said quietly. 'I don't get to meet many new young people in the village, perhaps we could catch up sometime for a drink and I'll introduce you to more of the locals. This is Hannah McDowell.' He turned to gaze at the pretty woman sitting opposite them, beside Edina. She had a mass of honey-coloured curls which tumbled down her shoulders and a pair of cool green eyes that were narrowed at Sam. 'We used to be childhood sweethearts,' Sam said but Theo knew he was actually saying, 'hands off'.

'Many, many years ago now,' Hannah drawled. 'Until Sam here decided to join the army when we were both eighteen and left Christmas Village without mentioning it to me.'

'Call that a youthful mistake...' Sam said softly, his jaw tightening. 'One I regret.'

'I call it a sign.' Hannah's tone was ice. She turned her attention back to Theo, deliberately twisting her body away from the younger man. 'I've recently moved back to Christmas Village and I work in Rowan's Cafe on the high street and help out in the school on Wednesday afternoons. I'm currently single, and I have an eight-year-old son called Ace, courtesy of my ex-husband who is completely out of the picture. I'm available for dates.' She offered him her hand. 'Just in the interests of total transparency.' She smiled again, and fluttered her eyelashes as she sipped her white wine.

Theo heard Sam make a growling noise under his breath. Hannah was obviously trying to bait her ex and he had no intention of getting between them. There was chemistry there, he could feel it – but there was also hurt and he understood that too.

'I didn't know you were into quizzes?' Kirsteen asked Theo, leaning forwards, ignoring the couple who were now shooting daggers at each other. 'I'd have invited you to join us weeks ago if I had. I've mentioned these evenings to Jared a hundred times but he prefers spending his nights tucked up in front of the fire wearing fluffy slippers and mooning over his cows.' She hissed air between her teeth. 'That man is old before his time...'

'Um,' Theo said, unsure of how to respond. Was the receptionist interested in Jared? Could the vet be interested in her?

'Aye, but never say never, lass.' Next to Kirsteen, Edina winked as she dipped her head towards Tavish and lowered her voice. 'I thought my romance days were long gone until sparks flew with this one last year.' Her cheeks flamed pink and she took a long sip of her bright blue cocktail.

'Before I forget.' Kirsteen jangled her bracelets as she reached into the handbag by her feet, pulled out a white paper bag and waved it. 'Jared mentioned Simba, the cat Ava Armstrong's niece is taking care of, is about to run out of his diabetes medicine. Merry was supposed to pop in and pick it up but she's a couple of days overdue. Jared – the eejit – was planning to drive over to deliver the pills himself this afternoon even though his leg is still bothering him. So when Tavish mentioned you were coming tonight I insisted on bringing it here. I wondered if you'd mind dropping it in to the lass since it's on your way home?' She handed the bag over without waiting for Theo to agree. 'I'd do it myself but it's miles out of my way and the roads down there are spooky.' She shuddered.

'Sure.' Theo took it from her. 'I'll pop it in after the quiz.' If Simba was a diabetic, he'd need that medicine. Was Merry even aware? He'd skimmed all the animals' notes the other day but had been more focussed on teaching her how to take care of the hens, cow and pigs. Then the crazed turkey had attacked them and he'd been distracted. He closed his eyes. He was supposed to be staying away from the woman but he couldn't until he was sure she could handle things herself. As a vet, he wasn't going to leave a host of helpless animals at her mercy. If anything happened to them it would be on him...

'Be careful of the turkey,' Kirsteen whispered, leaning forwards again.

'What about it?'

A man by the bar picked up a microphone. 'We'll be coming around to take the names of your teams in a minute,' he yelled.

'Jared told me Henry hates men,' the receptionist confided as Tavish conferred with Edina on team names, scribbling ideas onto his pad. 'Something to do with its first owner. I believe the man was a bit unkind. When Jared first started visiting Ava he was attacked by the turkey a few times. Didn't he mention it?'

Theo shook his head. 'It would have been helpful if he had. It does explain a few things, though.' Like why Merry hadn't been pecked.

'The man's so busy mooning over those cows sometimes it's a wonder he remembers to breathe.' Kirsteen rolled her eyes. 'Take a handful of cranberries. Feed them to Henry and it'll help get you as far as the front door. Offer them every time you visit and it'll help build trust. That's the best advice I can offer.'

'Any idea where I could pick up cranberries at this time of night?' he asked.

The older woman shook her head. 'You could try the high street, but it might be too late. Sorry, I should have thought about Henry before now.'

'I'll take my chances,' Theo murmured. He'd already put a spade into his car boot ready for the next visit. But now he knew the turkey had a good reason for his behaviour, he wasn't going to use it in case it made the bird even more skittish.

A man who'd been serving behind the bar collected their team name as Tavish pulled off his coat, revealing a garish red Christmas jumper with a picture of Santa Claus on the front.

As he undressed Hannah began to chuckle quietly and a few people a couple of tables down joined in.

'Aye, you all get it out of your systems,' Tavish grumbled as Sam snorted into his hand.

'I'm sorry, it's just...' His son shook his head. 'Usually when you dress up you're wearing a uniform and your medals. I had no idea you'd developed a fondness for festive sweaters.'

'Your da got it last year from the village's Secret Santa,' Edina explained, giggling too. 'Whoever comes up with those presents has a good sense of humour, but they always seem to get them just right.' Her eyes glittered.

'Secret Santa?' Theo asked, sipping his beer. 'Isn't that for kids?'

'Nae, lad.' Tavish plucked the hair on his chin, looking offended. 'It's a tradition in the village. On Christmas morning, we all meet up to sing carols around the tree at the end of the high street, near where your cat disappeared. A sack of presents is left in some nearby bushes and a few of the villagers are gifted something. We take it in turns to hand them out.'

'Who's Secret Santa?' Theo asked.

'That's the point. No one knows,' Hannah said, lowering her voice and furtively looking around. 'It could be anyone. But whoever it is knows the villagers well enough to choose the perfect gift every time. It's uncanny.'

'I've always suspected Ava Armstrong,' Tavish confided. 'I've never known a woman receive so many parcels through the post.'

'Don't be daft.' Edina snorted. 'She's far too busy with her animals to be involved in any of that.' She leaned forwards and cupped a hand around her mouth. 'I've long suspected Morag Dooley who runs the post office in Lockton. She's always been a font of village gossip, and she knows everyone's secrets. That woman would know exactly what gifts to choose.'

Tavish frowned. 'Ach, it's nae Morag, lass, she lives miles away.'

'Does everyone get a gift?' Theo interrupted, thinking of the boxes that had arrived at Chestnut Cottage the day before. Perhaps Tavish's guess was on the mark?

'Nae, they're given to the people who've done good deeds throughout the year. There are too many of us living in the village for us to all receive something.' Edina pointed to Tavish. 'This one helped me when I hurt my ankle last December and he got that jumper as a reward. He wore it right into January.' She beamed.

'Aye, well it was a cold winter.' Tavish rubbed his hands together, his cheeks flaming. Then he picked up one of the pencils from the table and tapped it onto a pad. 'Will this quiz be starting anytime this year?' he roared as the rest of the team shifted back in their seats and grinned.

Theo sat in his car, inspecting the front of Chestnut Cottage. Merry must have been busy this afternoon because there were now Christmas lights hanging around the porch and a brightly lit reindeer ornament sparkled to the right of the blue door. He pressed his nose to the glass of the driver's window and stared into the inky blackness. He'd driven through the high street after the pub quiz had finished, wondering if by some miracle he'd be able to buy cranberries. It wasn't much past nine thirty, but all the shops were shut – so he'd turned the car around and decided to just go for it. He couldn't leave Simba without his medicine so he'd have to take his chances with the turkey.

'Hold on, Dot.' He pushed the door open and got out, looking left and right. Theo grabbed the bag of medicine Kirsteen had given him from the passenger seat before trotting around to the back. He'd never been afraid of an animal in all his years of working as a vet, but his heart beat like a set of bongo drums when he heard a sudden rustling sound – then Henry came charging out of the darkness, squawking and warbling.

'Dammit!' Theo snapped, immediately unlocking the boot and grabbing the dog's lead. He felt the peck from a beak on his behind and yelped in pain as Dot began to bark. 'Stop!' He twisted around and waved the medicine bag like a weapon while helping his dog to the ground. 'Calm down, I'm not going to hurt you!' he yelled. Then he closed the boot and half ran, half slid towards the door of Chestnut Cottage, feeling like a fool. He saw a light go on in the hallway and then Merry was nudging her face through a sliver of a gap at the door. Her eyes widened when she saw him. Dot started to tug and Theo dropped the lead – then the dog skipped in between Merry's legs just as he slipped and plunged onto the icy driveway, scraping his hand on something hidden by snow. Theo felt a sharp peck on his back and leapt up, sprinting to the house. Merry stepped out of the way and he lurched past before helping her slam the door in the turkey's face. 'For God's sake!' Theo spluttered as he let out a shuddering breath. Outside the door he could hear gobbling and what sounded almost like an evil cackle of laughter. 'That thing needs to be served up with Brussels sprouts, gravy and roast potatoes,' he said angrily.

'I'm not sure what Aunt Ava would think about that – especially since she's a vegetarian.' Merry frowned and reached out to take his hand. 'You're bleeding, did Henry do that?'

Theo shook his head. 'I cut it when I fell in the snow. It's just a scratch.' He pulled away as the contact sent something wild and unexpected skidding up his arm. 'How's your knee?'

'Mostly better,' Merry said.

Theo took a moment to look at her. She wore a yellow dressing gown, hot pink pyjamas, fluffy grey slippers and she'd wound her hair into some kind of bun thing which was coming loose.

'I wasn't expecting visitors.' Obviously embarrassed, she wrapped her arms around herself and stomped down the hallway towards the kitchen.

The fire was roaring, the Christmas lights were on and Theo couldn't help comparing the space with his own stark kitchen where the cupboard doors were still piled up next to the counter and all his decorations – the few Miranda had let him take – were still packed away in the loft.

'I've been writing,' she explained when he paused beside her open laptop. She'd unpacked the rest of the boxes and there were mounds of eclectic items piled up on the table. The tiara; a small sewing kit; a plectrum; a silver tankard; two necklaces, each with half a broken heart; a knitting pattern for a bird's nest that seemed a little random; a magnetic tool belt which was the right size for a man's wrist; a snow shovel; a gold eyeglass chain; two pink and green swimming hats; an apron; a small painting of a cow; a large torch; and a Christmas hat with gloves that matched the jumper Tavish had been wearing in the pub. That was sixteen items in all and there were four more packages still obscured by bubble wrap which added up to twenty. He stared at the presents and then back at Merry, remembering what Tavish had suspected. Was it possible Merry's Aunt Ava had left her in charge of sorting out the village's Secret Santa gifts? If she had, why weren't they all wrapped?

'You look stressed,' he said, taking in the lines around Merry's eyes and across her forehead, the way she kept nibbling her fingernails. He was frustrated that he'd noticed – that he could feel that familiar tug in his chest that told him he wanted to fix whatever was bothering her.

'I've got lots on my mind.' Merry's eyes moved back to the presents and she frowned. Then she grabbed a couple of tea towels from one of the kitchen drawers and draped them over the top of the pile without saying why. 'What are you doing here? I'm guessing it's not just to fight with Henry...'

Theo held up the battered white bag. 'Apparently Simba's run out of his diabetes medicine. You were supposed to pick more up from the vet.'

She paled. *'That's* what the pills were for. I saw the box in a drawer, saw his name and tried to put it in his food. Not that he ate any of his dinner.' She gritted her teeth. 'I ground the dose up really small but it's like he knew.' Her eyes swept the room. 'I planned to call the surgery tomorrow morning to see if the medication was important...'

'It is,' Theo murmured, glancing around the kitchen. The cat was curled up on the sofa half asleep and he went to scratch behind his ears. 'A couple of days without it and Simba might be a little sluggish. He'll also be extra hungry. Has he been trying to steal your food?'

Merry looked troubled. 'He jumped onto the counter earlier and tried to eat ham from my sandwich. I thought it was because he'd refused his meal. I was cross.' She looked stricken. 'Poor Simba, I feel awful.' She nibbled her thumbnail, her face ashen.

'It's not your fault,' Theo said automatically, then frowned. This wasn't working out as he'd planned. He was supposed to drop the bag with Merry and leave – but he couldn't bring himself to go. 'I'll show you how to give him the medicine – there are a few things you can try. It's not uncommon for cats to turn their noses up at anything that smells or looks different, it's just the way they are,' he explained. 'It's not your fault. They can be stubborn.' His chest fluttered when colour returned to her cheeks.

Chewy scampered from behind the sofa and Merry raised an eyebrow at the rabbit. 'Stubborn beats destructive hands down. I'll bet Aunt Ava told me all about Simba's medicine and left me tips on how to give it to him, but of course *somebody* ate all my notes.' Her attention drifted to Theo's hand when a trickle of blood dripped onto the tiles. 'I'm going to clean that wound. It's the least I can do. A thank you for another emergency visit.'

'I'm fine.'

'You're bleeding on Aunt Ava's kitchen floor.' She held up a palm and went to grab a first-aid kit from one of the kitchen cabinets before signalling at him to sit. When he didn't, she marched over and pressed a fingertip to his chest. 'I've got three brothers – bossy, interfering and over-protective brothers who never let me help with anything. You're beginning to remind me of them,' she said sweetly.

Theo huffed but he sank back into the chair because, dammit, his hand hurt and it wasn't just the floor now; blood had dripped on his jeans.

'My point is, even they'd let me apply a plaster and I thought they'd cornered the market in macho and stupid. I'm not going to mess it up,' she said quietly.

Theo didn't comment as he watched Merry dip a piece of cotton wool into antiseptic and carefully dab the graze on his hand. The cut was deep but didn't look serious. It burned like hell, though, and he gritted his teeth instead of crying out. Merry had to move closer to study it and Theo smelled a tantalising mixture of gingerbread and cinnamon. It was such an innocent scent but he knew that every time he walked past a bakery from now on he'd think about her – and she was a million miles from the type of woman he wanted to think about.

'The good news is, it won't kill you. Does it hurt?' she asked as he sucked in another breath as she dabbed it.

'No,' he said tightly.

'You're not going to admit it feels better either,' Merry mocked as she covered the cut with a plaster. 'You are exactly like my three brothers.'

'It feels better,' Theo replied stonily because for some reason he didn't like being compared to her siblings. 'How are you getting on with the rest of the animals?' he deflected.

She pulled a face. 'Well, they're still alive – just – but the hens didn't lay again today.'

Theo frowned. 'There could be dozens of reasons for that. I'll pop back tomorrow in daylight and take a look.' After he'd tracked down some cranberries. 'I can check up on Simba too.'

'You really need to stop visiting.' Merry frowned. 'I mean, I'm grateful obviously but...'

'I'd rather keep an eye on the animals.' Theo cleared his throat. 'It's all part of the service. Remember...' He pointed a finger at his chest. 'Vet.'

Merry gazed at him, looking torn. 'Okay, but make sure you put all these call-outs on my account. I'm supposed to be handling the animals and everything else by myself. It's important to me.'

Theo dipped his chin. He wouldn't bill Merry for any of it. He probably should, but the idea didn't sit right. Nevertheless, he wasn't going to argue – it wasn't as though she was likely to chase the missing invoice before she left for home.

'You wouldn't need to keep helping if I had my aunt's instructions...' Merry's gaze drifted to the pile of gifts on the table again and her shoulders sagged – making something in Theo's memory click.

Was that why the presents weren't wrapped? Was it something to do with the shredded notes?

'Do you want a drink? I need one.' Merry wandered to the fridge and pulled out a bottle of white wine, waving Theo away when he tried to get up.

'I had a pint in the pub earlier so I'd better not, but I'll take some black coffee if you have instant.' He scratched his chin, torn between wanting to leave before he did something he regretted and that irritating part of himself that wanted to fix whatever was bothering her.

Merry put the kettle on and poured herself some wine before settling into the chair opposite. Her eyes scoured the array of gifts partially hidden by the tea towels, her lips thinning before she dragged her attention away. 'How long have you lived in Christmas Village?' she asked.

'A little over two months,' Theo said. 'I'm still finding my feet, getting to know the locals.'

Merry got up when the kettle boiled and busied herself taking out a mug and spooning in coffee granules. 'Where did you move from?' She poured water into his mug.

'London.'

'That's a big change. Don't you miss being around lots of people?' Wind whistled outside and her whole body stiffened. 'I'm still not used to the noises,' she murmured. 'If my brothers knew how remote this house was they'd take it in turns to drive up and babysit. Assuming they could find it.'

'Haven't they visited here before?' Theo asked, surprised.

'Aunt Ava is a little eccentric. My mum died when I was five and Ava wanted to get involved in raising me. She asked if I could at least spend my holidays in Scotland – but Dad wouldn't agree. He was very over-protective.' She shrugged. 'They fell out and... we lost touch until a few months ago.' Wind rattled the window again and Merry winced. 'I honestly don't know how Ava stands living here.' She brought the mug of coffee to the table. 'It's so lonely – we could be the last people on earth.'

'A lot of people move here *because* it's so remote,' Theo said.

'Is that why you came?' Merry asked, pulling out her chair.

He let out a long breath. 'I wanted a new start,' he admitted but didn't elaborate even when she looked at him expectantly. Instead, he wrapped his fingers around his mug.

'I did, too.' Merry filled the silence and leaned forwards. Her dressing gown fell open and Theo could see a hint of smooth, olive skin at the top of her pyjamas. He swallowed an unwelcome flood of lust.

'I wanted to prove I could do anything I wanted.' She

sipped more of her drink and leaned back in her chair. Light from above caught the edge of her face and he saw a silvery scar that ran from her right eye downwards. He hadn't noticed it before today; perhaps she'd covered it with make-up. More secrets? It was unnerving how badly he wanted to ask.

'How's that working out?' Theo watched her expression as she considered the question, ignoring the visceral pull he could feel arching between them.

'Let's see.' Merry tapped her chin. 'Chewy died before his startling resurrection, and let's not forget Simba missing out on his diabetes medicine.' She waved a finger at him. 'I slipped on a patch of ice and nearly broke my leg, *oh* and my aunt's hens have stopped laying. The worst thing is, Chewy ate most of my aunt's notes and now I can't do something that I...' She trailed off and sipped another mouthful of wine, pressing her lips together.

It definitely sounded like the rabbit had eaten more than just the animal instructions. Theo leaned back in his chair, trying not to look too interested. It was obvious Merry wasn't going to confide in him, which was for the best. He'd only come because of Simba; he wasn't responsible for anything else. Still, the fact that she needed his help niggled at him.

'You know, I met someone today in the village who wears tiaras.' The words slipped out before Theo's brain could catch up with his mouth.

Merry's eyes widened. 'Is that so?' she asked. 'Um, who was it?' Her voice was unnaturally toneless.

'Edina Lachlan – she lives in Evergreen Castle,' he said slowly.

He watched relief glide across Merry's face and felt a corresponding warmth in his chest. Nothing beat that feeling – the one that said you'd made someone's day better, fixed whatever was troubling them. If only people didn't use it to take advantage. He waited, expecting Merry to say more – perhaps even to ask for his assistance – as he considered whether he'd agree and decided he couldn't anyway.

Merry's lips glued together and she deliberately turned away from the pile of gifts, picking up her glass and glugging the rest of her wine. Then she rose and tracked to the bag, drawing out the packet. 'Can you show me how to get Simba to take his medicine before you leave? It's getting late, you ought to get going soon.'

Theo gazed at her, wondering why his gut felt like he'd been sucker-punched. This was what he'd wanted. He wasn't here to be a hero; he was done with rescuing women. He could walk away now with a clear conscience, leave Merry to sort out her problems for herself. But as Theo took the pack of medicine from her fingers he wondered if walking away was going be as easy as he hoped.

8

Chewy lay on the velvet sofa with his legs facing skywards when Merry headed downstairs the following morning. The instant she saw him her heart rate kicked up, but then she stopped in her tracks and narrowed her eyes, watching him carefully for signs of life.

'I know what you're up to,' she said, wandering to grab the rabbit a bowl of food and putting it on the floor before turning to Simba, who was regarding her solemnly through narrowed eyes. 'It'll be your turn next.' She eyed the bag of medicine. Theo had stayed for a while longer the night before and shown her how to gently rub the cat's nose to stimulate swallowing so he'd take a pill before Merry had whisked him out of the front door, keeping an eye on the vet until he made it to his car. She was attracted to him, too attracted, because instead of trusting her to solve her own problems, he kept trying to *help*...

'I was going to tell Theo everything,' she confided in the rabbit, who was still lying prone on the sofa. 'The heroine in my novel, Carmel, would never do something like that. She'd work out who the presents belonged to and Dan would stand aside and let her do it herself.' She squinted at Chewy again and took a step forwards, suddenly nervous she'd got it wrong when his ears didn't so much as twitch. Then she saw his chest rise and fall and her whole body relaxed. 'Which just goes to show I haven't learned anything. Then again...' She skipped across the kitchen and put the kettle on. When she turned, Chewy had jumped off of the sofa and was slowly approaching the bowl. 'I *didn't* tell him.' She'd wanted to, though, it would have been so easy. A problem shared – only it wouldn't have ended there. How long would it have been before the vet had taken over, just like her brothers always did, until she was just a shadow of herself again? This was *her* problem to fix, *her* life to reclaim, and she'd do it alone.

She made a cup of tea and brought it to the kitchen table, taking in the pile of unwrapped presents. She'd wrapped the tiara after Theo had left the evening before and scrawled 'Edina Lachlan' onto the label in black. She picked it up before placing it in the empty red sack. 'One down, nineteen to go.' She groaned. 'I'm going to have to visit the main high street today so I can meet the villagers and work out which of these gifts belongs to whom.' Her blood ran cold when she thought about being around a bunch of strangers and she pressed a fingertip to her scar, running the pad from the edge of her right eye all the way down to her chin. It was just a small bump now and she hardly noticed it most days – make-up could disguise it pretty well. But it still caught her off guard sometimes.

Her mobile buzzed in her pocket and she pulled it out. *How's it going?* Noah had messaged.

Great!!! she immediately typed back, hoping the triple exclamation marks would encourage him to believe her.

My weather app says there's a storm brewing, it might be best if you didn't go out. Whatever happens, don't even think about driving.

'As if.' Merry snorted. But she knew Noah would call in an hour to check up on her. All three of her brothers would – like they were taking part in a telephonic relay race. They'd be worried – and they'd try to extract a lot of promises she was determined not to make.

Merry stared at the message for a few moments before putting her mobile back into her pocket. There would be hell to pay later, but if she was going to change, take back control of her life, she had to start now. She'd become too passive, too malleable to other people's whims and too afraid to take risks, scared of what might happen. She checked her watch: she needed to write a few pages of her novel, then feed the animals outside before heading to Rowan's in time for lunch. The cafe should be busy by then, especially since it was a Friday. If she sat in the corner, she could study some of Christmas Village's residents and fix her Secret Santa problem for herself. Suddenly fired up, Merry sat at the kitchen table, switched on her laptop and loaded her manuscript before scanning the last few paragraphs and frowning at the screen. As Merry's fingers flew across the keyboard, she was instantly immersed in the world of Dan and Carmel.

Carmel whisked her long black plait behind her right shoulder and her eyes were drawn to the syringe of medicine in Dan's large hand as he frowned at the snake, his indigo-blue eyes troubled. They were in a small wooden hut in the African jungle which doubled as a temporary veterinary clinic and a young boy had asked them to take care of his poorly pet. The problem was, the medicine had to be swallowed by the snake, and it was far from an easy patient.

Merry looked up from the keyboard. The day before when she'd been writing, her hero Dan had suddenly morphed from a policeman into a vet. Merry had tried to change him back, but the character kept taking her in new and unexpected directions. She'd go with it for a while, see where the story took her. She set her fingers back on the keys.

'You hate snakes. Let me do this,' Carmel offered, swiping her suddenly sweaty palms on her green cargo shorts. 'You hold it, that way you can control the head and you won't have to look it in the eye.'

'I'm really not sure,' Dan growled, his expression darkening.

'Trust me,' Carmel said, staring up at him. She thought he might refuse, those bone-deep protective instincts might take over. Instead, he nodded and handed her the syringe but his full lips, the ones she'd been dreaming about recently, pressed together.

An hour later Merry looked up from the keyboard and rolled her aching shoulders. She'd lost track of time as she'd written about Carmel using a credit card to unfasten the snake's jaws so she could pry its mouth open and slide in the syringe. Merry's stomach had been in knots as the scene unfolded, overcome by Dan's quiet acceptance of Carmel's desire to put herself in harm's way when all his instincts would have been screaming at him to make her stop. This was the kind of person she needed in her world. Someone who'd support her in her quest to live her own life instead of suffocating her with their own protective impulses. Her mind drifted to Theo and she shook her head. Dan might have transformed into a vet, but that was the only similarity between her hero and Theo – and she would do well to remember that.

Rowan's Cafe was halfway along Christmas Village's main high street and snow was falling heavily by the time Merry arrived.

She'd briefly considered driving her aunt's Jeep but just the thought of getting behind the wheel made her want to throw up. She stood at the window of the cafe, peering inside. Someone had strewn gold and red tinsel across the ceiling and steam from the hot drinks of customers who were chatting around the tables rose into the decorations, making the place look warm and welcoming. Merry pressed her nose to the glass, ignoring the chill in her bones, and stamped her snow boots onto the ground, dislodging an avalanche of ice. Then she grabbed hold of the door handle, took in a bracing breath and stepped inside.

The shop was cosy, with a large glass counter positioned at the back which displayed a mouth-watering spread of sandwiches, cakes and festive pastries. Behind the booth, Merry spotted Rowan taking an order from a customer and a girl with curly honey-brown hair wrestling with a silver coffee machine which was puffing out steam. There was a door behind them that led to the kitchen – and Merry could hear the clatter of utensils and someone yelling orders from inside. She approached the counter and stood behind a tall shapely woman wearing a bright pink minidress.

'Diet Coke and a salad please,' the woman said in a strong American accent. She leaned on the counter and when Rowan looked up from her order pad she spotted Merry and beamed.

'Ach, you made it, lass! Good thing too, I was going to give you one more day and then come and get you myself.' She waved her forwards. 'This is Kenzy Campbell who runs The Workshop just along the high street. If you need any beauty treatments while you're here, this is your woman. She's dating Logan Forbes, who takes care of most of the gardening and odd jobs in the village,' she confided.

'Logan also takes care of me.' The woman turned to Merry and winked. She was stunning with long blonde hair and the type of face that inspired poetry. The good kind. 'It's awesome to meet you. I'm friends with Belle Albany and she mentioned you were staying in the village,' Kenzy said, her voice warm. 'Why don't you join us for lunch? Belle's meeting me here soon.'

'Oh, I'm—' Merry felt her cheeks flame. She wasn't used to socialising any more and the woman's friendliness was a little overwhelming.

'What a wonderful idea,' Rowan interrupted before Merry could refuse. 'I'll get Hannah to bring you over a Christmas coffee and order you our soup of the day – on the house.'

Merry allowed herself to be steered towards a bright green table in the corner of the cafe with a tiny Christmas tree adorning the centre. Seconds later, the woman with curly hair who'd been wrestling with the coffee machine approached them with a tray. 'Hi there, I'm Hannah. Rowan said I should take my break. Do you mind if I join you?'

'Please do!' Kenzy pulled out a chair and made space on the table for the drinks.

'I think you met my son Ace at the school? I volunteer there in the library on Wednesday afternoons. I'm sorry I missed you when you came.' Hannah beamed at Merry as she sat, sighing with pleasure as her bum connected with the chair. 'Ace said you really helped inspire his class. He was very excited about his Christmas story when he got home and he's already planned a festive car chase.' She snickered.

'It was only one lesson.' Merry flushed.

'I've always wanted to write,' Hannah confided. 'I've just never found the time, or maybe I'm just too afraid it wouldn't be any good.' She handed Kenzy a glass of Diet Coke and her salad and placed a huge mug topped with whipped cream and sprinkles in front of Merry along with a bowl of soup before putting the tray on the floor.

'You should come to the pub with us on Monday night,' Kenzy said suddenly. 'We have a monthly cocktail evening – women only.' Her shapely eyebrows performed a mini dance.

'Yep, definitely no men,' Hannah hissed. 'Especially not—'

'Sam Doherty,' Kenzy jumped in, turning to wink at Merry. 'Long story. Hannah will tell you all about it when she's got several cocktails inside her.'

'Nothing to tell,' Hannah muttered airily.

'Oh, I'm not sure I'll be able to come...' Merry faltered.

'I'll pick you up.' Belle's voice rang out from behind them and the schoolteacher sat in the seat beside Merry, putting her large leather bag onto the floor. 'Logan usually drives us all home, too.'

'My hero.' Kenzy sighed, tapping a hand on her chest just as Rowan appeared with a tray of food.

'Ach, lass, it's good to see you out and about. Your aunt was worried you'd squirrel yourself away and left us strict instructions to make sure you mingled.' She moved the tray she was holding into her right palm, exposing a long white apron with the words '*Complain at your peril*' printed across the front in black lettering.

Merry stared at it. She'd seen a chef's hat in with the Secret Santa presents yesterday afternoon and had unwrapped it, giggling when she'd read the slogan across the top: '*Warning, my knives are even sharper than me*'. She cleared her throat. 'Have any of you heard of the local Secret Santa?' she pried, wondering if she might discover more about the tradition if she asked a few careful questions. 'My aunt mentioned something about it in some notes she left...'

'Aye,' Rowan said, putting a hand on her hip. 'It's a custom in the village. I'm not surprised Ava mentioned it, it's a big deal here.'

'Is it?' Merry asked, trying not to look too interested. 'So what happens?'

'A sack is left somewhere in the clearing by the fir tree at the end of the high street on Christmas morning and the villagers gather to sing carols and to hand out the gifts.'

'Does everyone go?' Merry asked, thinking about Theo and the present he'd seen.

'Not really. Mainly it's the villagers who've lived here the longest, or those with a family history,' Hannah said. 'Because they know about the tradition. Newbies rarely come.'

Which meant the vet probably wouldn't be there. So even if Theo saw the gifts at Chestnut Cottage, he was unlikely to connect them with Secret Santa. Merry blew out a breath, relieved. At least she didn't have to keep hiding them from him. 'Who buys the presents?'

'No one knows,' Kenzy said and Merry's stomach dropped. 'Belle got colouring pens last year.'

'A huge pack,' the teacher agreed.

'And who gets presents?' Merry asked. Would Rowan have a solution to her dilemma?

'Could be anyone. But all the villagers who receive gifts have helped someone during the year,' Rowan explained, lowering her voice.

'Belle's always helping people,' Kenzy said, her eyes shining with pride. 'She usually gets something.' The women all smiled.

Merry frowned, knowing that wouldn't help her work out what Belle's gift was this year. There weren't any colouring pens in the piles of presents and she guessed her aunt was unlikely to get the same thing again. 'When did Secret Santa start, how long's it been going on?' she asked, picking up her drink and taking a sip, trying to look nonchalant.

'Around two hundred years. The same year we had a flood in the valley,' Rowan explained.

'Aye,' Hannah murmured. 'A lot of families lost everything but the rest of the villagers rallied around, helped them to rebuild and replace what was lost. That same Christmas, all those who helped received a Secret Santa gift. The tradition's been continued since then, but whoever's responsible has never been identified.'

'It must be one of the families who lost everything, surely?' Kenzy asked but Rowan and Hannah both shrugged.

'Could be, but there were a lot of families and they've all multiplied so it's almost impossible to guess now,' Rowan said. 'No one ever has and a lot have tried.'

'People are always gossiping about who it might be in my salon.' Kenzy scoured the tables in the cafe. 'Everyone here is being watched just in case they do too much shopping or ask too many questions. Especially around this time of year.'

'Wow.' Merry picked up her drink again. She knew a bit more about Secret Santa now but it wasn't going to help much. She did understand she'd have to be extra careful. Make sure she didn't arouse suspicion – which would make working out what belonged to whom even more difficult.

Still, she knew the tiara was for Edina, the chef's hat was definitely for Rowan and she'd wrap that one later. Now she just had to figure out who the other eighteen presents were for...

9

Fiona Price was absolutely stunning. She had blonde hair which she'd tied into a neat bun that was sans any of the usual tendrils that type of 'do' typically involved – and she wore a purple blouse and cool grey suit with no creases. Perhaps she had one of those hotel suit presses in her car boot? Theo should have been on his knees with his jawline hitting him somewhere mid-chest; he should have been scrawling through his calendar so he could pin her down for a date. Instead, he sat with his hands pressed into his lap as she clicked through a presentation on her laptop, explaining all the stunning things she'd like to do to his... *kitchen*.

The woman oozed efficiency and confidence but Theo found himself losing focus as she talked him through the various options. On one level, he knew he should be excited. This was exactly the kind of thing he'd envisioned when he'd first seen Holly Lodge on the estate agent's website. But his mind kept skimming over the layout, unit and colour scheme options before wandering to Merry. Where was she? He looked out of the picture window at the end of the kitchen to check the weather again and his chest tightened. A snow storm had been brewing all afternoon and the large grey clouds that had been sitting on the edge of the horizon above the loch had grown exponentially in the last hour. What if she'd gone for a walk again and been spooked by Bob the donkey? She'd been so afraid of the slightest noise the evening before – how would she cope with a Scottish storm? He let out a long puff of air, irritated. It really was none of his business...

'Mr Ellis-Lee.' Fiona interrupted his thoughts, her refined voice calm as she paused, probably waiting for him to focus.

'Theo,' he said as he turned and met her cool blue eyes. He could still see a glimmer of interest in them. Had the minute he'd opened the door to her. He should have felt a similar attraction, a punch of lust right through to his bones. Fiona was exactly the type of woman he'd been hoping to meet when he'd split with Miranda and left London. *Professional, independent, self-sufficient.* Instead he just felt... indifferent.

'Sorry.' He cleared his throat and pointed out of the window. 'The weather's getting worse. Would it be better if we rescheduled? I don't want you getting stuck in Christmas Village. I appreciate you taking the time to do a face-to-face visit but it's a long way back to Inverness.'

Her lush red lips spread wide. 'I've lived around the Highlands for a few years now, Theo. I can handle a little snow.' She chuckled in a way that suggested his gesture of concern was sweet but unnecessary. 'I'm really quite the grown-up.' Her eyelids fluttered.

He fidgeted on the stool. If he left now before the bad weather really got going, he'd make it to Chestnut Cottage and have plenty of time to drive home. A phone call wouldn't be enough to settle this knot of anxiety in his throat. He wanted to check on Merry and help her to feed the animals so she didn't have to do it herself. It wasn't just for her: he had a responsibility to make sure she took proper care of her aunt's pets.

'I'm sorry.' Theo found himself rising from the chair as if a puppet master were controlling his limbs. He watched Fiona's eyebrows shoot skywards but couldn't bring himself to change his mind. 'I'm...' He cleared his throat. 'I've remembered I have another appointment.' His attention darted to the window again. Were the clouds even bigger? 'Please forgive me, I love *all* your ideas.' He waved at her laptop as her expression clouded. 'Really,' he added when she stared at him, clearly shocked. 'Can you email me a copy of the presentation and we can arrange a way forwards?' He started to head for the front door. Fiona had pulled a shiny Mercedes-Benz up beside it an hour earlier when she'd parked. Dot scampered ahead, as if she were in a hurry to show the woman out too. Had his dog sensed where they were headed?

'Well, okay,' Fiona said quietly. 'I'd be happy to come back another time.' She pushed the laptop shut and dropped it into an elegant black shoulder bag and then picked up her practical black coat, shrugging it on soundlessly.

'I'll email you,' he said tonelessly, opening the door. The blast of icy wind almost knocked him sideways. 'Take care on the drive back, won't you? The hill up from this valley can be perilous. Do you want to message me when you get home so I know you made it safely?' The offer was instinctive.

Fiona chuckled as she pressed a button on the keys and the lights on her car winked on. 'I'll be fine, Theo.' She gazed back at him. 'I suggest you take care of whatever it is that's bothering you. When you want to discuss your kitchen again, you know where I am...'

Theo watched the kitchen designer walk to the car, waited until she'd up fired the engine and eased her Mercedes out of the drive, wondering exactly where his head had gone. Had Jake been right? Was he really just the equivalent of a German Shepherd in human form? Was this more about nature than nurture – was he capable of fighting this instinct, his need to protect? He let out a long breath as he went to pick up his veterinary bag and keys.

The weather was worse than Theo had expected and he drove at a slow crawl as wind and snowflakes the size of building blocks battered the window of his old Range Rover. Even Dot was crouched in the boot – she'd whined a couple of times and he suspected even now, his dog had one of her paws pressed against her eyes. He shouldn't have come. He knew he shouldn't. But once the idea had taken hold, the uncomfortable tightness across his chest, he couldn't settle. But he'd had time to think on the drive. He'd check up on Merry and the animals, make sure they were fed, maybe give her some hints on another of those Secret Santa gifts, then he'd head back to Holly Lodge before the weather got worse. When he arrived, he'd give Fiona a call about the kitchen and apologise again. Maybe even ask her on a date...

The gate was closed when he arrived at Chestnut Cottage and it took him a couple of tries to heave it open because a small drift had piled up in front. Once he'd coasted his car onto the drive and shut the gate again, he realised the heavy snowfall would probably make it harder to reopen when he left later. He considered leaving it ajar but knew he couldn't risk Henry making a break for it, no matter how tempting the idea. He could see Christmas lights sparkling inside the house and felt the tension in his shoulders drain out because it meant Merry was probably home and safe. As he drew closer, he spotted a set of boot prints leading from the front door across the garden towards the pig enclosure. They were fresh, which suggested Merry might be outside. He got his veterinary bag from the car and followed Dot, holding onto her lead as she scampered ahead, following Merry's tracks. There was no sign of the turkey who was probably more sensible than him and had already holed itself away from the storm. Theo had bought some cranberries in the village earlier and one of his coat pockets was stuffed full so he kept his eyes peeled and dropped a few in the snow as he walked.

Merry had hung a lantern torch inside the pig pen and even from where Theo was walking now, he could hear her voice. She sounded annoyed and he picked up his pace when he heard the low buzz of a man's voice. Did she have someone in there with her? The powerful wave of jealously took him by surprise.

'I'm fine,' Merry grumbled from the barn. 'Please Ollie, stop fussing. You know why I have to do this...'

'I really don't.' The man snorted. 'Look, someone's at the door, give me a minute, this conversation isn't finished!'

Theo stopped at the entrance of the barn and stayed out of sight. He could see Merry through the gap at the edge of the doorway as she shovelled corn into one of the troughs. She was wearing a coat that was too big for her, snow boots, a pink bobble hat and what looked like her pink pyjamas. She was so bundled up she reminded him of one of those cute LEGO mini figures he used to play with when he was a boy. The comparison should have put him off, but he felt inexplicably drawn to her. Her mobile phone lay on a crate which had been upended at the edge of the space and she'd put it on speaker – she'd obviously turned the volume up to maximum because he'd been able to hear every word of her conversation. Merry finished shovelling and stepped back as three plump, pink pigs snorted and charged past her, immediately dipping their snouts into the trough. 'Well Larry, Curly and Moe, you guys were hungry.' She grinned, watching them eat.

Theo pressed his face closer to the gap, holding Dot behind him and praying his dog wouldn't bark and give them away. He scanned the pen – it looked clean and Merry had clearly followed his instructions precisely. She'd fed the pigs just the right amount of food, proving she didn't need him as much as he'd expected. He fought the surge of surprise, ignoring the disappointment that swiftly followed it.

'You can't stay there.' Ollie's voice suddenly boomed from the mobile again, picking up the conversation and startling Merry. 'You're not thinking straight. You were in a coma two years ago – you've got that scar on your face as a reminder for us all.'

Theo saw Merry wince and felt a punch of anger. He understood bluntness, but drawing attention to her injury seemed unnecessarily cruel. Who was this idiot? He waited as Merry pushed her spade into the ground, expecting tears or recriminations. Instead, she spun around so her back was to him – then she lifted her head skywards as if she were praying for patience.

'I know the accident was hard on all of you. I'm your sister and I get it.' So this was one of Merry's brothers! Relief washed through him. 'But I'm better now,' she continued in a tone that was far calmer than her sibling deserved. 'The only thing that needs fixing is my life.'

'I know you think you need to do this.' Her brother's voice filled the pen, his tone kinder than before, which was some-thing. 'But you were doing okay at home. The weather up there is treacherous and you're alone. We're all so worried...'

Merry hissed. 'Which is exactly the problem. I already told you, I'm twenty-five. I have to stand on my own feet sometime. I love all of you, but you're not responsible for me...'

'Dad asked us to take care of you,' another male voice piped up from the phone.

'Noah,' Merry groaned. 'Dad should never have put that on your shoulders. He was always over-protective... even more so after Mum died. Maybe because I was the youngest and the only girl? As much as I appreciate it, all this anxiety about my whereabouts and safety has been holding me back. It's not your fault but I've become afraid to take chances or to do anything for myself.'

'You don't need to do things for yourself – you have us!' another deeper voice grumbled from the speaker. Merry's other brother, Theo guessed. She'd mentioned she had three and that they were domineering. Right before she'd compared them to him – his brow furrowed at the realisation. How would she feel about him spying on her now? Feeling uncomfortable, he started to ease away from the door.

'So you're here too, Liam,' Merry said softly, turning so Theo could see her face as she banged a palm onto her forehead and shut her eyes. He stopped in his tracks because suddenly he couldn't bring himself to leave. This wasn't the woman he'd been expecting when he'd set out from his house. Merry was far less vulnerable, far more determined to do things for herself, far less like Miranda than he'd supposed. His ex would have dropped to her knees and begged Merry's brothers to come up and help, before asking them to stop by Waitrose to pick up some emergency champagne and foie gras.

'I'm just asking for a few weeks. I'm writing again for the first time in ages, doing a good job of taking care of myself and Aunt Ava's pets. I'm not so scared of my own shadow here.' She looked around the pen and trembled. 'At least, I'm working on it – and I'm helping at the school, I've made some friends...'

A gust of wind howled and something banged in the distance, making Merry recoil and her eyes grow saucerish – she looked terrified but didn't give it away.

'What was that?' Liam snapped, sounding concerned.

'Just a storm. Nothing to worry about.' Merry's voice didn't betray the fear plastered over her face.

'We've had a family meeting and we've decided we should all come up. Each of us has holiday owing and we can take it in turns to stay and help,' one of the brothers offered as Merry scowled.

Theo balled his fingers into his palms, forcing himself to stay where he was. His instinct was to get involved, but he had to stay out of it.

'I don't—'

'You're taking care of a lot of animals by yourself, think of it as free labour. Besides, none of us like the idea of you spending Christmas alone.'

Merry let out a whimper and tugged off her pink bobble hat, scrunching it tightly in her hands. 'Look, I don't want you to come. I'm—'

There was another sudden gust of wind and Dot unexpectedly pulled hard on her lead. The leather slipped from between Theo's fingers and the dog charged, shoving him through the door and making Merry cry out before she glared at them. 'Dammit. Theo, what are you doing here?' She bent to stroke the Dalmatian's head as the dog batted her face against Merry's thigh.

'Who's *Theo*?' a voice he suspected belonged to Noah growled. 'You didn't tell us you had a man with you!'

'This is Doctor Ellis-Lee. He's not a man, he's...' Merry scowled at him, screwing up her nose. 'Aunt Ava's vet,' she finished, looking annoyed.

Theo did his best not to look offended.

'Are you dating?' a gruff voice demanded.

'Of course not!' Merry snorted. 'He thinks I'm as useless as you all do.'

Theo opened his mouth to protest and closed it when she zipped a finger across her mouth.

'I've got to go now – he's come to...' She raised an eyebrow.

'I've been helping your sister take care of the animals,' he said softly. 'So you don't need to worry about coming here too.'

Merry narrowed her eyes, clearly realising he'd overheard at least some of the conversation.

'What are you doing there at this time of night?' Ollie asked, his voice filled with suspicion.

'I've come to check on the hens,' Theo said, holding Merry's gaze. She was glaring daggers at him now, no doubt intent on skinning him alive if he said the wrong thing in front of her brothers. 'Your sister mentioned they haven't been laying and I need to check it's not serious.'

Merry searched his face before her expression softened and she jerked her chin. 'Theo's right, they haven't. Look, I'll call you later, if I keep Dr Ellis-Lee for too long he's going to bill me overtime. Please don't worry – and for goodness' sake don't come up. I'll never forgive you if you do!' She walked to the mobile and hung up as they all started yelling. Then Merry spun round and took a step towards Theo, her pretty mouth making an odd series of angular shapes. 'You were listening to my call?'

He shook his head vehemently. 'Not really. I overheard by accident: I was coming to find you.' Theo held his breath, hoping Merry wouldn't ask exactly how much of the conversation he'd eavesdropped on.

Her face cleared and then she frowned. 'You told me it wouldn't matter if the hens didn't lay for a couple of days? As you can see...' She arched a finger at her mobile. 'I don't need any more people keeping an eye on me.'

'That's not why I'm here,' Theo said quickly, knowing if he was going to help Merry – and after listening to the latest performance from her brothers, he wanted to – she couldn't suspect it. Which meant he'd have to make up a plausible excuse for his visit. He cleared his throat. 'Um, there's this thing, this...' He searched his brain. 'I checked at the surgery earlier. There's a parasite that can get into the coop. It can stop the hens from laying. I just need to check it isn't that. If it is, it can be... um, really bad.' He was grasping at straws, praying she wouldn't be able to read his face. He'd never been a liar; that had always been more Miranda's thing. But if you told a few white ones for the right reasons that made it okay, didn't it?

Merry continued to look suspicious, then her shoulders sagged. 'Fine. The hens haven't laid again today so I suppose you ought to check on them since you're here.' She marched outside and shut the door to the pig pen, batting flakes of snow from her eyelids as she headed for the hen house. 'But you should have called instead. Told me what to look out for.' She looked up. 'No one should be out driving in this storm.'

Theo sighed. 'The parasite can be hard for a novice to identify. Besides, I was in the area.' The untruth made his stomach pitch. He kept up with Merry as she trooped across the garden, keeping his hands to himself when she almost tripped on some protruding shrubbery. It felt wrong not to reach out and take her arm, to ensure she didn't fall, but he guessed she wouldn't appreciate it and he didn't want to get any further on her bad side. When they arrived, she pulled the gate open and stared at him.

'Do you need to see inside? Shall I get a torch so I can shine some lights on the hens?' she offered.

'No.' Theo shook his head. He didn't want to disturb them. 'I should be able to tell just from smelling their bedding.' Feeling uncomfortable, he leaned his head towards the entrance of the chicken coop and took in a breath before pulling a face. 'I think it's possible that might be our problem,' he said.

'What have they got?' Merry asked, her eyes widening.

'Um, Egg Drop Syndrome,' he fibbed. It was a real virus, but Ava's hens didn't have it. Most likely they were just feeling out of sorts because her aunt was away. 'It's not serious if you catch it in time, so don't worry,' he said quickly when her cheeks paled. 'I brought the correct medicine with me just in case. You just need to feed Cluck, Eggitha and Hennifer a handful over the next few mornings and evenings. If we go into the house, I'll write up the instructions.' He wandered out of the chicken coop, tipping his eyes skywards, hoping he wasn't about to be hit by a bolt of lightning. If Merry checked up on the internet once they were inside, he was in for the roasting of his life.

He still wasn't sure what had driven him to lie. Perhaps it was listening to her brothers? The way they'd ganged up on her, how she'd fought back. He'd expected Merry to welcome their interference; instead, she'd put her foot down and insisted on fending for herself. He'd already liked her, but he hadn't expected to admire her too. She was out of her element here, clearly terrified, but she had no intention of asking for help, which made him even more determined to offer it... She was nothing like his ex. Nothing like he'd expected. The knowledge left him feeling surprised and confused.

Merry opened the front door of Chestnut Cottage and wiped her feet, standing back so Theo could enter. Dot scampered ahead as soon as he unhooked the lead. She'd already found her way to the fire and slumped beside Simba before he and Merry made it to the kitchen. Theo scanned the room – the gifts were all still piled on the oak table without the tea-towel covering today. A few more had been removed from the safety of their bubble wrap and, while he couldn't see the tiara anywhere, the rest appeared untouched.

'Do you want coffee?' Merry asked, tracking over to put on the kettle without waiting for a response.

Theo watched her take off her coat and drape it over the sofa, trying not to notice the way the pink pyjamas clung sexily to her shape. He swallowed and put his bag on one of the chairs and opened it. He had a bottle of vitamin powder in here somewhere and an empty pot he could tip it into. If Merry fed a handful to the hens, it wouldn't do them any harm and he'd have an excuse to visit again. He waited until she turned away to finish off the drinks before he decanted the powder into its new container, feeling a wave of discomfort that told him what he was doing was wrong. But it was for a good cause, which was the only justification he had.

'I'm sorry about my brothers,' Merry said as she brought him a mug.

Theo shrugged. 'You told me they were controlling.' He wanted to ask about the accident, but knew he couldn't admit to overhearing any more of their conversation. Instead, he took the coffee, put his bag onto the floor and sat. Wind whistled outside and something banged in the chimney, making Dot whine.

'I wish they'd just trust me,' she said quietly, walking up to peer out of the window.

Theo winced. Did he trust Merry to take care of the animals without him? Did he trust her to work out who the Secret Santa presents belonged to without assistance? Perhaps she could. But it would be easier if he helped – and she didn't have to know. 'Why don't they trust you?' he asked.

She shrugged, still standing with her back to him. 'An unquenchable need to defend. Also, none of them are in long-term relationships yet, so I'm the full focus of all those protective genes.' She fell silent for a moment. 'I was in a car accident two years ago and almost died. They're not really over it.' She drew in a breath and let it out slowly.

'I guess I can understand that,' Theo admitted but when Merry's shoulders tensed, he guessed he'd said the wrong thing.

'This storm is getting worse, you should probably get going.' She spun around to look at him, her expression shuttered.

Theo didn't want to leave – he knew Merry was okay but there was still that odd sense that she'd be better off if he stayed. But he rose, drinking the coffee down quickly before handing her the mug. 'Thanks for the drink,' he said, turning towards the hallway. Maybe this was for the best.

'Don't you need to leave the medicine?' she asked, sounding suspicious.

Theo swallowed and turned before reaching into his bag

and handing Merry the bottle. 'Sorry, I almost forgot. Just sprinkle a handful in with the hen feed for the next few days and that should fix it. But I will be back to check up on them tomorrow.'

'Surely that's not necessary?' she snapped. 'I can do it myself; you really don't have to come back.'

'I'm thinking of the hens.' Theo didn't look her in the eye, he couldn't. He felt a little sick as he made his way down the hallway towards the front door. Even Dot held back, as if she could feel the tension coursing through his veins. Or maybe she just didn't fancy another drive on the snow-plastered roads?

But when Merry opened the door they saw the driveway was now knee-deep in snow, which had piled up in front of the gate, making it impossible to open. She let out a frustrated moan. 'I'd better make up the spare room,' she said, her lips tightening. 'You're not going anywhere tonight.'

Theo grimaced, wondering if staying was such a good idea. He liked Merry more than he wanted to. If he stayed, would that complicate things even more? But when he looked back out at the driveway he realised he really had no choice.

10

Theo was here in her Aunt Ava's house, probably stark naked under the duvet in the spare bedroom. Merry's pulse fluttered wildly as she imagined all that smooth skin, the layers of hard muscle she'd been doing her best to ignore, and tried to make herself comfortable. She tugged up the cover on her bed before pushing it down because she felt too hot, then scraped a hand through her hair. She'd barely spoken to Theo after realising he'd be staying the night. There was a part of her that was delighted to have him around and another that was mortified. After the scene with her brothers, realising he'd overheard some of what they'd said... Merry shut her eyes. She was drawn to him – he wasn't just a gorgeous face and body, he was vet who rescued animals on a daily basis. A testosterone-fuelled hero who'd probably be on hand to save her from any situation she found herself in.

Dead rabbit, tick.

Crazed turkey, tick.

Injured knee, tick.

Sick hens, tick.

He'd managed to free her from the uncomfortable call with

her brothers and even inadvertently helped her work out who one of the Secret Santa gifts belonged to. If she wasn't careful, she'd just roll over and let him take charge, falling back into the negative patterns she'd been following for the last two years. Letting herself be rescued and taken care of. Having no real life of her own. Which was why she wasn't looking for a hero, and she suspected that was the only type of man Theo knew how to be.

She opened her eyes and lay in her bed staring at the ceiling, listening to the storm battering the roof. Would the animals be all right? She'd tried to find Henry earlier, but he'd obviously holed himself up somewhere safe. If the turkey knew what was good for him, he'd stay there. She turned to look at the window to the right of the bed with its floaty pink curtains. They were so flimsy they didn't block the tiny slivers of light from the moon poking between the clouds, although it was a wonder she could see anything considering the ferocity of the storm. She closed her eyes again for a few moments before sitting up in bed and switching on a lamp. She'd brought her laptop upstairs earlier and half an hour of writing would be the best cure for insomnia. The only possible distraction from Theo. She powered it up and quickly read through the last scene.

Chemistry had been brewing between Dan and Carmel over the last few chapters and they were sitting at a bar on a beach drinking beer, making eyes at each other, on the cusp of their first kiss. Tingles fizzed through Merry's limbs as she set her fingers to the keys. Would Carmel be brave enough to initiate and see the kiss through? And, if she was, how would Dan react? Her whole body heated as she began to type.

Carmel dared herself to be bold and reached up a fingertip so she could brush it down Dan's face, stroking the rough surface of stubble on the way. For a moment she wished the stubble was Braille so she could read it, know if he wanted to kiss her

*too. Her heart thumped louder in her chest and she deliber-
ately leaned forwards and pressed her lips to Dan's.*

*If he was surprised, he didn't show it. He didn't pull back
or push her away. Perhaps they'd been moving towards this
moment since they'd met? Dan hadn't touched her and
Carmel suspected he'd been waiting for her to make the first
move. Their connection was tentative at first, but then his
mouth moved under hers and she knew she'd done the right
thing. Felt another layer of her old self peel away...*

Merry slammed the lid of the laptop shut and puffed hair
from her eyes. Woah, she was hot, despite the gale still howling
outside, rattling the windows. Thirsty, too. She ran her tongue
across her gums, wondering why she could taste beer, then
eased out of her bed and put on a pair of slippers, ignoring her
dressing gown before creeping out of her room to the hall.
Merry took care to tread carefully on the polished oak floorboards as she passed the bedroom Theo was sleeping in. She
didn't want to wake him – the thought of seeing the vet now in a
half-dressed state made her uncomfortable. Sure, he'd seen her
in her pyjamas earlier, but they'd got dirty outside and the
nightdress she'd changed into was flimsier and stopped mid-
thigh. Halfway down the stairs, she noticed a multi-coloured
glow from the kitchen, suggesting the Christmas lights had been
switched back on. She stopped at the bottom of the stairway
and spotted the vet sitting at the kitchen table, inspecting the
pile of unwrapped presents. He'd moved a few aside, although
the bottle of lavender oil was sitting in front of him. He had a
pen and one of her aunt's Post-it notes in front of him too –
while one hand nursed a bottle of beer. The Dalmatian snored
quietly in front of the fire which Theo had obviously reignited
because it was flickering again and Simba was curled up on the
sofa close by.

Merry cleared her throat and padded into the room.

'Couldn't you sleep?' she asked and her voice came out husky, making a flush shoot up her cheeks.

Indigo-blue eyes shot to her, startled, then Theo ripped the top few Post-its from the pad and shoved them into his pocket, looking guilty. 'I'm sorry, I got distracted,' he murmured. 'Long to-do list,' he explained, clearing his throat.

Merry waved him down when he started to rise. 'You don't need to stop, I just came to get a drink. I couldn't sleep either.'

'Beer?' He shook his bottle. 'I hope it's okay that I helped myself but it can help with insomnia.'

'Is that your professional opinion?' she asked, wondering if she was flirting with him. She hadn't flirted for years. Had writing about Carmel made her bold, or was it just her hormones bursting back to life at the sight of Theo?

He chuckled, relaxing a little. Theo had rarely smiled in her company but it suited him. Added a layer of humour Merry was attracted to. 'Sort of, but I only give it to the animals if it's an emergency.' He studied her and she felt goosebumps rise across her skin. 'Is that a yes?'

Merry thought about her heroine. 'Why not?'

She watched him rise from his chair and pluck a bottle of beer from the fridge. Saw the open bottle of wine in the door and almost asked him for a glass of Chablis instead, before deciding to just go with it. It was what Carmel would do. She pulled out the chair opposite and pushed more of the presents aside, sighing because there were still so many to match with their owners and wrap, and she was running out of time. Then she watched Theo pop the lid from the bottle before handing it to her. He sat again and started to push his own drink back and forth between his fingers.

'Bad day? I didn't really ask earlier.' Merry watched something skate across his eyes before he shrugged.

'Interesting – I...' He puffed out a breath before leaning across the table and picking up a hand-painted cow in a silver frame from the pile of presents. Merry hadn't bothered to cover them – after her conversation in Rowan's Cafe she knew the vet was unlikely to attend the carol service on Christmas morning. 'You know Jared, my partner at the surgery, loves cows? This would be the perfect gift for him. Any idea which shop it was from?' He studied her intently.

'No, it was in with all the things my aunt had delivered.' Merry cupped her chin in one hand, trying to look indifferent. Theo had just identified another Secret Santa recipient. Now she knew three. Then the vet's eyes moved to the bottle of lavender bath oil and he picked it up.

'This isn't for you, either?' he asked, his eyes shifting away from hers.

Merry shook her head. Why all the questions? Had Theo guessed something? She swallowed.

'It's just a weird coincidence because Logan came into the surgery earlier and told me his girlfriend Kenzy's favourite bath oil is this exact scent,' Theo said, looking surprised. 'He wanted to get her some for Christmas and asked Kirsteen if she knew where he could find it. I don't suppose you know?' He sipped more of the beer and put the bath oil with the other presents, pushing them aside.

'That's, um, no, sorry,' Merry muttered. 'Maybe we should mention it to Tavish so he could order some for The Corner Shop?' She waited for Theo to ask more questions and when he didn't, she took a long sip from her bottle, feeling relieved. Another recipient had just been exposed. That was four in total now – talk about good luck. She waited, wondering what else the vet might reveal before drinking again. Theo looked around the room, the pile of gifts forgotten, and she let herself relax.

The Christmas lights on the tree in the corner of the room twinkled, throwing shadows across the edge of Theo's face, picking out the dark patch of stubble on his chin. Would it be prickly, or soft? Merry's fingertips traced her cheek as she imagined touching him. Wondered how it would feel to be that brave. How it would feel to be more like Carmel? If she was, would it be easier to achieve her goals and would Theo morph into Dan – like her fiction had cast a spell in real life?

The vet's eyes gleamed and he stop playing with the bottle and leaned forwards, his large body almost covering the table. Merry could feel the heat of him from the other side, could smell the scent of mountains and apples each time she breathed in. Wind howled outside, battering against the windows, and she flinched, then found herself leaning forwards too. What would it feel like to kiss this man, to run her fingers through his hair? If she were Carmel, she'd already be doing it. He was flawed, and she really wasn't looking for a relationship but... there was that tug in her chest every time she looked at him, a pull she couldn't explain. It was why she'd wanted Theo to leave earlier: it felt too dangerous. But he was here now and she wasn't sure if she'd be able to stop herself. Or even if she wanted to.

For a nanosecond Merry considered reaching out to run the pad of her finger along Theo's cheek, mirroring what her heroine had done. She steeled herself to step out of her own box and bring fiction to life. She leaned forwards a little and saw Theo echo the movement, watched his eyes drop to her mouth and felt her stomach flip-flop. She licked her lips and was about to rise from the chair, but just before she worked up the courage, she noticed his gaze drop to the edge of her cheek and trace the scar, saw his expression switch from lustful to sympathetic. It was a like dose of icy water, a reminder of why she was here and her hand shot up to cover it.

'It's from the accident,' she said, her voice betraying none of the emotions swirling in her chest.

'Sorry, I barely noticed it before, I didn't mean to...' Theo's breath whooshed.

'It's why my brothers are... like they are. It's a reminder for them,' she explained. 'I think in some ways they're more hung up on it than me. Or at least less willing to move on.'

Theo's eyes filled with understanding. 'We all have wounds, things that are difficult to get over.'

'What are yours?' She choked back her immediate embarrassment at asking the question. 'You know so much about me, it doesn't seem fair.' She made her voice softer. But it was true. Theo might just be her vet, but she'd spent more time with him than anyone else in Christmas Village. He knew a lot of details about her life and she knew almost nothing about his.

Theo frowned and for a moment, Merry thought he was going to refuse. 'Well, okay.' He swigged from his bottle and leaned back in his seat, spreading his legs in a gesture of openness. She had to tug her eyes away from the pure symmetry of his thighs. 'What do you want to know?'

She pondered the question – there was so much she wanted to ask. 'I don't know. Where are you from, do you have family?'

He puffed out a breath. 'I'm from London originally. Both of my parents have passed and I have a brother called Jake who's surfing his way around Australia. He's my only family, aside from Dot.' He waved at the Dalmatian.

'That must be awful. I mean, I've lost both my parents too,' Merry said gently. 'Mum years ago when I was five and Dad when I was in the coma.'

'That's tough,' Theo said.

'It was hard. I didn't get to say goodbye. I woke up and...' Tears prickled the backs of her eyes. 'I still expect Dad to call me on the phone, or to turn up at the house unannounced.' She tried to clear the emotion wedged in her throat but couldn't. 'Do you miss your parents?'

Theo looked thoughtful. 'Sometimes... certain days are difficult, Christmas isn't great. It was odd when I graduated; I was the only one without any parents there celebrating. That wasn't a good day.' His voice dipped.

'I can't imagine being alone.' What would the world be like without her brothers? They were domineering, sure, but they loved her, she knew that, knew they were there if she needed them. That she always had a safety net.

'You get used to it after a while,' Theo said softly, looking at the table rather than at her.

Sympathy roared inside her, an odd protectiveness. She wasn't used to being the one that wanted to look after others, the strong one. 'What made you want to be a vet?' she asked because he looked uncomfortable.

Theo met her eyes. 'My father and mother were doctors – they wanted me to follow in their footsteps, but I always preferred patients who didn't talk back.'

'Ah.' Merry chuckled softly. 'A control freak. You really would get on well with my brothers...' Surprise flashed across Theo's face, then something that could have been hurt and Merry immediately regretted the comparison. 'So, no girlfriend, partner?' She quickly moved on.

'Nope,' Theo said, then grimaced.

'What?' she asked.

He looked uncomfortable. 'I was engaged until recently.'

Merry ignored the instant frisson of jealously. 'What happened?'

He jerked a shoulder and his mouth twisted like it was a bottle-top he was trying to undo. 'You know, these things don't always work out,' he said flatly.

'Mmm,' Merry said and put her palms on the table, wondering if she should let it go but she didn't want to. Didn't like the unhappiness now shadowing Theo's eyes. She gulped. 'Why?' That one word felt like a departure – like she'd just crawled out from under a rock. She was so out of practice with being around new people, especially men, had forgotten basic etiquette, but pushing him felt right. Pushing him was exactly what Carmel would do. Perhaps she'd just peeled a layer of her old self away, too? Merry held her breath, waiting for his response.

Theo took a moment to respond. He took another sip from the beer bottle and put it back on the table before swallowing. 'She wanted a knight in shining armour and I was happy to deliver that over and over again, but when I stopped and wanted something in return, she found someone else.' He rubbed a hand across his brow.

'Was she stupid?' Merry spluttered, widening her eyes.

Theo laughed. 'Nope. She's a vet too, very accomplished, beautiful...' He shrugged.

'Figures.' Merry swallowed, imagining long blonde hair, endless legs and scar-free skin. Without thinking, she pressed a fingertip to her cheek again and skimmed the length of it.

Theo watched, then leaned forwards so he could carefully pry her hand from the edge of her eye. 'You're beautiful,' he said quietly and she snatched it away as tingles hip-hopped across her skin.

'I wasn't fishing.' She sighed, rubbing the prickles of awareness from her hand. 'I don't need to be built up or complimented. I've had a lifetime of it. I came here to...' She pressed her lips together. 'Find myself, take care of myself, move on. I'm writing a book – I've been doing it for years. I'm going to finish it and send it off.' She heaved in a breath, feeling the weight of it, the importance of what she was sharing. 'And Theo, I don't want to be rescued or taken care of. If anything, I want the opposite.'

He raised an eyebrow, the indigo-blue eye underneath an unreadable pool.

'I want to help someone.' Merry answered the question she guessed he wanted to ask. She wanted to be like Carmel. She couldn't explain it any better. She watched his lips purse and then morph into a smile and something flared inside her – another stroke of lust. Suddenly she wanted to kiss him again, wished she could make the first move – but she hadn't changed that much yet.

'As in, scale a mountain freestyle then give someone a fireman's lift all the way down?' he joked.

Merry snorted, enjoying their game. Theo was smiling again, and she realised she liked it, liked that amused look in his eyes. 'I was thinking of something tamer, at least to start with.' She tapped a fingertip on her chin as if she were considering. 'Like fighting off a crazed turkey with a spade.' She tipped her head towards the window. 'Offering a stranger a bed and a beer in a storm.'

'Ah,' he murmured, clearly entertained. 'I had no idea I was your first rescue.' He rolled his large shoulders, rippling muscles she wanted to explore. 'That's quite the honour. You might need a special name if you're going to make a habit of it.' He raised his eyes to the ceiling before nodding. 'SuperMerry – that's short and to the point. So what's next on our super-heroine's agenda?'

Merry grinned. 'I was thinking breakfast in the morning. Unless you have any snakes that need medicating?'

'What?' Theo's brow knitted.

She shook her head. 'Joke, it would take too long to explain.' Besides, what would Theo make of Carmel? Would he like her? She wasn't ready to share her heroine with him just yet. 'Seriously, you've done a lot to help me since I arrived.'

'All part of the service,' he said smoothly.

'I'll believe that when I get my invoice.' She met his gaze steadily but couldn't read what it meant. 'Seriously, what can I do for you? I can help with that to-do list you were writing. Think of it as part of my personal growth.'

'I...' He looked a little shaken and his eyes skirted the room before sweeping back to her face. They lingered on her lips and every cell in Merry's body went still. Then she leaned forwards as if she were being guided by an invisible thread. But Theo must have realised he was staring because he looked back up into her eyes again. 'I've no idea.' He closed his own, considering, and then nodded suddenly. 'Well, there's this cat I saw the other day that's injured one of its eyes. I want to find it so I can make sure it doesn't need any treatment. You could help me with that?'

'A cat-hunting expedition. Okay,' Merry gushed, feeling buoyant. She sipped the rest of her beer and rose. 'Thank you,' she said, gazing at him – feeling a rush of something in her chest. Not attraction this time, but gratitude. Because he'd taken her seriously, because he hadn't tried to take over or help. She knew enough about Theo to realise that could be difficult for him. 'I thought you were just like my brothers, but I was wrong...'

Theo cleared his throat and frowned, rubbing his jaw. 'You're welcome,' he said roughly as something unreadable slipped across his face.

11

'There's a call for you.' Kirsteen poked her head through the door of Theo's consulting room and pointed to the black phone sitting on his desk. 'Be quick. You've got precisely ten minutes until you have to leave for your next house call. Make sure you sneak out before Jared tries to beat you to it.' She waggled her eyebrows. 'The eejit is still convinced his ankle isn't badly sprained. He's still limping but he tried to pry the boot off it this morning so he could apply arnica. I've a good mind to put sleeping pills in his camomile tea to make sure he rests.'

'I don't think our patients would appreciate him falling asleep during appointments,' Theo warned.

'Shame.' Kirsteen rolled her eyes and waved a finger at the phone again. 'Pick up when it buzzes.'

'Who is it?' Theo shouted, taking a swig of coffee, but Kirsteen had already disappeared. He knew the mystery caller wouldn't be Jake, because his brother would have called his mobile. His mind wandered to Merry. He hadn't seen her since Saturday morning when she'd made him breakfast and coffee and they'd hatched a plan to go searching for the one-eyed cat... He'd already decided to return to Chestnut Cottage this afternoon to check on the hens and to give Merry another Secret Santa clue. He'd made a note of all the presents on Post-it notes before she'd discovered him in the kitchen – and had a few ideas already. After overhearing Merry's conversation with her brothers and having her confide her hopes to him, he knew he had to help. It wasn't about rescuing Merry, it was more about... facilitating. Pointing her in the right direction so she could work things out for herself. He'd toyed with the idea of walking away all weekend, but she'd been so earnest, so determined to make her own way. What kind of man would he be if he just left her to struggle by herself? It had nothing to do with the attraction he could sense burning between them.

The phone finally rang and he scooped it up. 'Doctor Ellis-Lee?'

'Is that Theo?' The voice at the other end of the line sounded familiar but he couldn't place it. 'This is Noah McKenzie, Merry's brother,' the man said. 'You were at my Aunt Ava's house with her on Friday night.'

The breath whooshed out of Theo's throat. 'Is everything okay with your sister?' Was she hurt? Theo rose and paced the office as he imagined Merry stuck in a snowdrift – or maybe she'd slipped again and broken something while feeding the animals outside? He should never have left her. 'What happened and how did you get my number?' He grabbed his coat from the hook by the door and scrambled through the pockets, searching for his car keys, almost dropping them in his haste as his head pounded and his blood pressure surged. He could be at Chestnut Cottage in ten minutes, at the closest accident and emergency unit in less than an hour.

'My sister's fine, don't worry,' Noah soothed, clearing his throat. 'I used Google to find you. You've got an unusual name and there's only one of you in Christmas Village. You're named as a partner on the Furry Friend's veterinary surgery website so I decided to call you at work. I wanted to talk to you in private.'

'About what?' Theo asked curtly. Was he about to be warned off?

'I'm worried about Merry,' Noah confessed. 'I don't know what she's told you but she shouldn't be living in the middle of nowhere alone. She wants to do this whole independence thing, I get that.' He sighed. 'But... she was in a car accident a couple of years ago, a bad one—'

'She told me about it,' Theo interrupted.

'Right.' Noah didn't sound particularly happy to hear that. 'Well, then I expect you can understand why my brothers and I would be far more comfortable if someone was keeping an eye on her.'

'I don't think...' Theo started, shaking his head.

'We've discussed it. You're the vet, it would be easy for you to visit her regularly to check up on Aunt Ava's animals and Merry would never suspect anything,' Noah continued as if Theo hadn't spoken. 'I'm not asking much – just look in on her from time to time.'

'You mean you want me to spy and report back?' Theo stopped pacing and looked out of the window. It was snowing again and he'd put the lights on in his office. He could see a reflection of his face in the glass, see how his mouth had twisted. He turned away. Theo hadn't been able to look himself in the eyes properly since he'd lied to Merry about the chickens. But at least he could convince himself that had been the right call – making up excuses to help her keep the animals safe while assisting with her Secret Santa quest was all about helping Merry to achieve her goals. But if he spied on her for her brothers, he'd never be able to justify it. 'I can't do that I'm afraid.'

The man let out a long-suffering sigh. 'I thought you might feel that way and of course, I understand. I might even like you more for saying no. But I wanted to see if you'd be amenable before I booked any holiday.'

'You're coming up?' Theo guessed, grimacing.

'Just for a week. Liam and Ollie will tag-team with me. Between us, we'll be able to help her until Christmas. By that point there'll only be a few days until Aunt Ava is due to return home and Merry will be back here not long after that,' he said.

'But your sister doesn't want anyone to join her,' Theo said urgently. 'I mean, she told me she needs to do this herself. It's important to her...'

'You seem to know a lot about Merry, considering you're just the vet.' Noah's tone turned suspicious and any warmth that had been in his voice had gone.

'I *am* the vet,' Theo said. 'But she's here in Christmas Village alone. We talk while I'm helping out or checking up on the animals. I'm just being neighbourly.'

'*Exactly!*' Noah sounded relieved. 'Neighbourly is all I want. Someone making sure my sister is okay and she doesn't do anything dangerous like try to drive or, I don't know, burn down the house or something stupid.'

'Is that likely?' Theo thought about the fairy lights she'd left on the other day and dismissed it. Merry was perfect capable of taking care of herself. If he wasn't careful, he'd start behaving exactly like her siblings. He'd already gone too far down that road by lying to her about the Egg Drop Syndrome.

Noah huffed. 'I don't know. I'm just concerned. She's always had someone looking out for her. I get that she wants her independence. Obviously I support that, she's twenty-five. But this is about running before you can crawl. You have no idea what it was like when Merry was in hospital.' His voice cracked and he stopped for a moment, gathering himself. 'I have to know she's safe. That's all,' he croaked. 'We're going out of our minds here, she's our little sister, the only one we have...'

Theo let silence fall and dropped back into his chair, thinking about when his parents had died in a fire and he'd taken on the responsibility for Jake. He'd only been nineteen and Jake five years younger. It had been a difficult path to travel

– that constant urge to protect and guide without smothering him. Even now, he couldn't settle if he didn't know that Jake was safe or what he was up to – if he didn't hear from his brother for a few days, he was always the first to get in touch. Was it really so different?

There was a knock on the consulting room door and Kirsteen poked her head through the gap and pointed to her watch before retreating.

'You just want me to check in?' Theo sighed into the handset. He was planning on doing that anyway. 'I'm not going to spy on her.'

'I'm not asking you to.' Noah's voice brightened. 'Just check in each day and I might call the surgery every now and again for a chat. Just two guys chewing the fat and if my sister comes up from time to time, that's just natural, right?'

Theo considered the options. If he said no, Merry's brothers would drive up to Christmas Village, destroy any chance she had of being alone, of making the changes she so desperately wanted to make. The German Shepherd inside him snarled at the idea. He was planning to help with the animals anyway, to assist with Secret Santa – and she was going to be his partner in his quest to find the one-eyed cat.

He'd be seeing a lot of her so would it really hurt? He wouldn't be spying – and when Noah called, he wouldn't have to tell her brother anything except that she was thriving and alive. That was all her brothers needed to hear, the one thing that would stop them from coming up and ruining everything, from stopping Merry doing the things she needed to do.

'Fine,' Theo said but there was a tightness across his chest. An uncomfortable sense that all wasn't right. Even after they'd said their goodbyes and he hung up, Theo couldn't help wondering what Merry would say if she ever found out.

12

Merry was gazing at the cherry-red Jeep parked up to the right of the house when Theo pulled his car into the drive of Chestnut Cottage later that afternoon. He hopped out, scattering a handful of cranberries into the snow as he checked for signs of Henry before releasing Dot from the boot and tramping across the driveway. Merry looked pretty today: she was wearing black trousers, a bright orange jumper and her aunt's coat and looked impossibly small and delicate. An image of him picking her up with one arm and hugging her into the safety of his chest flashed through Theo's mind and he shoved his hands into his pockets, dismissing it.

'Hi,' he said brightly. 'I thought I'd pop in and check on the hens since I was in the area.' At least, it had only been twenty minutes out of his way.

'They laid this morning!' Merry did a charming happy dance and pointed to the coop. 'I'm still feeding them the medicine though because I wasn't sure if I should stop. Clearly you are a genius vet.' She beamed – making something inside Theo spin – then pulled a face. 'I keep sniffing their hay but... You obviously have to be specially trained to know what to look for because it smells exactly the same to me. Maybe you could teach me so I know what to check for if they stop laying again?'

Theo looked down at his boots. 'That can be difficult to explain.' He glanced up just in time to notice her attention stray back to the Jeep. 'Is that your aunt's?' he asked, aiming to distract her.

She nodded, puffing out a breath. 'I've been thinking about driving it.' She chewed her bottom lip. 'I haven't been behind a wheel since the accident. My brothers hated the idea and, well, I suppose I wasn't ready to put myself through it... which seems cowardly now.' She put her hand to the scar on her cheek. 'I've been considering it all weekend, wondering if I should just try... you know, back on the horse and all that.'

Theo saw her hands tremble and stepped closer. 'You could drive to the high street with me. We could have a quick look around for the cat.' He checked his watch. 'I've got eighty minutes until my next appointment so I have time now.' Being able to drive would be the next step to Merry reclaiming her independence. Theo hated the idea of her trying it for the first time alone – but he definitely wouldn't be mentioning it to her brothers when they called.

'I'm not sure.' Merry chewed her lip again and shoved her hands into her pockets. 'It wasn't my fault – the accident – someone hit me and...' She shrugged. 'The car rolled because I was on an incline. It was plain old bad luck, but a part of me is afraid if I get behind a wheel again I'll freak out and somehow cause another crash. Then again...' She sighed, tossing her head. 'That wouldn't stop Carmel...'

'Who's Carmel?' Theo asked, bemused.

She blushed. 'Um, no one. It doesn't matter, just...' Her lips tugged down. 'Okay.' Her chest heaved. 'I need to do this. But I only want your moral support – no help, guidance or positive chit-chat. The last thing I want is that.' Her brown eyes were serious pools. 'I need a warm, silent body beside me – no speaking, you understand.' Her mouth flattened as she waited for him to say something. 'Because if you can't promise me that, I'm going to have to do it alone.'

Theo could hear the nerves in Merry's voice and knew he'd have to agree, but before he got a chance she started to shake her head.

'I shouldn't be asking.' Her attention swivelled back to the Jeep. 'I'm supposed to be doing this by myself.'

'Doesn't every superhero need a sidekick?' Theo asked, imagining Merry taking her first drive alone, knowing he had to join her or he'd go out of his mind with worry. 'I promise I won't say a word.'

She wrapped her arms around herself. 'Are you sure?'

He mimed zipping his lips as Dot hopped over to stand beside him. 'Let's go now before you change your mind. I'll come back and check on the chickens after my appointments.' He waved at the car. 'Is there a place for Dot in there?'

'She can go in the boot – there's a cage thing to stop her jumping into the back seats. Looks like Aunt Ava is used to transporting her pets.' Merry unwound her arms and pulled at her sleeves, glowering at the car, but she didn't move.

'Do you have keys?' Theo probed.

Merry pulled a keyring with silhouettes of multiple animals from the pocket of her coat and jangled it. 'I've been carrying these around all weekend. Rowan told me I'm insured to drive, so nothing's really stopping me except...' She paused. 'I'm scared.'

Every instinct encouraged Theo to encircle Merry in the safety of his arms before advising her to leave it, to insist she didn't need to drive. But he knew he couldn't. Firstly, she'd probably thump him if he tried – and secondly, she had to do this on her own if she was going to move on from the accident. 'Let's go.' He tramped towards the car, snapped on Dot's lead and opened the boot before helping the dog to climb in. Then he unfastened the passenger door and waited while Merry stared at him. 'It'll be easier once you get going,' he said gently. 'Remember, you're SuperMerry! You can do this, you can do anything.'

'I need to lock the front door,' she croaked before wandering out of sight and Theo took a moment to check the car to make sure it was roadworthy. The driver's seat had been pulled up to the steering wheel, suggesting Merry had already adjusted it to fit her small frame. Had she sat in that same spot over the weekend, willing herself to just do it? Theo could imagine that, wished he'd been around to help her earlier. But he'd been trying to give them both some space. To regain control over his growing feelings.

Merry opened the door and shoved her handbag onto the back seat, then she climbed inside and slowly shut the door. She put trembling hands on the steering wheel and squeezed it until her knuckles paled. It took everything Theo had to stop himself from trying to talk her out of it. Letting Merry drive went against all his natural instincts, but he'd made a promise and knew he had to keep it. He wasn't here to rescue her: he was here to help her to save herself. She silently put on her seatbelt and murmured something under her breath before starting the engine. The chords of muscle across Theo's neck and shoulders began to throb as she sat silently.

'I'm not sure I can do this,' Merry said suddenly, unfurling her hands from the wheel and wiping them on her jeans. Theo opened his mouth to tell her she didn't have to, but before he could, she put a fingertip over his lips. 'Don't!' The word was delivered in a rush. 'Give me a moment. I don't need a pep talk, not unless I'm giving it to myself.' She took in a long breath and let it out slowly, then did the same again. 'Time to channel Carmel,' she whispered.

Who was this woman Merry kept mentioning? Theo kept his mouth shut as she put the car into reverse. He could feel the knots of tension in his shoulders bunch as they slowly glided backwards out of the parking space.

It was a lesson in restraint and for the first time Theo wondered if helping, taking over from someone, was actually easier than letting them do it for themselves. It was an uncomfortable realisation, one that didn't sit particularly well – because it would mean in some ways he'd enabled Miranda, given her all the space she needed to take advantage of him... Perhaps it was time for him to own his part in the downfall of that relationship?

'Oh boy,' Merry hissed as the car went over a bump and the steering wheel jerked. Theo gripped his hands into bunches, willing himself not to intervene as the air rushed from between her lips and she put the car into first gear and began to ease it slowly forwards along the driveway. 'I can do this,' she muttered through gritted teeth.

'I'll look after the gate,' Theo offered as they drew closer, unlocking the passenger door and jumping out so he could pull it open. He stood and watched Merry move the car inch by inch onto the lane before he closed and relocked the gate. She was sitting with her head angled forwards and her eyes fixed firmly ahead when he joined her again. She didn't say a word or move a muscle, but as soon as he'd refastened his seatbelt the car began to creep forwards – although Merry kept it securely in first gear. It took fifteen painfully slow minutes until they reached the main road that would join Christmas Village high street. They'd encountered no traffic and Merry still hadn't changed gear – nor had the speedometer crept above ten miles per hour. Even Dot had whined and poked her head up to look out of the back window as if she were questioning the delay.

As they reached the T-junction Merry slowed to a stop and applied the brake before licking her dry lips. 'I don't know if I can do this any more,' she said, her voice tight with tension.

Theo fought the urge to tell her that was okay, that he'd take over. Instead he put a hand over hers, feeling the tautness in her muscles ease a little at the connection. He cleared his throat. 'I know I'm not supposed to say anything,' he said gruffly. 'So I'll keep this brief. Merry, you can do it, believe in yourself.'

Her hand flinched but he kept his palm in place, wondering if he was doing the right thing. Knowing if Merry didn't drive now it might take her months before she had the courage to try again. By which time she'd probably be back living with her brothers who'd most likely try to talk her out of it. 'Keep looking forwards,' he said sternly. 'I'll be here with you every step of the way.' Theo forced himself to lift his hand and break contact, his stomach churning with a myriad of conflicting emotions as he sank back in his seat and kept his eyes forwards, waiting for her to decide. The German Shepherd inside him was up on its haunches now, barking wildly, desperate to tear its way out and save Merry, but Theo knew he couldn't give in to it. Not today. He heard her let out a long sigh, watched her carefully check the road for any other vehicles before she put the car back into gear, indicated and turned right.

The road to Christmas Village was quiet and Theo hoped it would remain that way for the rest of the short journey. He was on tenterhooks, scouring the road for danger as Merry continued to crawl the car. She changed gear and moved into second, gasping as she pressed her foot on the accelerator and sped up until they were travelling at twenty miles per hour. The tension was palpable and Theo tried to force himself to relax. But as they approached the last bend which would lead to the start of Christmas Village high street something flashed in the corner of his eye and he watched in horror as the one-eyed cat came skidding from the nearby rows of trees before cutting in front of them and disappearing under the car.

'No, no, no!' Merry yelled, slamming her foot on the brakes as they both watched the black and white demon dodge from beneath the wheels and scoot to the other side of the road before disappearing into more trees. The car had been moving so slowly it barely wobbled as it stopped but Theo could almost hear the pump of blood as both their pulses went wild.

'*Shit*,' he snapped and placed a hand over Merry's. 'Are you okay?'

As soon as she nodded he jumped out of the car and jogged over to where the cat had vanished, circling the clearing just before the trees thickened in case he could see any prints. There was nothing, so he ran back to the car.

Merry was still sitting in the driver's seat, but her hands were shaking.

'Shall I take over?' Theo asked quietly.

'No!' She restarted the engine before he'd done up his seatbelt. 'It's only a little further. If I give up now, I'll never get back behind a wheel.' She tensed and let the car roll forwards, keeping it in first. A few minutes later they pulled up beside the pavement at the edge of the high street and Merry put on the brake. Then she leaned her head on the steering wheel and let go of a long, shuddery breath.

Theo willed himself to stay silent. Nothing in his life had felt as hard as this moment. Every cell in his body was poised to soothe but he held himself back. It wasn't his place to rescue Merry. She didn't want his help and he'd promised he wouldn't offer any.

Finally Merry straightened and undid her seatbelt before twisting around to gaze at him. 'Thank you,' she said quietly. 'That was... awful. But I did it.' She shivered and gave Theo a half smile. 'And I wouldn't have made it here without you.'

'I didn't do anything,' he said, clenching and unclenching his jaw.

Her brown eyes considered him. There were flecks of gold in them – an arresting palette of colours Theo hadn't noticed before now. Hidden depths or parts of Merry that were only just emerging?

'I can only imagine how hard you found that.' She offered him a full smile. 'There's a certain power in doing nothing, especially when it doesn't come naturally to you. I know my brothers couldn't have done it,' she added. 'You were my hero today and I owe you.'

Theo cleared the lump that had formed in his throat, unsure of how to react as guilt ate at him. 'You did really well.' His voice sounded gravelly. Their eyes held and Theo could feel that tug again, an almost visceral need.

Then Merry cleared her throat and broke eye contact. 'Shall we look for your cat? At least we know it's still living around here.' She waved a hand over her watch. 'I'm guessing we don't have long before I have to drive you back to Chestnut Cottage and we're going to need *lots* of time to get there.' She flashed him another shy smile, before unplugging the keys from the car and stepping out.

'I still can't see it,' Merry said as Dot nuzzled her nose into the undergrowth at the end of Christmas Village's main high street. They'd already searched the trees closest to where the one-eyed stray had jumped into the road earlier. Now Theo and Merry searched the small clearing where a huge fir tree stretched into the sky. Someone had decorated it with colourful baubles and glittering fairy lights, then wrapped a shiny silver ribbon around the trunk. A series of stubby trunks had been chopped into stools and scattered around the hollow – and the whole area was framed by tall bushes, thick forest and various snow-laden greenery.

'I can't either,' Theo said, feeling disappointed as he circled his way back out of the cluster of trees. He wasn't sure what he'd been expecting – but the one-eyed cat was nowhere to be found. 'Have you heard of Secret Santa?' he asked, wondering if Merry would own up to knowing about the tradition.

She paused at the edge of the opening. 'Rowan mentioned something in the cafe the other day,' she said carefully, pointing to a cluster of pretty evergreens at the edge of the space. 'I think this might be where his sack gets left on Christmas Day.'

Theo let out a sigh. 'I wish Santa would deliver the cat to us, too.' He was joking, but the mention of Secret Santa had given him an idea. 'Perhaps we should ask Tavish Doherty who runs The Corner Shop if he's spotted anything. We know the stray is still in the area and he promised he'd keep an eye out.' If he was lucky, the older man would be wearing his Christmas jumper – if Merry saw that, she might put two and two together and that would be another Secret Santa gift matched with its owner. As long as she made the connection he wouldn't technically be helping...

'Good idea,' Merry said, walking ahead in the direction of the shops. Her gait was determined and there was a confidence in her step that hadn't been there before the drive.

The Corner Shop looked empty when Theo and Merry walked inside after tying Dot's lead to a large metal ring close to the entrance. They passed shelves stacked with tins of fruit, soup and vegetables, jars of curry pastes and pâté alongside numerous everyday condiments. A fridge lined the whole of the right side of the shop and Theo spotted milk, cheese, ham and various fresh foodstuffs and promised himself he'd make a point of returning soon. Tavish was standing behind the long counter at the far end of the shop. There was a till to the left of him and newspapers had been laid out on racks in front. He wore the same Christmas jumper he'd been wearing in the pub and Theo let out a silent cheer and held back, letting Merry walk ahead. He watched as she picked up a packet of mints and went to pay. He saw the exact moment she spotted the red jumper, watched her head snap up as she connected the pattern with the matching gloves and hat from her Aunt Ava's purchases. There were still a lot of gifts to allocate and Theo knew they'd have their work cut out to match all of them with the correct villagers before Christmas. He wished he could confide in Merry, tell her he knew and wanted to help, but after everything she'd told him he suspected she'd tell him to get lost – and he couldn't risk that.

'Um, can I check, is your name Tavish Doherty?' Merry asked softly, her cheeks reddening.

'Aye, lass, why?' Tavish rang her sweets up on the till.

'No reason.' Merry shook her head. 'I'm Ava Armstrong's niece, she mentioned your name. I just wanted to check I had the right Tavish. Looks like I do.' She grinned.

'Your aunt's a good woman. You still looking for that cat?' The older man turned to Theo once Merry had paid.

'Yep, it just jumped out in front of our car and disappeared into the woods.' He picked up a tin of soup he didn't need and placed it on the counter. 'Have you seen it?'

'Aye, it was hanging around the Christmas tree earlier this morning. I was going to message you straight away but then it spotted my dog Iver and scampered off.' He pulled a face. 'Its eye looked gammy – I'm guessing the creature could do with looking over. I'll take another walk down there later and I've mentioned the cat to some of my customers, they promised to keep a lookout too.'

'Thank you,' Theo said, feeling frustrated. 'If its eye is infected I'll need to treat it soon.' He grimaced.

'We could come back tonight?' Merry suggested.

'Ach, no, you can't!' a woman's voice cried out from behind.

Merry turned and her face lit up. 'Hannah and... is it Ace?'

She walked past Theo, then leaned down to speak to a small boy with curly brown hair who was holding on tightly to Hannah's hand.

There was a sudden thump from the stairs behind the shop counter and then Sam appeared, his face shining, clearly out of breath. 'I thought I heard your voice,' he managed, his attention fixed on the young woman with long curly hair. Theo watched as Hannah's eyes flashed with annoyance.

'I popped in to get some carrots,' she said. 'I'm not here to see you.'

Sam leaned on the counter, his eyes bright. 'Well, it's lucky I was in because we're all out. We've a delivery coming later – I could drop some by your house?'

'We'll make do with something else,' Hannah snapped, her eyes narrowing. 'If I wait for you to bring my veg, chances are it'll never turn up. Ace, lad, will you grab us a stalk of broccoli please?' She patted the boys head but he stayed where he was, gazing at Merry.

'You came to my school,' he gushed. 'You write stories. Did you put a car chase in your book yet?'

Merry chuckled. 'No, but I'm thinking about it.'

'I've got all my characters worked out,' he continued. 'When you come back to school, can I tell you about them?'

'Of course. I'd love that,' Merry said and her attention shot to Theo. She'd spoken about her novel, but hadn't discussed the details with him. Why did she look so embarrassed? Perhaps when they were alone again he'd ask.

'And will you read us your car chase when it's finished?' the boy begged. 'I'm going to put one in my book too.'

'Aye, that'll be quite the Christmas tale,' Hannah joked, beaming.

'I'm still working on it,' Merry admitted. 'Mind you.' She peered out of the window into the high street at her aunt's Jeep. 'After today I have some inspiration – although I'm hoping my heroine will manage to get above second gear.' Her eyes rose to meet Theo's again and this time they shone.

Hannah rubbed the boy's curls. 'Ace has been so excited since you came to the school. I think we might have a regular Roald Dahl on our hands because he hasn't stopped planning his story. It's so good of you to give up your time to teach the children.'

'I loved every minute,' Merry said softly. 'I've hardly spoken about my book for years. It's been inspiring for me to have such an enthusiastic audience.' She shoved her hands into her pockets. 'I didn't realise how much I needed that. I've written so much more since I got to Scotland.'

'Are you still on for the pub tonight?' Hannah asked Merry. 'Remember: you, me, Edina Lachlan and Belle have a date with some cocktails?'

'Oh.' Merry pulled a face. 'I was supposed to be helping Theo search for a missing cat.'

'Ach, I'll keep a lookout for that, lass,' Tavish offered. 'I'll message the lad if it turns up.'

'That would work,' Theo agreed. He didn't want to get in the way of Merry going out.

'Well, okay,' she said.

'Are you planning on driving, because I can give you a lift?' Theo asked as his mind conjured Merry trying to get to the pub herself. She might get stuck in the snow, try to drive alone – the chances of disaster suddenly seemed endless. Merry didn't say no, but he could see she was disappointed which affected him more than he expected.

'Belle is going to pick you up, remember – and Logan always drops us all home so you don't have to worry about driving or lifts,' Hannah said.

'Why don't you join me for a drink in Christmas Pud Inn tonight?' Sam turned to Theo. 'Sounds like it's going to be a busy night.' He ignored Hannah as she made an irritated huffing noise.

'Of all the pubs in Scotland,' she scoffed. 'Mind you, I won't hold my breath.' The younger woman fixed Sam with an unfriendly glare. 'Chances are you'll find somewhere else you'd rather be and you won't turn up.' With that, she headed towards the back of the shop where Tavish kept the vegetables, leaving the younger man gazing after her with a look of pure longing on his face.

13

The kitchen was quiet when Merry came down from her bedroom later that day. She'd spent the last half an hour getting ready for her evening in Christmas Pud Inn, but her mind had been drifting over and over again to her book. She was awash with emotions after the drive with Theo – eager to somehow translate her feelings onto the page. Merry checked her watch. She had about forty minutes before Belle arrived to pick her up, enough time to do some work on her latest chapter, perhaps to put Carmel behind the wheel of a car too? She had an idea about a car chase; perhaps if she started writing it now when all these emotions were bubbling inside she could make it work? Merry pulled out a chair at the table so she could sit, then she opened her laptop and got to work...

> Carmel sat in the cherry-red Jeep and squeezed her hands around the steering wheel. She hadn't driven since the accident that had changed her life two years before and could feel fear burning its way up her throat, making every molecule in her body shudder.
>
> 'Time to get moving,' Dan said, hopping into the passenger

seat and putting the canvas bag with the jewel in it onto his lap. He fixed Carmel with an unreadable look, those bright blue eyes filled with expectation. 'Okay?' he asked when she didn't start the engine. 'You can do this,' he added softly, as if he'd read her mind. Carmel dismissed the tingles of fear creeping up from her feet and turned the key...

Merry let out a long breath as she closed the file half an hour later and put her laptop to one side on the kitchen table. Dan had been so supportive, giving Carmel all the space she needed to drive. Even when a car had squealed onto the road behind them, then chased them through the jungle, he hadn't tried to take over or intervene. The fact that Theo had behaved exactly like Dan wasn't lost on Merry. Nor was the realisation that her imaginary hero was becoming more and more like the vet each time she placed her fingers on the keys.

But this wasn't all fiction. Theo had surprised her today. Instead of trying to convince her not to get behind the wheel, he'd offered support and encouragement. Allowed her to take those baby steps by herself. If he hadn't arrived when she'd been staring longingly at the Jeep she knew she'd have driven the car at some point – but his warm body beside her, his quiet belief in her, had made it easier to follow through. She wondered again how it would feel to kiss him. He'd be in the pub tonight, was she ready to take another leap? Was she ready to put herself out there again?

She checked her mobile for messages and frowned before tracking to the canary-yellow phone on the other side of the kitchen so she could pick it up, almost tripping over Chewy who was lounging in the middle of the floor. The dial tone told her it was definitely still connected but it was almost six o'clock and not one of her brother's had texted or called. Her chest compressed. Were they about to appear on her doorstep? She didn't trust the silence and concern knotted her insides as she considered what they might be planning.

'It doesn't make sense.' Merry bent to scratch behind the rabbit's ears and frowned. 'One of them always checks up on me, usually all three. They haven't gone a full five hours without contact since I woke from the coma.' She rose and narrowed her eyes at the mobile before putting it on the table. Or perhaps she was making too much of it? Hope bloomed. Maybe they were finally coming around?

She wandered back across the kitchen to the unwrapped Secret Santa presents still piled on the table then picked up the hat and gloves and waved them at the rabbit. 'I'm sure these are for Tavish Doherty, Chewy. I'm beginning to think I might be able figure out who all the gifts are for. That's five down once this is wrapped, then I've only got another fifteen to go...'

Everyone in Christmas Pud Inn was enjoying a busy Monday evening. Merry watched Belle balance a tray of blue cocktails on one arm as she approached the table they'd taken in the middle of the main pub. 'First round's on me!' she declared, grinning as Kenzy grabbed two of the drinks and placed one in front of Merry and another in front of Edina before taking one for herself.

On the other side of her, Hannah seized a cocktail and swirled a fingertip around the top of the glass. 'What shall we toast to, lasses?' she yelled. 'A life without men?' She brushed a few random tendrils of curly brown hair away from her face and drank.

Kenzy shook her head before sipping her cocktail. 'I'd rather drink to my six-foot-two handyman.' She winked.

'I'll be drinking to Bob and Tavish.' Edina took a swig from the glass, righting her tiara as it started to slip off her head.

'Aye, and I'll toast to Jack Hamilton-Kirk, my – slightly less handy but wonderful – boyfriend.' Belle blushed. 'Maybe you should give Sam another chance, Hannah. Put the poor lad out of his misery and go on a date?' She shrugged. 'He made a mistake... maybe he could make it up you?'

'And how would he do that – by turning back time?' Hannah puffed air from her cheeks, looking upset. 'I'm not going down that road again, Belle. I've got Ace now, his da walked away soon after he was born. I need a man I can rely on, a steady pair of hands.'

Merry cast her eyes around the pub as the pretty woman made herself comfortable. It had low ceilings and a long bar on the opposite side of the room to where they were seated. Lights and tinsel glittered across the ceiling and all the tables were packed with customers, while more villagers were lined up around the busy bar. As she scanned the unfamiliar faces, her attention caught on a set of indigo-blue eyes that were currently fixed on their table.

Theo was sitting with Sam, Kenzy's boyfriend Logan, and Belle's partner, Jack. The other three men were chatting but Theo's eyes were trained on her. Attraction danced across Merry's skin and she turned away because she didn't know what to do about it. Wasn't sure she was ready to take that leap. She was getting closer, could feel desire for Theo burning under her skin. But when they kissed, she knew she had to make the first move.

'I think you've got an admirer in our vet,' Kenzy said, leaning closer so she could whisper in Merry's ear. 'If I wasn't loved up with Logan, I'd give you a run for your money all right.'

'Mmmm.' Hannah frowned, sipping some of her cocktail. 'I practically threw myself at the man the other night but he's obviously so smitten with you I don't stand a chance.' She pouted even as her eyes slid to Sam who was still busy talking.

Merry tried some of her cocktail, feeling her stomach

bunch. She hadn't kissed a man since before the accident but it was one more hurdle on her list. Would she find a way to make it happen tonight?

'He's coming over,' Hannah gasped, her eyes widening. 'My God, those muscles are to die for. What do you think he looks like under those clothes?'

'You need to stop dribbling, girl,' Kenzy said dryly. 'Or I think Sam Doherty is going to combust.'

Hannah sniffed, but Merry saw her mouth soften. She didn't turn, but knew Theo had reached their table because her body instantly reacted, like metal filings being drawn towards a magnet.

'Can I buy anyone a drink?' he asked softly.

'We're all good. But feel free to join us.' Belle beamed, hopping up so she could grab a chair before shuffling over and squeezing it in between her and Merry. 'I've got something for you. Edina here mentioned you'd done such a great job of looking after Bob when you gave him his vaccination, I baked you a batch of mince pies to say thanks.'

'Aye, that donkey means the world to us,' Edina said. 'Belle here is dating my grandson and I asked if she'd help me to thank you properly.'

Belle shuffled in her bag before drawing out a silver tin and handing it to Theo.

'Thank you, mince pies are my favourite,' he said, sounding surprised. 'I'll join you for a minute.' He slumped down and placed the tin under his chair.

'Don't let those out of your sight,' Hannah warned. 'Belle bakes the best desserts in Christmas Village. She's a genius with sugar. Doesn't matter what she touches, it turns to *yum*.' She licked her lips, and her attention darted momentarily to Sam who was now openly ogling her while Logan chatted happily to Jack. How would it feel to have someone adore you that much? 'Trouble is, Belle gives so many treats away she's constantly having to buy new containers!' Hannah angled her seat so she could keep an eye on Sam without making it obvious.

'Really?' Theo turned to gaze at Merry as her mind wandered to the pretty flat boxes decorated with cupcakes which had been packed in one of her aunt's parcels. Were they for Belle? It sounded like the right match, so she'd put them aside later. She smiled and nodded, then watched Theo's mouth curve too.

'Aye,' Hannah said. 'Belle is far too trusting for her own good. I was the same – once.' Her eyes were drawn across the pub to Sam again just as he picked something up and wandered over to join them.

'I got you this.' He handed Hannah a grocery bag, looking awkward.

'Is it a goodbye note?' she shot back, her eyes firing. When Sam didn't respond she dug into the bag and drew out a sack of carrots. Her face immediately softened before it hardened again.

'It might take me a few years, but I'll prove to you I can be trusted,' Sam murmured.

'Delivering vegetables I didn't ask for isn't going to make up for you breaking my heart,' Hannah hissed before calmly placing the carrots back in the carrier. 'It's not that easy. I told you before – you can't waltz into my life after ten years and expect to pick up where you left off.'

'I made a mistake.' Sam cleared his throat, looking around the pub. 'But this isn't the time.' He gazed at Hannah, his expression intense. 'I'll make it up to you, I'll figure something out.'

'There isn't a gesture big enough. You should just give up.' Hannah put the shopping bag on the floor before turning her back.

14

'You didn't have to drive me home,' Merry said as Theo steered his car through Christmas Village high street, stopping momentarily beside the clearing with the Christmas tree so he could quickly check for the one-eyed cat out of the window.

'Logan was dropping Belle, Edina and Kenzy off and Chestnut Cottage is in the opposite direction,' he explained. 'You're pretty much on my way.'

Merry briefly wondered if Theo was making it up, perhaps finding an excuse for dropping her home so he could make sure she got there safely. 'If you live that close, I should probably come and visit. Isn't that what good neighbours do around here?' She'd like to snoop in Theo's space, find out more about what made him tick. She brushed a finger through her hair. She'd worn it down but had been fiddling nervously with it so much during the evening it was probably a mess. 'What's the address?' she tested, tracing a fingertip across her lower lip which felt strangely sensitive.

'Holly Lodge, by Holly Loch. It's about ten minutes from your aunt's but it's not the easiest drive,' he murmured. 'You might want to walk it the first time you come, get a feel for the proportions.' He looked uncomfortable. 'The track is basically a narrow, rocky incline and...' He puffed out a breath.

'Not for the faint-hearted?' she finished. 'That's fine, I'm guessing it'll be a picnic if I do it in fifth gear and just floor the accelerator. Plus, if I close my eyes while I'm driving I won't get scared at all.' She laughed when he sucked in a breath. It was fun teasing him, poking the bear – but even better that he wasn't immediately jumping in with a million reasons why she shouldn't take stupid risks. She'd probably walk, but Theo didn't need to know that.

'No cat,' he grumbled as he wound the window up again and restarted the car before heading along the main road. 'Tavish messaged earlier to say he'd wandered down to take a look but there was still no sign...'

Merry twisted so she was facing him. 'We can both try searching again tomorrow. I've got some of Simba's treats and they might help. Why does the finding the cat matter so much to you?'

He considered the question. 'Maybe because I hate the idea of it being out here alone, especially when I know it might be injured and I could probably make it better.'

'Tell me about the first animal you saved.' She closed her eyes and leaned back on the seat again, listening to Theo's voice. It was deep with an underlying huskiness that made him sound like he might be coming down with a cold. The pitch was pleasing and amplified the warm buzz in Merry's veins that lingered from the cocktails.

'When I was ten I saved a field mouse after it had got caught in our lawnmower. I kept it in my bedroom and nursed it back to health.'

Merry turned to glance at Theo's profile and saw him frown.

'I liked how that felt.'

'Saving something?' she asked, knowing she admired that

about him. So long as he wasn't aiming all that protectiveness at her...

He shrugged. 'My brother Jake says I can't help myself. He says it's in my blood, that no matter how hard I try I could never escape my own nature.' He sounded sad.

'What do you believe?' she probed.

He shrugged. 'I think we can become more than our experiences or genetic alphabet. It's what sets us apart from animals. We can learn and grow, or at least we can try...'

Merry nodded. That was what she was doing here, how she planned to change her life. 'Are you close to your brother?'

'Less so now he's older. Our parents died in a fire when he was fourteen. I was nineteen at the time and we lived together until he was old enough to move out.' His jaw tightened. 'After that I went to university to study to be a vet.'

'So you raised him?' she asked, suddenly in awe.

'I think we raised each other,' he said quietly. 'He's nothing like me, we're nothing like each other – but we rubbed along. I may have been a little too interested in keeping him safe...'

Woah, so now Theo wasn't just a potential cat saviour, he'd adopted a three-legged dog and taken on an orphaned brother. The fact that he was letting Merry push her boundaries without trying to step in made her like him even more. Showed a strength of character she admired. Her brothers could learn a lot from Theo. 'I'm sorry about your parents,' she said softly. 'I know how hard it can be. Especially if you don't get to say goodbye.' She swallowed as emotion coursed through her chest and she took a moment to steady her breathing. 'You never really get over it...' Perhaps knowing that about him helped her understand Theo a little more? Or at least, it made her feel closer to him.

They didn't speak again until they pulled up beside the gate that led to Chestnut Cottage. Theo was clearly happy with his own thoughts and Merry was lost in hers, thinking how every time she found out something new out about this man it made her want to know him even more.

'The lights are all off, did you do that?' Theo said as he hopped out of the car to open the gate. When he got back inside, Merry was gazing at the house.

'No, I left the lights on in the porch, hallway and front room.' A frisson of fear glided up her throat.

'It could be an intruder, but more likely a fuse has blown – unless Chewy's been up to his old tricks and gnawed his way through some wires. I seem to remember an incident with one of your aunt's lamps in his notes at the surgery.' Theo drove the car through the gate and nipped out to shut it. 'I'll come in to help you check.'

'I know where the fuse box is,' Merry said. 'So I can look at that – you can find Chewy, and make sure a Yeti hasn't broken in and run amok.'

She was serious but Theo obviously thought she was joking because he chuckled as he peered out of the car, listening for signs of Henry. Then he carefully got out and scattered a handful of cranberries in the snow before releasing Dot from the boot. Merry had seen the turkey this morning, but guessed he must be getting used to Theo's visits, or perhaps the gifts the vet was leaving were having the intended effect? She understood the easing of defences, how easy it was to let Theo get under your skin, to let down your guard no matter how hard you tried to fight it...

Merry blindly searched for her keys and it took a while to find them because it was so dark. She had to take a deep breath and channel Carmel before she took the first step into Chestnut Cottage. It was gloomy and there was almost no ambient light. Theo tried to dodge ahead but Merry pushed him aside so she could lead. She didn't walk too fast though because she liked knowing he was close. They wandered slowly towards the kitchen listening for strange sounds. Theo held onto Dot but the dog didn't bark or make a noise. He stayed right beside her like an avenging angel and watched Merry pull her aunt's toolbox out from under the sink so she could find a torch. But when she switched it on, it didn't work. 'Dammit.' She bashed it against her hand to no avail. 'Maybe it needs new batteries.'

'Didn't I see a torch in with the things your aunt bought?' Theo asked quietly.

'Of course!' Merry said, feeling her way to the kitchen table so she could search amongst the presents and pick it out. It wasn't packaged so whoever it was intended for would never know it had been used. When she switched it on she let out a relieved breath as a bright beam illuminated the kitchen.

'I remembered seeing the torch because Duncan Knox at the stables showed me his and it's exactly the same design,' Theo explained, his voice soft. 'One of his horses stepped on it and it hasn't worked properly since. He told me it was such a good torch he couldn't bear to get rid of it, but half the time it won't switch on.'

'Duncan Knox,' Merry repeated as she wandered slowly towards the stairwell next to the kitchen where the fuse box was located, trying to remain calm. That was yet another Secret Santa gift matched; once Theo had left she'd be able to wrap it. She eased down to check the fuse box, using the torch to light it up. 'It must have been tripped by something.' Merry let out a long breath as she flicked one of the switches, triggering all the lights. The microwave beeped and Simba looked up from where he'd been sleeping on the sofa and yawned.

Theo turned and trailed back to the kitchen before bending to check under the kitchen table. 'Chewy's right here and there don't seem to be any chewed wires anywhere so the rabbit probably isn't responsible.'

'Maybe it was the wind?' Merry suggested. Her aunt's notes probably would have warned about the likelihood of power outages, but without a simple explanation for them she felt weirded out. Feeling tense, she put the torch back in the pile of presents and then she walked to the fridge and pulled out a bottle of wine and waved it at Theo. 'My cocktails have worn off, I think I'm going to need a glass of this or I'm not going to be able to relax. Do you want one?' She cleared her throat, hoping he wasn't about to make an excuse and leave. She wasn't ready to be alone but didn't want to ask him to stay. 'Unless you need to get going?'

'I'm okay to stay for a while, a small one please.' Theo knelt in front of the fire and lit it while Merry poured them both a drink and took them to the table before taking a seat. Dot immediately settled onto the rug and once it started to catch, Simba wandered over to join her. The lights on the Christmas tree flashed on and off, throwing multi-coloured shadows over them both. 'They look like they're at a disco,' Theo said, wandering back to the table to join Merry. His eyes shifted to the presents piled on the table and his gaze paused on the torch and flat-packed cake boxes Merry had decided belonged to Belle. If she counted the torch, that meant seven gifts had now been matched with their rightful owners.

Merry stilled as Theo continued to stare, wondering if he'd somehow guessed about Secret Santa – *but how could he? No one in the village knew.* Then his attention moved on to the swimming hats and she relaxed.

'Jack was telling me about a loch not far from here where people go wild swimming.' He pulled out a chair and dragged his wine glass closer before sipping some.

'What's wild swimming?' Merry asked.

'It's when people swim outdoors, in nature.' He shuddered. 'Even at this time of year. People say it's invigorating.' He pointed to the hats. 'Does your aunt swim in the lochs?'

'Um...' Merry sipped some wine. 'I've no idea. She's got a wetsuit upstairs in her wardrobe. Any idea who from the village goes?' If she was lucky, Jack had provided Theo with a list of names.

'Nope. Why?' He leaned his elbows on the table and scoured her face. 'Do you fancy trying it?'

Merry ground her jaw; she couldn't imagine anything worse. But if she was going to work out who those hats belonged to, she'd have to at least turn up.

'I can take you?' Theo offered. 'I mean, I've always wanted to try wild swimming but I'm not sure I'll actually get into the water unless I've got someone to go with. Someone really brave.' He flashed a grin.

'Because you're afraid?' Her voice dripped scepticism.

'No...' He paused. 'There are trout in the loch, I've heard they bite. If I take someone with me, maybe they'll act as a...'

'Decoy?' She snorted. 'You're serious?' Her brow knitted as she tried to read him. There was no way a man like Theo would even consider putting someone in harm's way to protect himself. 'You're not serious. What are you up to?'

He looked amused. 'Nothing, I just thought with all that sweet coffee you're always drinking you'll probably taste a lot better than me. If you swim beside me in the loch I'll feel a lot safer.' His mouth curved. 'I'm just offering SuperMerry a new adventure. Another chance to rescue me.'

'Right.' She laughed. He was playing with her, teasing her – but the question was, what would he do if she agreed? 'Fine, I'll come with you.' She'd kill two birds with one stone. Work out who those swimming hats belonged to and do something new. Prove to herself just what she could do.

'It's a date,' he said, looking pleased with himself.

'A date,' she repeated, mulling it over with her tongue, realising she liked the idea. A floorboard creaked upstairs making her flinch and Theo looked up at the ceiling.

'Do you want me to investigate?' he asked, frowning.

'Nope,' she rasped. 'It's just house noises. Or a ghost. I'm sure they're coming from the airing cupboard on the landing, but I'm not going to look.' She rolled her shoulders, trying to push off the weight that had settled onto them. 'If I still had my aunt's notes I'd probably have the explanation. I only hear the creaks at night. It freaked me out for the first few days, along with the owl and rumours of a Yeti, but I'm getting used to the sounds now.'

'Brave,' Theo observed.

She choked back a yelp when the floorboards groaned again. 'If I really was brave, *I'd* go and investigate.'

Theo started to rise and she put a hand out to stop him.

'Please don't. I'm working myself up to checking it out, I just need a little more time.' His skin was warm and the buzz of attraction instant so she tugged her hand away. She thought he was going to ignore her but something inside her clicked when he sat down again. He sipped more of his wine and tapped a finger on the table as if he wasn't sure what to do with his hands. Theo didn't look like he wanted to leave and Merry wished she knew what he was thinking. 'I'm sorry, I just...'

'Don't want to be saved.' His mouth curved down. 'I should probably get going.'

'Please don't.' She reached out to press her hand to his arm again, felt his biceps flex, and left it resting there. Let her fingertips explore the warm, rock-hard muscles.

'What do you want, Merry?' Theo asked, looking down at their joined limbs. His voice was as rough as it was confused.

'I want to be braver – more like Carmel,' she murmured. She didn't move; instead, she leaned into the table and held Theo's gaze.

'There's that name again,' he said. 'You've talked about Carmel before. Who is she, a friend?'

Merry sighed. 'I made her up, she's in my book,' she whispered. 'She's everything I want to be. All the things I came to Christmas Village to become.'

Theo placed his other palm flat over her hand. It was a signal that he was listening, a sign she should continue. That he wasn't here to judge her or laugh. 'What do you like about Carmel?' He moved his other hand, started to caress a fingertip over each of her knuckles, and every stroke felt like the tick of a hypnotist's clock. She felt herself sag in her chair before she realised he was leading and she was supposed to be the one in control.

She puffed out a breath and tugged her hand away so she could place it on his cheek. Until that moment, Merry hadn't realised she was capable – although the knot now growing inside her throat told her she was miles out of her comfort zone. That this didn't come naturally to her. 'She's courageous and confident.' She brushed her finger down the edge of Theo's cheek, feeling like it didn't belong to her. His skin felt rough – like warm sand on a beach, and she wished she could just close her eyes and sink in. But that felt like cowardice – she had to stay fully present in this moment if she was going to change. 'She doesn't take crap from anyone.' Her chest heaved. 'No one tells Carmel what to do and no one saves her.'

'I see,' he said, his mouth barely moving. She continued her slow slide and let her fingertip trace his bottom lip, moving from rough to smooth – it felt like she was caressing sandpaper then weathered glass.

'So if Carmel were here now, what would she do?' he asked, tipping his chin to give her better access.

'She'd kiss you,' Merry blurted without thinking. 'On the lips.' She let her eyes rise to explore his face, drifting down the chords of his neck to the tops of his wide shoulders. 'You're just her type.' She sighed.

'What's your type, Merry?' Theo asked seriously, watching as her fingertip stilled.

Merry inhaled, feeling a wave of something growing inside her, something that had probably been building for years. 'I don't know,' she gasped, meeting Theo's eyes. His lids were heavy now and his pupils had widened.

He leaned closer. 'Do you want to know mine?' he asked, his eyes dropping to her mouth.

'I'll go first,'' Merry offered. If she let Theo take over now, she'd lose the ability to form words. 'I like vets with muscles you normally only find on Olympic swimmers.' The look on his face made her insides flame. 'Who have smiles that could power a lighthouse. I like heroes who know when to help and when to take a back seat.' She opened her mouth to continue and he pressed a fingertip to it as a crease inched across his forehead.

'I like you,' Theo said, looking conflicted. Perhaps because he didn't want to?

Merry rose so she could lean over the table, close enough to press her mouth to Theo's. She knew if she didn't do it first, they were moments away from him making the first move – and it was important that she do it. Theo started to stand too although Merry guessed he was probably crouching otherwise he'd be towering over her now. The edge of the table was digging into her stomach and she had a sudden urge to hop onto the top and shimmy across so she could sink into him.

Theo tasted as good as she'd expected. He wasn't sweet, more... fresh. The wine must have evaporated on his tongue because Merry could only think of a crisp wind that stirs your blood after a long walk. She let her tongue explore his and pushed her fingertips into his thick hair, combing her way through the silken locks, trying to ignore the annoying wooden barrier that was keeping them apart. Then suddenly, Theo leaned closer and scooped Merry from the floor before lifting her over the table until she was kneeling on the far edge – her body moulded to his. Now they were the same height and their faces were level.

'That's better,' Theo said and put his mouth on hers. Merry countered by pressing her body – from her thighs to her collarbone – against his. She dropped her hand so she could lay it on his shoulder and stroked her fingertips across the muscles she'd been admiring. They flexed under her touch. He was huge and made her feel tiny, but his caresses were gentle and, despite the contrast in their sizes, Merry still felt in control.

She moved her mouth so she could nibble at the corner of his and felt the rough stubble chafe her cheek. Her fingers continued to wander across his shoulders, laying claim, memorising every flawless inch. Theo was obviously holding back because his hands remained resting on the curve of Merry's spine. Was he waiting for her to decide what to do next?

She took a moment before letting her hands glide lower until they skimmed the bottom of his T-shirt. Merry paused for a beat before taking a deep breath and tugging the material out of Theo's jeans. Then she pressed her fingertips to his skin and felt the bunch of those hard muscles she'd been admiring. Even without looking she could tell Theo was glorious. A million nerves inside her simultaneously liquefied and contracted until she was forced to squeeze her legs together. She moved her fingertips upwards, marvelling at the sheer perfection of his chest, feeling the corresponding pump of heat fizz through her veins as she continued to explore. 'You're gorgeous,' she murmured against Theo's mouth, keeping her eyes shut. If she opened them now she might wake up or lose sight of the person she'd become. The woman who took control and wasn't afraid of anything. But she had to concentrate hard to hold on to this moment.

She felt Theo smile against her lips, then his hand moved to her bottom and he eased her closer until she could feel the evidence of his attraction press against her hips.

'I'm trying to hold back here,' he whispered as his mouth slowly drifted from her cheek to her ear. 'But if you keep on touching me like that...' He inhaled sharply when her fingertip found a nipple and she stroked the sensitive skin. 'I'm going to lose it.' She could feel the tension hardening his body, feel his muscles straining. Then he bit the lobe of her ear and she shuddered, knowing she was seconds from letting him take over, seconds from losing herself. Perhaps it was a warning, but it was enough to wake her. Enough to stop the dream. Merry pulled away so she could look into Theo's face.

'We should stop.' She cleared her throat. Things were moving too quickly, she was losing her ability to think. She had to regroup. 'I'm sorry,' she said as he stared at her in surprise.

'It's okay,' Theo said, softly easing away, dropping his hands, leaving her feeling empty and bereft. He stroked a finger down her cheek. 'You're in control.' He blinked. 'We have plenty of time. I can wait until you're ready.'

With that, he stepped away and tucked his T-shirt back into his jeans before shrugging on his coat.

All the while Merry's body was screaming 'no!' and the sliver of Carmel inside her was attempting to crawl back up her throat so she could tell Theo he didn't need to go. Instead, Merry watched as he dressed and gathered his things, wondering if she'd ever be ready for Theo Ellis-Lee.

15

The phone buzzed in Theo's consulting room at the surgery and he immediately picked it up. 'Doctor Ellis-Lee.'

'How's Merry?' Noah demanded and Theo felt his shoulders sag.

'Fine. Great,' he said as his body immediately recalled how she'd felt pressed up against his chest the evening before – how sweet she'd tasted. But he was pretty sure Noah wouldn't want to hear about that.

'So she's safe?' her brother probed as Theo got up from his desk so he could pace the room. The desire to put Noah straight, to tell him to butt out, sat heavy in his throat but he knew if he did it, all three of her siblings would be in Scotland before the end of the day. This was the only way he could offer his invisible protection and help Merry to achieve the independence she craved.

'She's doing well.' He swallowed. 'The animals are great and she's been... making friends, getting to know the locals.' She'd got to know him pretty well last night and her scent still lingered on his skin, even after his morning shower.

'Friends?' Noah sounded suspicious. 'Male or female?'

'All women – she met them for cocktails,' he shot back.

'So she's not putting herself in danger, there's nothing for us to worry about?' Noah asked, the tension in his voice easing a little.

'She's been writing her book,' Theo explained, avoiding the question. He didn't want to lie and couldn't tell the truth, but the fine line between the two was delicate and perilous. He could only hope Noah hadn't employed another spy in Christmas Village; if he had, Theo was sunk. What would her brothers say if they knew he'd taken Merry driving? What would they think about the forthcoming swim? He planned to ask her to 'help' with some of his veterinary visits later, too. He'd made a list last night of clients from the surgery and had a few more Secret Santa clues he could point out, ready for Merry to solve.

'It's good she's working but please discourage her from sending off her manuscript to anyone,' Noah continued. 'Last time she shared it an idiot eviscerated her. If she does it again, I'm worried she won't get over it.'

Theo grunted because he knew he couldn't promise that – even if the idea of Merry being hurt sat heavy on his chest.

'When will you see her next?' a different male voice demanded. Theo heard the low buzz of voices in the background and realised he was on speakerphone. Probably all three of Merry's brothers were listening in. Had he been this over-bearing with past girlfriends, with Miranda and Jake? Hovering over them like a mother hen, not letting them make their own mistakes? The idea made him uncomfortable.

'Later this afternoon.' He was picking Merry up at lunchtime so they could go to the loch and swim. Apparently, on Tuesdays there was an afternoon meet. He'd fished out his wetsuit from the loft and planned to take a break in between appointments. He hoped Merry could swim. His shoulders tensed: he hadn't thought to ask. 'We're going to... get some fresh air,' he explained.

'Keeping her busy is a good idea. How's the weather up there?'

Theo looked out of the window as a flurry of snowflakes blew past on a gust. The wind was picking up and they'd want to be tucked up safe in their houses before dusk. 'Cold but there aren't any blizzards forecast at the moment,' he lied. The weather apps hadn't mentioned any but a few of the villagers had been predicting another big storm – although there was little news on exactly when it would arrive.

Noah sighed. 'Are you *sure* Merry's okay? Because I could book a flight, or drive and be there by tonight...'

'She's fine,' Theo said firmly, imagining her reaction if her brother arrived on her doorstep. All her carefully laid plans would be ruined. 'I told you, I'll have an eye on her and keep you in the loop. You know she doesn't want you to visit.' He shut his eyes. He felt despicable, but knew this was the best thing he could do. Theo hated lying, but knew Merry would hate it even more if her brothers descended. Besides, he was enjoying spending time with her, having her to himself. Learning how to be around someone without trying to rescue them from every tiny problem. Or at least being with someone who didn't expect that from him.

Someone knocked on Theo's door and Kirsteen poked her head around before he had a chance to respond. 'I need to go,' Theo muttered, not waiting for an acknowledgement before hanging up. He didn't want the receptionist overhearing, couldn't bear the idea of Merry finding out he was talking to her brothers – he wouldn't be able to explain it and, even if he could, she'd never understand.

'I wondered if you'd have time later to visit one of the local farms?' Kirsteen asked, handing Theo a scrap of paper with a scribbled address. 'There's a pregnant sheep who's a little testy. I just need someone to make sure there's nothing wrong.'

'Was that Isla McGavin?' Jared limped into Theo's office and leaned on the doorframe, frowning. His leg was still encased in the blue boot he complained about constantly. 'I could take a look, lad, if you're busy? I know those sheep well.' His expression was so eager Theo almost felt sorry for him. Jared had been stuck in the surgery for a few days now and it was obvious he was going out of his mind.

Kirsteen turned to glare at the older vet. 'Aye, and how would you do that? You can barely make it across the car park on your own.' She shucked in a breath and shook her head. 'Besides, Robina Sinclair, the headmistress from Christmas Village primary school, is due any moment with her sick guinea pig and she asked especially for you. The poor wee creature hasn't eaten for days.'

Jared frowned. 'That woman scares me,' he said hoarsely, turning back to glance into the empty waiting room, the wrinkles edging his eyes deepening. 'Last time she came to the surgery she left her glasses in my room, then when she popped in to pick them up she invited me to lunch.' He pulled a horrified face.

'Imagine that,' Kirsteen said dryly, although Theo detected a bite of jealousy in her tone. 'Tell her you're already taken if she asks again,' she said, sweeping out of the room.

'Taken by whom?' Jared asked, watching her go and looking perplexed.

'I'm sure you can work that out for yourself – it has four legs and its favourite word is "moo",' the older woman snapped and she marched into the waiting room. Jared shook his head and turned back to Theo, scratching his jaw. 'I don't know what's got into the lass. She mentioned bringing me a casserole over to the house yesterday evening and I told her I wanted to watch a documentary on cows – she's barely spoken to me since.'

Theo looked at the ground and shoved his hands into his pockets. 'Well.' He pulled a face – was pointing out the error of the vet's ways the same as getting involved? 'It's possible you hurt her feelings,' he explained because he felt sorry for Kirsteen.

Jared turned around to look into reception, his eyes wide. The man was still young, not much older than mid-fifties but his demeanour was so much older sometimes. 'How? I'd never want to do that.' He turned back to stare at Theo. 'What did I do?' He looked shaken.

Theo shrugged. 'You turned down a home-cooked meal from an attractive woman because you wanted to watch TV,' he said, watching as Jared processed the words and his cheeks paled.

The vet put a hand on his chest. 'Aye, I can see how that might...' He blew a breath between his teeth. 'I never was that good with the opposite sex; it's why I became a vet. I always get things wrong with anything that has less than four legs.'

'Join the club,' Theo murmured, thinking about Merry's brothers. Thinking about that kiss. He didn't regret it but knew it had been a bad idea. What if Merry discovered he'd been lying to her? He'd have to hope she never would. It was unlikely, as long as her brothers stayed away. But the dread was still there, nibbling at the edge of his mind.

Jared moved so he could stare into the waiting room again, his eyes following the receptionist as she busied herself behind the desk. She'd coiled tinsel around her computer screen and reflections from the pretty decorations glimmered across her cheeks. 'I never thought... I never imagined...' Jared twisted to look at Theo, his hazel eyes alight. 'The woman's far too good for the likes of me...'

'It's possible she doesn't agree.' Theo reached out to pat the older man's shoulder, feeling awkward.

'But what do I do now?' Jared asked.

Theo considered the question. He should walk away, refuse to help, rein in the German Shepherd inside who was so desperate to assist, but the baffled look on his partner's face was too much for him. 'Ask Kirsteen somewhere, take her for a meal, prove she means a lot more to you than any cow,' he suggested.

Jared rotated towards the reception area again, looking thoughtful. 'Aye.' He tapped his chin. 'I could try that, I suppose,' he said before slowly limping out.

16

Six women in various stages of undress were standing by the small loch when Theo pulled up in his car. He'd spent the last half hour checking the McGavins' sheep which had complained bitterly throughout the examination. He couldn't find anything wrong, but he planned to keep his mobile on in case anything changed – and had promised to pop in to see it again later today.

Beside him, Merry stared out of the window with her hands wound tightly in her lap. She'd not spoken much on the journey but he wasn't sure if it was because she was nervous about the impending swim – or perhaps it was because of their kiss?

'Um.' Theo cleared his throat. 'I wondered if you'd be free to come on a few of my call-outs later?' he asked, waiting while Merry considered the request.

'Why?' She sounded suspicious. 'Don't you have people at the surgery who could help with that?' She swallowed. 'I don't want to be patronised, Theo. I want to help, but please don't invent ways of keeping me occupied. That would be insulting to us both.' She sounded upset.

Theo felt something in his stomach tip and spin. Merry had read his intentions perfectly, which meant he'd have to elaborate, dig himself deeper into the lie. 'Jared's hurt his ankle and he needs Kirsteen to help with the clients at the surgery. I wouldn't normally ask, but—' He grimaced as the words caught in his throat. He was doing the right thing, just pointing Merry in the right direction, helping her to complete her Secret Santa quest. He'd feel good about this eventually and she'd never find out. No one knew what he was doing, so how could she? 'Sometimes it's helpful to have another person with me. But if you don't have time...' A part of him hoped she'd say she didn't.

Merry puffed out a breath and turned to face him. 'I'm sorry, I didn't mean to doubt you. It's just...' She shrugged. 'It's the kind of thing my brothers would do. Ask for help when they don't really need it, just to keep me busy and to make me feel useful. So they get to control all of my experiences.'

Theo's insides chilled.

'I'm free later and of course I'd be happy to assist. Although, as you know, I don't have a lot of experience with animals.' She gave him a shy smile.

'I just need another pair of hands. I appreciate you giving up your time,' Theo assured her, but the words felt like they were coated in barbs. He stopped the car and watched as Merry opened the door and hopped out. She was already dressed in her aunt's wetsuit which was obviously too long for her because she'd rolled the bottoms up. Theo got out of the car too and locked it before striding over to join Merry, trying to shake off his guilt. They approached the small huddle of women and he immediately recognised Moira McGregor – the landlady of Christmas Pud Inn. She waved as they strolled up to join them and he watched as Moira scraped her hair from her face so she could put it into a ponytail. 'Kirsteen said you were coming to join us today.' Moira beamed, pointing to the water. 'Have you done any wild swimming before?'

'No,' Merry said, her eyes scanning the lake. Theo watched her bite her lip, her expression filled with trepidation. The water covered less area than Holly Loch by Theo's house, and the whole pool was fringed with high-sided banks of shingle and snow-covered trees which sheltered the area, making it feel a little cosy. But the water in the loch was dark blue and looked deep. Merry took in a shuddery breath. 'Is it safe?'

'Aye, as long as you know how to swim,' Moira joked as a woman with red hair cut into a pixie style wandered up to join in.

'Hi, I'm Julie Knox, I help my husband run the riding stables a couple of miles out of Christmas Village.' She offered Merry and Theo a hand before stroking it through her crop of hair. The other people milling around were all wearing swimming hats so Theo guessed these two were the intended recipients of the Secret Santa ones. He watched Merry's face as she narrowed her eyes and deduced she must have reached the same conclusion. On the back of the cake boxes and torch which had been allocated last night, he estimated Merry probably knew nine of the gift beneficiaries now. 'We come here for a quick splash every Tuesday lunchtime and on Sunday mornings,' Julie explained. 'It's very cold, so make sure you're careful when you get in. I wouldn't take too long but don't get in too quickly either because it'll be an awful shock. You okay?' Julie asked Merry when she continued to stare at their heads.

'Yep.' She gazed at them, her brown eyes bright. 'I've not been swimming for a while, but...' She tried to smile. 'I'm looking forward to it.' Her eyes shot to Theo – they were filled with challenge and he bit down on all the warnings circling his head.

'Me too,' he lied.

Another, taller woman with a long angular face came over from her car to join them. She wore a calf-length wetsuit, and seemed to be knitting.

'You going to put that down before you swim?' Julie joked. 'This is Rachel Brun; she's a whizz with a set of needles and wool, makes all sorts of blankets and things for our local animal charities.'

'That's amazing,' Merry said after a short pause and Theo wondered if the bird's nest knitting pattern he'd seen amongst her Aunt Ava's things were intended for Rachel. He waited to see if Merry would make the same connection, holding himself back from finding a subtle way of pointing it out. 'What sorts of things do you knit?' Merry's voice was guileless.

'Ach, beds, hats, clothes, all sorts,' Rachel said, as her fingers continued to stitch. 'I've promised I'll finish twelve dog blankets by the end of this week – it's a challenge, which is why I'm knitting now.' She dipped her head towards her blue and pink creation. Theo saw Merry's mouth quirk and guessed she was trying to hold in a smile. She'd obviously connected the dots, which meant yet another Secret Santa recipient had been identified.

'You can't swim and knit at the same time,' Moira teased, pointing to the needles.

'I'll put these in the car now, I need to grab my hat anyway. Good to meet you, Merry. Nice to see you too, Theo.' Rachel flashed them both a grin as she headed away.

'Don't you two wear anything on your heads?' Merry asked Moira and Julie as she tugged the black swimming hat she'd been carrying over her hair.

Julie sighed. 'I got a hole in mine last month and Moira here lent hers to Lennie, one of her twins, and he lost it when he was at a swimming lesson.'

'Aye.' Moira raised her eyes skyward. 'I've been meaning to order a new one but I've got my heart set on something specific – it's pink with a green flower on the side.' She patted the edge of her head. 'It's always going out of stock in the one place I can get it. Julie wants the same design. I'm signed up to the mailing list and we're waiting to hear.'

Merry looked back at the loch, obviously fighting a grin.

The two hats on the table back at Chestnut Cottage were both pink with green flowers.

Now she'd solved another Secret Santa clue, Theo hoped Merry would find an excuse to back out of the swim. 'Do you still want to do this?' he asked and she shot him a curious look.

'Of course, why wouldn't I?' she whispered, taking a step forwards.

'Shall I go first?' he offered, matching her step.

'Better if I do it.' Her voice was tight. 'If there are any trout in there, we'll want to make sure they catch my scent first.'

He cautiously followed Merry to the edge of the water, holding himself back. He'd make sure he swam beside her and kept her within arm's reach, but he wouldn't interfere unless she looked like she needed help. It was the least he could do, considering he was supposed to be keeping an eye on her. He shook his head, imagining what Noah would say if he could see them now. Merry was wearing swimming socks but when she stuck her foot into the loch, she shivered.

'Cold?' Theo asked, dipping his sock in too and gasping as icy tentacles of water slithered between his toes.

Merry flapped her arms by her sides, warming herself up. Then they both watched as the six women wandered to the water's edge and gradually submerged themselves one by one. There were a few shrieks, a torrent of laughter, then they were all swimming – their arms lancing into the clear pool.

'Are we really going to do this?' Merry turned to stare at Theo. Her voice was calm but he could hear the uncertainty in it now. He gripped his hands by his sides, fighting the part of himself that wanted to make an excuse or say no.

'Carmel would,' he said instead – and his insides lurched when Merry gave him a grateful smile.

'She would.' She hissed air between her teeth. 'That's exactly what I needed to hear.' Then she turned and waded into the water, flinching as the dark liquid slithered up her calves.

'You coming in?' she yelled, turning so she could look at him. Theo had made it up to his knees, but the cold had stolen the breath from his throat.

'Right behind you,' he gasped, speeding up as he cursed himself for encouraging Merry to do this. He watched her stop when the water reached her waist. Then she glanced back suddenly, winked and dived in. 'No!' The panicked word shot from between Theo's lips and he was glad Merry was under the surface so she didn't hear. His heartbeat went into overdrive and he dove too and swam, matching its pace. He ignored the slither of frigid loch water as it reached his shoulders and neck, then slunk underneath the body of his wetsuit, flooding across his chest. Did people really do this for fun? He wanted to laugh, but couldn't seem to form the sound. Instead, he dived under again and in two quick strokes caught up with Merry. She was halfway into the lochan, treading water, looking around, her eyes wide.

'This is... different,' she gasped as he stopped and paddled closer then started to tread water too, attempting to catch his breath. 'If my brothers could see me now...' She rolled her eyes.

'I'm guessing they'd perform an intervention – before making me "swim with the fishes" permanently.' Theo cleared his throat. 'I don't think I've ever been so cold.' He shivered and Merry grinned.

'I'd never have pegged you as a whiner,' she teased. 'The love interest in my novel, Carmel's—' Her lips pinched. 'I'm not sure of the right word – let's call him a boyfriend, or perhaps partner in crime? No, he's her sidekick.' She nodded. 'Yep, that works.' She looked back at him and arched an eyebrow. 'He never whines.'

Theo swam closer, feeling curls of water whisper against his limbs. 'What's his name?'

'Dan,' Merry said. 'It's a good name, no-nonsense.'

'What does he do?' Theo guessed he was a spy, or something just as adventurous.

'He's a vet,' Merry said, then she looked away, avoiding his eyes. 'At least, he might be, I haven't completely decided on that yet.' She began to swim away, clearly embarrassed and Theo held back, giving her space, as something inside him warmed along with the understanding that what she'd just told him might not be a good thing. Was Merry developing feelings for him? That definitely complicated things, especially since he hadn't told her about his informal agreement with Noah. Then again, wasn't he developing feelings for her too?

Theo started to swim again, aiming to catch up. He wasn't trying to rescue Merry but he wasn't happy leaving her alone when she was out of her depth. What would her brothers say? He wished he didn't care, wished he could be more carefree, like Jake.

Theo swam faster as Merry made her way further into the lake, trying not to think about the creatures lurking underneath them. Then something bumped against his knee and he gasped in surprise, losing his rhythm and swallowing a mouthful of icy water. He coughed and stopped swimming so he could gather himself. He still had one eye on Merry so saw her turn and frown.

'Are you okay?' She swam towards him with Julie and Moira following at speed.

'What happened?' Julie asked as she placed a gentle hand under Theo's arm, making sure he kept his chin above the water.

'I'm okay.' Mortified, Theo spluttered and coughed again. Where had all the liquid come from? Why couldn't he catch his breath?

'We should probably go back in, I'll come with you,' Merry said, reaching for his wrist.

'I'm okay.' Horrified, Theo tugged himself away from the

women. He wasn't used to being rescued, this whole situation felt wrong.

He trod water as Julie and Moira checked him over. 'Ach the lad's fine – Merry, keep an eye on him in case he tries to drown again.' Julie winked and the two women swam off.

'Are you sure you're okay?' Merry asked, paddling closer. 'I know you're embarrassed, but that could have happened to anyone. I'm a pretty good swimmer. When I was younger I used to compete for my school.'

'Might have been useful to know that earlier,' Theo growled, still treading water as something in the depths slithered against his leg. *Jeez*, he'd only been joking about the trout. This time he didn't go under, but his attention fixed on the shore. 'Maybe we should get out. It's getting cold and I need to change and get to work.'

'I'll come with you, just in case you need rescuing again.' Merry's eyes glittered with humour when he frowned.

Theo started to swim towards the shore, feeling like the world was turning on its axis but he no idea what it all meant.

'We've got a couple of places to visit,' Theo explained a few hours later. He'd been home, showered, eaten lunch then picked Merry up from Chestnut Cottage and planned to stop off at a few clients' houses so he could point her in the direction of more locals who should be recipients of the Secret Santa gifts. He had to take it slow to make sure she didn't get suspicious, so wouldn't risk highlighting more than one or two. The road was layered in snow and Theo had to slow the car as it skidded a little. 'First we'll check in on the sheep Isla and Clyde McGavin were worrying about.' He'd heard Isla complain about her husband's cold feet on his visit to the farm early this morning and guessed the heated slippers he'd seen in with the rest of the Secret Santa gifts were intended for him.

'Sounds good,' Merry said, looking out of the window. After a mild start to the day, it had started to snow and flakes were now flinging themselves at the car. 'What's that?' she asked, leaning forwards to peer out of the windscreen. 'Is a car stuck?'

'Maybe.' Theo pulled up behind the truck he knew belonged to Logan Forbes before carefully stepping out. 'I won't be long, Dot,' he promised the Dalmatian, grimacing when Merry jumped out too. Instinct pleaded with him to tell her to stay in the car but he stopped himself just in time.

'Are you okay?' Theo heard Merry ask as he caught up with her. It was freezing outside; the wind had definitely picked up and it whipped past his head, worming its way under his coat so it could spread its icy feelers across his chest.

'We're fine,' Logan grumbled as he shovelled remnants of the blizzard from the rear tyres of a black Audi TT which was stuck a few metres down the road from his truck. 'Jack here insists on driving this ridiculous toy car regardless of the season. You'd think after a year of living in Christmas Village he'd have managed to buy himself a grown-up vehicle, or at least learned to pack something useful in that miniscule boot – like a snow-mobile, or a kilo of salt.'

Jack poked his head up from the front of the car and waved a shovel that had snapped in half, rendering it almost useless. His black hair was soaked and his cheeks were ruddy from the cold. 'Belle bought me a spade, but I broke it in the summer and keep forgetting to replace it. My car is grand, the weather is the problem.' He sighed, before bending to scoop more snow.

'Can I help?' Theo asked, tracking forwards.

'Nae, it's fine. Jack's lucky I spotted him when I was driving past, we're almost done,' Logan said. 'You settling in okay, lass?' he asked Merry as her attention fixed on Jack. There was a small spade amongst the Secret Santa gifts.

'Yes, thank you.' Her eyes drifted to Logan and then to the large shovel he was using. 'Do you carry tools wherever you go?'

'He'd strap them to his body if he could,' Jack said dryly, rising and waving the broken shovel at his friend.

Theo pursed his lips – was the wristband of tools for Logan? It sounded like the perfect match – he should probably have worked it out sooner. Who other than the village handyman would a tool belt be intended for? He couldn't risk looking at Merry because he knew his expression would say it all.

'I'm done. If you give me a moment, I'll see if I can move the car,' Jack shouted.

'I won't hold my breath.' Logan folded his arms. 'You two should get going.' He pointed at the sky. 'I'm not sure how long this break in the weather will hold.'

'You call this a break?' Jack snorted. 'Logan's right, though, I'm sure you've got plenty of better things to do. Thanks for stopping to help, maybe we'll catch up again in the pub soon?'

Theo nodded and followed Merry as she made her way back to the car. It only took ten more minutes to drive to the McGavins'. Merry didn't say much but he saw her pull her mobile from her pocket to make a few notes. Was she reminding herself of the latest gift recipients? He wanted to ask, but couldn't. He was already on shaky ground considering how many clues had been thrown her way in the last few hours. He couldn't risk her becoming suspicious.

As they drew up to a large farmhouse, Theo spotted Clyde opening the front door. Then he trotted out and waved. 'It's good of you to stop in again.' His green eyes surveyed the car as Merry got out too. 'And you've brought a visitor!' He grinned.

'This is Merry McKenzie,' Theo introduced them.

'Ach, you'll be that author my son, Adam, has been telling me about.' Clyde beamed. 'The lad has been writing stories ever since you came to talk to his class.' He held out a hand.

'It's great to meet you. Adam is a lovely boy,' Merry said, shaking it before looking around.

'Well, you've inspired him all right,' Clyde glowed. 'He

keeps talking about car chases and women saving men. My wife, Isla, is very impressed, we could barely get him to hold a pen until now.'

'Well, thanks...' Merry blushed. 'This is a pretty house.'

'It's bonnie, but it gets cold in winter.' The man shivered and stomped on the ground, shaking flakes of snow from his boots. 'My wife will tell you I'm always freezing.' He flapped his arms, patting his shoulders before waving at his feet. 'Especially my toes. She says I don't have blood down there, just ice!'

'Don't you have any slippers?' Merry arched an eyebrow.

'Aye lass, but nothing works,' Clyde lamented.

Theo watched Merry's lips press together and saw the almost imperceptible nod. After checking on the sheep, his work would be done for today. He'd drop Merry off, then head back to the surgery. He wouldn't risk taking her to see anyone else in Christmas Village – couldn't chance her growing suspicious. He had feelings for her, feelings he'd vowed he wasn't going to have – but it was already too late. Now he had to ensure Merry allocated every one of the Secret Santa gifts without ever knowing he'd helped. Perhaps then he could ask her on a proper date, maybe see if she'd consider starting a relationship? He only hoped it wouldn't be too much longer before he could.

17

Merry finished reading the extract including the car chase from her manuscript and fought to steady her shaky hands. The classroom was silent and she breathed deeply before looking up into the faces of the eleven children who were all now gaping at her. *They hated it* – Merry swallowed as tears pooled in the corners of her eyes. She had no talent, the anonymous critic had been right – her insides felt like crushed ice.

Then Ace McDowell rose from his chair and began to clap, then the rest of the class got up one by one to join in. Finally, Belle stood and put her hands together too. 'I enjoyed your story. The car chase was really cool,' the young boy gushed when the applause faded. 'I hope you'll read some more of your book when you come next week.'

Merry carefully placed the pages of her novel onto the table, feeling like someone had just pumped up her chest like a balloon. It was the first time she'd shared her work since she'd uploaded a chapter to the writing website a few months after her coma and her confidence had been shattered. On the heels of the car accident, months in hospital and weighed down by the over-protectiveness of her brothers – and their lack of faith in her ability to cope – she'd decided to give up writing for good. Until she'd seen Mrs Adam's obituary and later decided to come to Christmas Village. It was almost inconceivable how far she'd come. 'Of course I will. Thank you.' She gulped the bubbles of happiness exploding in her throat. 'The car chase was your idea, after all.'

Ace beamed and patted himself on the back as the class erupted into giggles.

'Do Dan and Carmel kiss?' Mazey Taylor asked when the noise died down. She'd sat through the short reading with her arms folded, sporting a frown. Merry had assumed the young girl hated the story, but she'd obviously misread the room.

'Um, yes they have,' Merry admitted, trying not to think about Theo's lips.

'My da told me kissing is really unhygienic,' Mazey said sadly.

Belle came to stand at the front of the class. 'Your da might have a point, especially since it's flu season, but...' She looked at Merry with humour in her eyes. 'I'm guessing Dan and Carmel must have decided it was worth the risk. Do any of you have characters or ideas you want to share with Ms McKenzie?'

A boy shot his hand in the air and wriggled on his seat.

'Yes, Adam,' Belle said, smiling indulgently.

'My hero loves sheep.' He brushed a thick lock of black hair from his eyes. 'But he's afraid of people.'

Merry perched on the edge of the desk and regarded the earnest young man. 'Any particular reason why?' she asked quietly.

Adam swallowed. 'Because sometimes they can be mean,' he said.

'Aye.' The rest of the class chorused their agreement and a few at the back started to chatter, perhaps sharing stories of their own unhappy experiences?

Belle looked at Merry expectantly. 'Well,' Merry started. 'I think the last time I came we talked about character traits we liked. Things like being kind and giving people the space to do what they need to grow.' Her mind moved to Theo and she tugged it away, trying to concentrate. 'I think sometimes we have to move away from other people's opinions, or at least recognise they might not be right.'

Merry's brothers had never been mean, but there was no doubt their assumptions about her fragility had held her back. She'd started to believe them – it had become so much easier to remain in her safe, cosseted world.

'Not everyone is unkind. Perhaps your character could find some people he likes?' she suggested. 'Characters in books can learn a lot from other people. Their friends can teach them so much about themselves – or give them the strength to change, to be braver and happier too.' Her mind conjured up Theo again, from his patience when she'd been driving the car, to the swim he'd clearly hated, to him asking for help with the one-eyed cat. 'Remember, you're making this up so invent whoever you want. Your characters don't have to be real, but they could share traits with friends, family or other people you know. How about if your hero has a friend with a soft spot for sheep too?'

The young man regarded her silently. 'My da likes sheep, I could write about him.' He winkled his nose. 'My mam loves sewing, I might write about that.'

'Sewing?' Merry's ears pricked. There was a colourful sewing kit in with the Secret Santa gifts.

'Yes, she's really good at it – her name is Isla McGavin,' the young boy said proudly. 'She'll make you something if you ask.'

'I went to your house yesterday with Dr Ellis-Lee but I only met your dad. I'll definitely think of your mum if I need anything made. She has a very pretty name, I won't forget it.' Merry made a mental note as her eyes skirted the room and she wished she could ask the children more about what their parents enjoyed. Then again, after spending yesterday afternoon with Theo, she'd managed to tick a lot more gifts off her list and only had six of the original twenty presents left to assign. 'A lot of writers take inspiration from the people they know,' she said, thinking about Dan's eyes, the way he smelled, of how many of Theo's traits had made their way into her hero now. She swallowed the sudden uncomfortable realisation that she might be falling for the vet. It hadn't been part of her plan when she'd left Hertfordshire, but it seemed she didn't have much choice. She'd never met anyone like him – he'd listened to what she'd wanted and supported her when so few people in her life had. He hadn't tried to take over or protect her; he'd let her make her own mistakes.

'My da is called Bram McGregor. He collects beer tankards,' Lennie said, suddenly putting up his hand and speaking at the same time. 'We live in the pub and he drinks from them sometimes, but no one else is allowed to touch.' He widened his eyes. 'I think the hero in my story is going to like tankards.'

'That's a good idea, Lennie.' Merry fought a grin. That was fifteen Secret Santa gifts identified now, meaning there were only five left to go... If only she could share the good news with somebody – then again, the only person Merry wanted to confide in was Theo and she couldn't tell him and break her aunt's trust.

Suddenly, someone knocked on the door of the classroom and opened it without waiting. An older woman with bushy eyebrows wearing a tidy blue suit wandered inside. 'Have any of you children seen my glasses?' she asked, patting her head. 'I can't find them anywhere. Honestly, I'd lose my own nose if it wasn't attached. Anyone?' she asked, scouring the room.

'No, Ms Sinclair,' the children recited.

'I'm sorry,' Belle said quietly. 'No glasses here. Perhaps you should try in reception?'

The older woman squinted at the door. 'Aye, I left them in

the library yesterday afternoon, I'll look there now.' With that, the woman headed out of the room.

Belle turned back to the class when the door closed. 'Does anyone else have a question for Ms McKenzie?'

The children looked at her blankly, then a young girl with a long angular face and stunning green eyes put her hand in the air.

'Yes Alison Brun, did you have any characters you wanted to discuss?'

'No, but I'd like to know what's going to happen in your story next,' she said. 'I really like Carmel. Are she and Dan going to get the diamonds to the museum on Tinsel Mountain in time?'

'I've not written the next part of the story yet, but...' Merry tapped a fingertip on her chin, thinking about Theo and what had happened in the loch the day before. It had made her feel good to help him and in an odd way braver – as if focusing on someone else's problems helped you face your own fears. Perhaps because it made them seem so much less important? 'I think Dan might be captured and Carmel will save him,' she said, thinking on her feet because she had no idea.

'I like that idea,' Mazey said. 'She'd have to be really brave because she'd probably be scared too. The heroine in my book is really heroic; she's going to save the hero when he falls out of Santa's sleigh – even though she's afraid of heights.' There were chatters of approval from the class.

'I'd love to read that,' Merry said, smiling.

'So would I,' Belle agreed. 'So, in a minute, we're going to talk about the elements of a good story. Then for the lesson next week, you're all going to write your Christmas story and Ms McKenzie is going to read them and choose the best ones to read out.'

Ace bounced on his seat. 'I've got a great idea. I bet you'll choose mine.' He grinned.

'I'm looking forward to seeing it,' Merry said.

'And you'll share the next part of your story while you're here?' Mazey asked again.

'Of course I will,' Merry promised as her mind drifted to Theo once more and she wondered how many more ways Dan might start to resemble the vet.

The weather had taken a turn for the worse when Rowan pulled her car up on Chestnut Cottage's driveway half an hour after the lesson.

'You need to feed the animals soon, lass,' she said worriedly, surveying the sky. 'There's a storm coming, a bad one. Even the weather apps are predicting it now. Make sure everything's locked up and get yourself inside, preferably under a duvet. Whatever happens, don't go back outside. There have been worse storms than this in the past years and your aunt's garden is well sheltered, so the animals will be safe. Just check on them in the morning and don't stray from these four walls. I've made you dinner.' She handed Merry a casserole dish, waiting as she got out of the car before shouting more instructions. 'Logan will drop in tomorrow when the weather is calmer to chop some wood. Tonight you're going to have to keep the fire fed – so make sure you use as much as you need.'

'I can chop wood myself,' Merry replied.

'Ach, but Logan will be happy to help. As you know, he's our local handyman and always keeps a special eye on everyone who lives around the village. Give him some eggs from the chickens as a thank you, that's what your aunt does. It's the only thing he'll accept. I'll call tomorrow to make sure you're okay.' With that, Rowan quickly backed the car out of the drive before closing the gate, leaving Merry staring at the sky.

It took half an hour to feed and secure the animals. Even Henry was happy to be locked in a pen and Merry gathered some of the uneaten cranberries Theo had dropped in the garden, leaving him a handful to keep him content. The turkey raised his beak when she dropped them, as if he were smelling the air, perhaps expecting Theo? Merry didn't think she'd just imagined the slump in the big bird's gait when he realised the vet wasn't there. Theo definitely had a way of getting under your skin, making you feel special, giving you exactly what you needed. It obviously worked if you had feathers too. As Merry did a final check to ensure the animal enclosures were properly locked, she looked up at the sky. The clouds had grown larger and darker even while she'd been busy – all the apps were predicting nothing short of a disaster movie, but perhaps they hadn't been exaggerating? Merry wondered where Theo was now. She hadn't heard from him since the swim yesterday afternoon and a part of her was worried. Would he be reckless enough to venture out in the storm? She guessed the answer was yes if he thought an animal was in need. Her stomach knotted.

Once inside, she busied herself putting the Christmas lights on and placing the casserole dish in the fridge before pulling her mobile out of her pocket to check for messages. 'Noah hasn't called in over a day. Neither have Liam or Ollie,' she confided to Chewy as he scampered across the tiled floor. 'It doesn't make sense. Do you think they're okay?' She tapped a quick message to check in, hoping she wasn't about to trigger a flurry of concerned responses. She was so used to their constant texts and calls, it would take a while to get used to the silence – even if a part of her was relieved they were finally coming around to the idea of trusting her, and giving her the space she'd asked them for.

The lights went off and her whole body froze, then she breathed out slowly when they flared back on. A floorboard squeaked in the ceiling and Merry forced herself to take a seat at the kitchen table and switch on her laptop.

'It's just house noises, right?' she said to the rabbit, her tone muted as she focused on the words on the screen. After her lesson with Belle's class, and all the children's questions and praise, she was filled with an overwhelming desire to continue writing her book. After today, she was determined the next scene would focus on Carmel rescuing Dan. Her hero was now locked in a dungeon because the Jeep had broken down and he'd been captured. Carmel had managed to escape with the diamonds, but her heroine had no intention of leaving him behind.

Merry stared at the computer, mulling over what might happen next as her mind drifted back to Theo. What was he doing, where was he now, was he safe – and what was she going to do about her growing feelings for him? She blew out a breath, realising she had no clue so decided to focus on her book instead. At least here she could control what happened next...

'What are you doing here?' Dan croaked from the back of the small, damp cell. 'I let myself get captured so you could get away.'

Carmel looked behind her, checking for guards, and then sneaked forwards. She could smell Dan's scent now and the fact that he still somehow smelled good comforted her.

'I'm going to get you out,' she whispered, glancing behind her again. 'We're a team. No one gets left.' She pulled a clip from her hair and straightened the gold-coloured metal before wriggling it into the large padlock securing the cell...

Everything went black. One minute Merry was typing and the next, all the lights blinked off. She waited as fear skidded up the back of her neck and her hairs performed a Mexican wave as she listened for sounds – but all she could hear was the soft crackle of the fire. She knew the cause of the power cut was probably her aunt's sensitive fuse box again, but there was something frightening about being here alone. Especially now the lights were off.

Pitter, patter, pitter, pat. Simba strolled across the kitchen tiles towards Merry, making her heart thump hard.

'Stay there. You too, Chewy,' she commanded although she couldn't see the rabbit anywhere. She got up so she could search under the kitchen sink for the toolbox and also find the torch, which was now working thanks to new batteries. Fortunately, there was just enough light from the laptop to guide her. She crept across the kitchen towards the stairwell, stalling momentarily when she heard another creak from above. 'It's nothing, Chewy, don't be afraid,' she whispered, knowing the soothing words were more for herself. 'I'll have the electric back on in a tick and we'll be fine.' A gust of wind howled and bashed against the windows, making Merry jump. She took in a prolonged breath and continued to tiptoe towards the stairwell. 'Almost there,' she said, opening the fuse box and pushing the switches back up.

Nothing happened.

'Dammit.' She shoved the switches down then heaved them up once more. 'This should work.' It had the other day. Wind battered the house. Was the storm getting worse? Was that why the fuse box wouldn't come back on? The weather app had indicated that Merry had an hour or two before the worst of the squall began. She searched the kitchen, squinting into the darkness. She could just make out Simba, who'd returned to the fire, but there was still no sign of Chewy. She slowly crept across the room, using the torch to search in the corners. The fire was sizzling, but it seemed unnaturally quiet. There was a loud crack as one of the logs ignited and Merry flinched. Could she really stay here alone? She let out a long sigh – she'd have to. She scanned the room, checking beside the fridge and underneath the kitchen table. 'Where are you, Chewy?' she asked, wandering behind the sofa to where Theo had found the rabbit on the evening they'd first met.

'*No, no, no!*' Her heart tumbled in her chest when she spotted the rabbit laying on its side, tangled in wires. 'Oh God!' she yelped, hurling herself to her knees so she could check on him. She pressed her fingertips to Chewy's chest and felt a faint *pat, pat, pat*. The wires underneath him, which led to a large grey lamp, had been nibbled right through. 'Chewy, what have you done?' Merry gathered the rabbit in her arms, but he didn't wake up. 'Please be okay,' she pleaded, running to the kitchen table and pulling out her mobile so she could call Theo, praying he'd be at home, but the phone immediately clicked to voice-mail. Perhaps the storm was messing with the signal?

'You're okay,' she said as Chewy twitched and his eyelids fluttered. 'But you're going to have to be checked out.' She couldn't risk leaving him. What if he died and she could have done something to save him? She peered out of the window. 'Rowan said all the animals will be okay if I leave them locked up.' There was another gust and a loud bang as a branch thudded against the side of the house. Merry breathed in a gush of air, looking around the kitchen, then at the rabbit again. 'I have to take you to Theo's.' But was she brave enough to drive alone through a storm?

Merry put Chewy carefully onto the sofa. Then she used a poker to spread out the wood and embers to help the flames die out, then found baking soda and threw the whole pot onto the fire, watching until the final sparks and embers spat and faded to black. She gathered Simba up mechanically, keeping her emotions in check as she placed him in a carrier, ignoring the cat's complaints. She wasn't going to leave him here on his own – besides, she had to give him his diabetes medicine. She put enough animal food into a bag to last a day in case they got stuck at Theo's, Simba's pills, and Rowan's casserole. Hopefully Theo would still have power, which meant she'd at least be able to feed him as a thank you for treating the rabbit. He hadn't invoiced her for any of his services so far and Merry suspected he never would. She took another slow look around the room and then, ignoring the roll of fear in her belly, grabbed the keys to the Jeep. She would drive to Theo's alone. She'd been okay the other day when she'd been with him. She'd driven slowly but they'd made it. Now she had to do it again. She wouldn't let herself think as she headed for the front door.

The Jeep was half obscured by a layer of snow when Merry climbed inside, placing Simba's carrier and the bag with the casserole and food for the animals in the back. She put Chewy carefully into the footwell of the passenger side. The rabbit was still breathing, but seemed unnaturally quiet. Merry sucked in a lungful of cold air before starting the car – then she sat for a few minutes, giving the engine time to warm and the worst of the snow to melt. She programmed 'Holly Lodge' into the satnav on her mobile. 'I'm going to be okay,' she whispered, feeling a little light-headed. Theo's house was a ten-minute drive which meant he hadn't been lying when he'd told her he didn't live far away. Merry put her seatbelt on, ignoring the imaginary chorus of dismay from her brothers which immediately crowded her mind. She eased the car from its parking spot.

It was one thing driving with Theo, and quite another doing it alone. Merry's hands shook as she steered and her mind was assaulted with flashbacks to the accident. To the car rolling and losing control, to the pain of the glass cutting her face – and then waking up three months later.

She focused on Carmel, thinking about how her heroine would deal with this situation. 'You can do this.' Merry checked Chewy again before turning the car until it faced forward. She had to hop out to open and close the gate at the end of the driveway and stopped momentarily to glance back at Chestnut Cottage. Everything looked secure, and the solar-powered Christmas lights scattered across the garden were still glimmering. She jumped back into the Jeep and sucked in a breath before pulling away and turning right. 'I hope Theo was joking about how difficult this drive was. I think he was just trying to put me off trying it alone.' She looked at the rabbit. 'You're going to be okay, Chewy, I'm going to get you to Theo and he'll make sure of it.' She ignored her shaking hand as she changed into second gear. Wind and snow were battering the windscreen now, obscuring almost everything, and she switched on the radio, changing it from a channel where a serious-sounding newsreader was warning everyone in the area to stay indoors to one playing Christmas songs.

Merry began to sing along to 'All I Want for Christmas is You' but stopped when she heard the wobble in her voice. 'I can't see much, Chewy,' she said. 'I know you can't talk but when I was in the hospital, my brothers used to take it in turns to sit with me. They said I was always happier when they were talking.' Merry indicated and took a left, joining another narrow road. She kept the car in second gear and didn't speed up. 'It might take me an hour to get to Theo's but slow is better than not making it at all,' she said. She didn't let herself think about what she'd do if the Jeep broke down, or she found herself facing a snowdrift, or worse. 'We're okay, Chewy, we're going to make it,' she repeated as she continued to drive blindly, moving into third gear before losing her nerve and shifting back down. 'We're not in a rush, are we?' she whispered. 'You're okay, aren't you?' She checked the footwell and saw the rabbit's ears twitch. 'Let's hope I can find Holly Lodge.' She followed the satnav and took a right, unpeeling one hand from the steering wheel as it began to go numb before doing the same with the other. Then she paused the car as they reached the top of a narrow, steep hill. Maybe Theo hadn't been lying when he'd warned her about the journey? The path looked perilous. She squinted and could just make out lights in the distance. 'It's okay, I think I see Theo's house.' Her chest filled with a flurry of relief. She started to edge the car down the hill, inching her way along the track. Snow was hurling itself at them and wind was pounding the windows, making it almost impossible to see. 'I don't think Theo's going to be happy to see me,' she muttered. She could already picture his face when she knocked on the door – could imagine his shocked expression, the hard clench of his jaw.

The car bumped over something and fear pinged against Merry's ribcage. She trained her eyes forward, feeling a sudden wave of exhaustion. The effects of all the concentration and stress? Her breathing slowed and evened as the car got halfway down the narrow track. The lights from Theo's cottage had grown bigger and brighter. 'I think we're almost here,' Merry said. 'Don't worry, Simba,' she added, although the last time she'd checked, the cat had been asleep.

When they arrived at the bottom of the hill, Merry pulled the Jeep up beside Theo's Range Rover and left the engine running so she could rest her forehead on the steering wheel and breathe. The song on the radio switched to 'Baby, It's Cold Outside' and Merry shook her head and laughed, feeling a little hysterical. 'No kidding!' She cut the engine and carefully got out of the car, pulling her coat tighter as she battled with the wind which had reached gale force now.

She grabbed Simba's carrier and the bag of food and medicine from the back seat, balancing it in one arm before scooping Chewy under the other. She leaned into the wind and made her way across the driveway to Theo's front door as furious clouds began to hurl what felt like snowballs at her face. 'I hope Theo's not as mad as you,' Merry shouted at the sky. Then she took a deep breath and pressed a finger on the bell.

18

Theo opened the door in less than thirty seconds and his jaw dropped, then he took Merry's arm and drew her inside. 'I've been calling Chestnut Cottage to see if you were okay. What the hell are you doing here?' he spluttered, checking behind her before slamming the door and taking the bag and Simba's carrier from her arms. 'Please tell me you didn't drive down the hill with your eyes closed,' he rasped. His cheeks were pale and he took a moment to check Merry over, probably searching for wounds.

'I kept them open the whole way,' Merry joked. 'Not that I could see anything; the weather's really bad. Chewy chewed through a lamp cable and electrocuted himself. Then the electricity wouldn't come back on.' She held the rabbit in her arms and watched Theo as he helped Simba climb out of the carrier. The cat immediately scampered down the narrow hallway towards Dot.

'Show me.' Theo held his hands out and gently took the rabbit.

She followed as he tracked along the passage, cradling Chewy, and made his way into the kitchen. The room was huge with a picture window at the far end which offered views of Holly Loch. It also boasted a front-row seat to the biblical storm now in full swing. Merry watched Theo place a mat onto the kitchen table and lay Chewy on top. Then he carefully examined the rabbit, checking his limbs, spine and eyes before scratching his head.

'Is he okay?' Merry asked, feeling her eyes prick. 'He looks all right, but...'

'He seems fine,' Theo soothed. 'Especially considering he's just been electrocuted, but I'd still like to keep an eye on him overnight.' Wind hammered against the windows and he glanced towards the loch. 'You'll have to stay here too – why the hell didn't you call? I'd have driven to you.'

'I tried,' Merry confessed. 'It went to voicemail and I was too worried about Chewy to leave a message.'

Theo grimaced. 'Isla McGavin rang my mobile earlier to tell me the sheep we went to see yesterday afternoon is starting to recover. You probably tried me at the wrong time.' He turned away and placed the rabbit on the floor before washing his hands.

Merry watched him for a moment before she took in her surroundings. Long white counters lined two of the walls and there was a large breakfast bar in the centre which was clear and clutter-free. Above and below the counters were multiple cupboards with their insides exposed – they showcased a sad array of kitchen utensils. Merry counted one pot, and one pan. A solitary bowl, single mug, cup and saucer were stored on another shelf alongside a lone glass. Then she noticed a pile of Barbie-pink cupboard doors leaning against one of the walls.

'What happened?' she asked, pointing to the doors. 'Did the wind blow them all off?'

'I'm not a fan of pink,' Theo said dryly. 'I have plans from a kitchen designer, I just haven't decided on the colours or layout I want yet.'

Merry paced the kitchen. 'You've only got enough stuff in this kitchen for one.'

'I left a lot in London when I moved.' He shrugged. 'New start.'

'I get it, you were looking for a new life without the commitment of multiple saucepans?' She turned to smile at him when he laughed.

'Something like that,' he admitted.

'Well, I hope you have a door on your oven, because I'm starving.' She pointed to the casserole dish. 'Have you eaten? Rowan made me dinner and I planned to cook it tonight but then... Chewy...'

'I haven't eaten.' Theo crossed the kitchen so he could switch the oven on. He was wearing jeans and a long-sleeved black shirt that hugged the muscles across his chest, giving Merry a tantalizing insight into what might be underneath. 'You really shouldn't have come.' He regarded her solemnly.

'I'm here now,' she said, exasperated. 'I know it was risky but I'm honestly happier now I know Chewy's going to be okay.' She studied the weather out of the window. 'I can't leave yet, the storm's getting worse.'

'You're not going anywhere,' Theo said. 'I've a spare room upstairs and I can make up a bed. I'd be a rubbish sidekick if I didn't occasionally offer to rescue you too.' His mouth twisted into a smile. Chewy scampered across the kitchen floor and sniffed his socks. It was on the tip of Merry's tongue to tell the vet not to bother to make up a bed because she was happy to share his, but she chickened out at the last minute. She wasn't Carmel yet. Although after tonight, she was closer to becoming the person she wanted to be than she'd ever imagined.

'The animals will be fine down here,' he continued. 'I'll leave the heating on.'

The oven beeped, indicating it was hot enough, and Theo put the dish inside. Merry went to take a seat at the breakfast bar so she could watch as he pulled out the single bowl and a plate, then dug into a drawer for cutlery. He seemed to have plenty of that.

'Where are your Christmas decorations?' Merry asked, checking around the room. It was a pretty space with a stunning view, but Theo had barely moved anything in.

'In the loft,' he admitted. 'I keep meaning to dig them out.'

Merry scanned the rest of the surfaces. Theo was a tidy man, but she could see piles of paperwork on a coffee table by the picture window, and on top of that a mound of multicoloured Post-it notes. Wind battered against the glass above as the storm reminded them it was still there – bigger and bolder than ever, unpredictable as hell. 'I'll put on some music,' Theo said then stopped as if he'd remembered something important – she saw his Adam's apple bob. 'Actually, did you know Matt, Rowan's son, plays in a band?'

Merry shook her head.

'Kirsteen mentioned it. I downloaded some of his songs, I'll find one.' He picked his mobile up from the windowsill and tapped the screen. Music began to play from some black speakers set into the far corners of the ceiling. 'He sings and plays guitar,' Theo added, giving Merry an intense look.

'He's good,' Merry said. 'I like it.' Also, she'd just recalled a silver plectrum in amongst the Secret Santa gifts – which meant once again, Theo had unwittingly helped to identify another beneficiary. That meant she'd matched sixteen gifts now, and only had four left to find – including the owners of a glasses chain, bangles and two silver broken heart necklaces. 'Is Matt's surname Taylor, the same as Rowan's?' she asked, thinking about the gift label she'd have to write.

'Yep.' If Theo thought the question was odd, he didn't show it. But his mouth crept up at the edge – perhaps because he was enjoying the song? He watched Merry tap her foot on the floor and something about the way he was studying her made the air rush out of her lungs. Suddenly she wanted to touch him, wanted to glide her fingertips over his cheeks. Perhaps it was because of the drive here and the fact that she'd found a way to harness her inner bravery; maybe she'd finally learned to let go of her old self and was embracing the new improved Merry? The one who could do or be anything she wanted? Take what she needed because she was no longer afraid?

She could feel a rush of something in her blood, as if Carmel herself were coming to life, slipping under her skin. Perhaps Theo felt it too, because his mouth tipped up. The storm raged and wind crashed against the windows, making Merry flinch and the lights flicker off and then on.

'Do you want to dance?' Theo asked. 'We've got the disco lights covered.' He pointed to a lamp when the lights blinked again.

Merry stared at him, considering. 'Are you trying to distract me?' she asked softly. 'Because I'm not afraid. Not now I'm here.'

One of his eyebrows winged. 'No kidding. Anyone prepared to drive down that hill in the middle of this is way braver than me.' He paused. 'Perhaps I'm scared, maybe I want your hands on me.'

'For protection?' Merry asked, surprised.

'No,' Theo said seriously, his eyes darkening. 'For body heat.'

Merry felt everything inside her go hot, as if someone had lit a fire in her pelvis. 'I...' She stopped, willing her mouth to co-operate with her brain – although she wasn't entirely sure what she wanted to say. Even Carmel had deserted her.

Theo smiled as if he'd read her mind and rose so he could walk slowly across the kitchen. He offered a hand and Merry waited a moment before she took it. The beat of Matt's song kicked in suddenly. This wasn't a slow and soulful tune intended to seduce, this was fast and furious and Merry found herself being swept around the kitchen, twisting and turning, spinning and dipping until she could hardly feel her feet. She could barely keep up, scarcely concentrate on the shivers travelling up her spine and she gripped Theo's shoulders, digging fingertips into hard muscle, marvelling at the perfect beauty of his frame.

Then the song rose to a loud crescendo of voices and instruments before it abruptly stopped. The room fell silent, aside from the chaos of the storm outside. Theo didn't let go and Merry kept her hands on him too. She could feel the lingering heat from his skin burning through her palms, and the pads of his fingers pressing against her waist. It was clear neither of them could bring themselves to let go. She took in a deep breath and inhaled that now-familiar smell of mountains and apples, then looked up into two clear, blue eyes. It was as if Dan himself were here and she could feel the spirit of Carmel too, pushing up from inside her again. She rose onto her tiptoes and pressed her mouth against his. It seemed fitting that she make the first move once again. She wanted Theo with a certainty she'd never felt before. He was everything she'd been looking for in a partner – someone strong and caring who knew when to give and when to hold back. Understood what was important to her but was happy to make sure she got it for herself – even though it went against every natural instinct inside him.

His lips took a moment to soften, and it was as if he were coming to a decision. Then again, when it came to Theo, Merry knew he had his own demons to conquer too. His mouth started to move against hers and his hands lowered, pulling her closer before he leaned down, grabbed the globes of her bottom and lifted her until their faces were level. Merry pulled away, prematurely ending the kiss. Her lips were tingling, but from here she could see into Theo's eyes, examine the curve of his cheeks, study his expression. She wound her arms around his neck and pressed her forehead against his, breathing him in.

'You want to dance again?' he asked.

Merry shook her head.

'You hungry?' His voice lowered. 'I expect the casserole will be hot enough soon.'

'I'm not hungry and I don't want to dance,' she whispered against his mouth. She sucked in a long breath before taking her next leap. 'I want to go upstairs to your bed. I want to feel your body against mine.' She swallowed her embarrassment, the uncomfortable sense that she'd gone too far. But that was old Merry surfacing again, the one she'd decided to leave behind. New Merry was brave and fearless; she knew what she wanted and wasn't afraid to ask.

Theo pulled back. 'Is that so?' he said, his voice hoarse. 'Because I'm fairly sure that can be arranged. If you're sure?'

'I am,' Merry said and this time she could hear Carmel's voice in the timbre of her tone. It was as if they'd become the same person, as if her fictional character was alive inside her now.

Theo nodded but didn't put Merry down. Instead, his eyes scoured the kitchen, pausing on Dot and Simba who were both sleeping before tracking to Chewy who'd found a corner underneath the table and looked content. He went to switch the oven off, hitching Merry higher on his hips before striding into the hallway and taking the stairs two at a time. She held on, enjoying the ride and his obvious haste to get upstairs.

Theo's bedroom was at the far end of the landing. It was a masculine room with dark grey walls and an enormous bed. He'd made it, so points for him, and the rest of the space looked neat. Even the small en suite bathroom – which she could see through an open doorway – was tidy. He wandered towards the bed without putting on the light or breaking a sweat. She obviously hadn't been exaggerating when she'd imagined Theo bench-pressing a tractor because he'd carried her all the way here and wasn't even out of breath. The curtains around the window to the left of the bed were open and he left them that way. Merry could see thick snowflakes dropping from the sky, egged on by an eager wind, and was pleased she wasn't alone with the noises in Chestnut Cottage tonight. The moon was still visible and threw slivers of light across the duvet, so when Theo lowered Merry onto it, the light shimmered across her legs. He blinked, looking down at her, his forehead bunched.

'Are you sure about this?' he asked again.

'Yes,' she said simply. 'I won't change my mind.'

He climbed onto the bed beside her and leaned onto his side, stretching along the mattress so he could look at her. He was so big, so gorgeous and she wanted to burrow her face into his chest. Instead, she reached out so she could trace the bumpy edge of his jaw.

'What are you thinking?' he asked as she continued to explore.

She chuckled, letting her finger wander downwards from his neck to his chest. 'Isn't that my line?' She sighed. 'I'm trying not to think – I'm going with the flow.'

'Being Carmel again?' He lifted an eyebrow and put a hand on her hip. 'Because I don't want her in my bed. If this is you proving something to yourself—'

'It's already proved.' She cut him off, charmed by the vulnerability she could hear in his voice. 'This is all about me and you. I think I've wanted this since I first saw you at Chestnut Cottage.'

He snorted. 'You thought I was there to rob you.'

She grimaced. 'Okay, maybe a few minutes after that. I was attracted to you, but then you helped make sure I could care for the animals, sat with me when I wanted to drive, didn't interfere or try to stop me from doing all the things I wanted. You named me SuperMerry and helped me to believe I could do anything,' she said huskily.

A knot marred Theo's forehead and he frowned. 'Merry,' he growled. 'I have to tell you something.'

She pressed a finger against Theo's mouth again. 'Then tell me later, because I don't want to hear it now – unless you're about to offer me a striptease?'

He chuckled, despite his obvious reservations. 'You might want to hear this.'

Merry shook her head before leaning forwards so she could kiss him again. He took a few seconds to respond and for a worrying moment Merry thought he might not. Then his hand moved down her hip and he tugged her towards him, pressing their bodies together. Into the bulge that signalled he was as on board with this as her. The kiss deepened and Merry moved her hands between them, starting to undo the buttons on his shirt. She wanted to feel his skin, wanted the sensation of flesh against flesh. She didn't break the kiss as she fumbled with his clothes, shoving the shirt from his shoulders, exposing his perfect skin. Theo was busy shoving up her jumper, and she had to lean back so he could pull it over her head. Her T-shirt followed and then she was just wearing her bra and staring at the most perfect torso she'd seen in her life. Even her wildest fantasies about Dan hadn't prepared her for Theo.

'You're lovely,' he said, echoing her thoughts as he gazed at her. Then he reached behind her to deftly undo the bra and tug it off.

'I've got scars,' she whispered, pressing herself to him. They weren't as severe as the one on her face but beside the perfection of Theo, she suddenly felt inadequate and shy.

Theo gently pressed her backwards so he could look at her properly, then shook his head and lifted his eyes to meet hers. 'Don't apologise for what you've been through, Merry. It's part of who you are – and you're beautiful.' He kissed her again, softer this time, and she stroked her hand down the side of his chest, feeling the ebb and flow of his muscles before dropping her fingertips lower to stroke his thighs. He was still wearing jeans so she tugged at the button, unfastening it and making quick work of the zip. She began to push the clothes over his hips, waiting while Theo took over until he was lying naked in front of her. It was her turn next and he tugged down her jeans and underwear, pulled off her socks before rising up to look at her, his deep blue eyes glowing. Merry wanted to hide herself again; instead, she lay still and let him feast on her – offered herself to him, no barriers, fully exposed. She was braver now and determined to stay that way.

'No secrets,' she said softly as she pushed her mouth to his. 'This is everything I am – take it, and I'll do the same.'

He murmured something into her lips, something she didn't understand, then he rocked them over so she was under his hips. He felt big and warm and Merry nuzzled her nose into his collarbone, breathing him in before kissing her way across his chest to his shoulders until Theo took her hands and lifted them above her head.

'My turn,' he said softly, blinking at her. Then he lay his mouth on hers, kissing his way down her cheek and neck, licking her skin, pausing to take a nipple into his mouth. By the time he reached Merry's navel she was soaring off the bed, so she grabbed his shoulders and pulled him up, encouraging their bodies to join.

Then Merry's breath caught in her throat because on some level, this was what she'd wanted since the moment she'd seen Theo and realised what kind of man he was. But she hadn't believed she was brave enough to have him until now.

19

It was cold when Merry woke and it took her a minute to remember she wasn't in her own bed at Chestnut Cottage. She could feel a warm limb pressed against her leg and when she turned, she saw Theo sleeping beside her and remembered why she was here. What they'd done last night. She smiled as she watched him doze, then pressed a soft kiss to his cheek, feeling her insides dance when he yawned and opened one eye.

'Good morning.' He smiled as he perused the bedroom and his eye rested on the window where the moon and stars glistened in the sky. 'Is it morning yet?' He sounded confused.

'It will be soon,' Merry said softly. 'I always wake up early. I was going to watch the sunrise, thought you might like to join me?' She held her breath, wondering if she should have left him to sleep, but she'd wanted to share this moment, wanted to be with him.

'Of course. I've seen it before, but not with you,' Theo whispered before twisting and pushing himself up on one arm so he could stroke his lips across hers. Merry rested a hand on his shoulder and stroked her way across the skin, marvelling that this moment was real – that she was actually here. At how far her life had moved forwards in a handful of days.

'I'll make coffee,' she promised and he grinned.

'Please brew vats of it, and make it strong,' he begged. 'I want to make sure I'm fully awake for the sunrise, and for what will come after.' He kissed her again, making butterflies cavort in her stomach.

Merry grinned and confidence bloomed in her chest as she rose from the bed and picked up a stray navy T-shirt from the floor before tugging it on.

'Looks good on you,' Theo growled. It was one of his and it was huge on her.

She sniffed the material, feeling her insides shimmer when she caught the scent of mountains and apples. The familiar fragrance made her feel content and she hugged her arms around her waist before padding quietly out of the room. 'See you soon,' she said as she reached the hallway.

It was quiet downstairs and the worst of the storm had passed. Merry could see that the ground surrounding the loch and house was covered in snow and trees leant under the weight of sparkling ice, but the clouds looked carefree now. She put the kettle on and searched the kitchen, spotting Simba on one of the comfortable cushions on the window seat. Dot was snuggled up beside the cat and the dog looked up when she wandered in, before placing her head back down to sleep.

'Chewy,' Merry whispered, crouching so she could search for the rabbit. She found him balled up in the corner of the kitchen with his back to the skirting board. He was snoring softly and she leaned down to stroke his ears, feeling relief wash over her that he seemed unaffected by his electric adventures. Score one for SuperMerry and her sidekick. She really could do this: survive away from her brothers; keep herself and her aunt's animals safe.

She rose and got out a mug and cup and saucer from an

open cupboard before tracking back around the kitchen, righting a cushion on a dark blue chair that faced the huge picture window. Was this where Theo did his paperwork? The pile of folders, papers and multi-coloured Post-its she'd spotted last night lay on top of a small glass coffee table within arm's reach of the chair. Merry made a big cafetière of coffee – black because Theo didn't have the ingredients for a gingerbread latte. She listened out for his footsteps and heard floorboards creak upstairs, suggesting he was out of bed. She went to sit, curling her legs up beneath her, ready for the sunrise. When Theo arrived, she'd make space beside her or sit on his lap.

Above her a clock ticked, providing a rhythmical backdrop to the stunning view. She leaned against the soft cushions, wishing she'd brought her laptop, but she'd been too afraid and too caught up in the Chewy emergency to think about packing that. Perhaps she could pop back to Chestnut Cottage later and finish her scene, help Carmel rescue Dan so they could complete their mission? There was a shuffling sound and Merry watched Dot jump from the bench so she could scramble over to wish her a good morning. She stroked the dog as Dot's tail whipped back and forth, creating a draught that swept up the paperwork balanced on the coffee table. Before Merry could rise, the pile slid from the table and separated – pieces of paper glided across the kitchen floor and under the table.

Merry jumped up so she could gather them as Chewy woke and began to make his way towards the Post-its. 'You're not eating those!' she snapped, grabbing a folder and placing it back on the table before picking up the Post-its.

It was then she spotted the words 'Hat and Gloves' scrawled across the top of the pink square with 'Tavish Doherty' written beside them. Merry's chest froze as she quickly scanned the rest of the notes, leafing through each of the Post-its, fighting the wave of emotions that threatened to choke her. All the Secret Santa gifts had been documented and beside them, the intended recipients – at least the ones Theo knew about – were written in the vet's messy scrawl. Robina Sinclair had been noted beside 'Glasses Chain' and Merry remembered the headmistress visiting Belle's class and complaining about losing her specs. She hadn't made the connection at the time, but Theo had obviously heard about the missing glasses. How did he know about Secret Santa? Had he been spying on her or had he somehow guessed? Why hadn't he said anything?

Feeling sick, Merry slumped back into the chair as she stared at the pieces of paper, trying to make some sense of what she was seeing. Theo had become her sidekick, he'd been on hand each time she needed help, beside her as she'd gradually solved the Secret Santa clues she'd stumbled across. But obviously they hadn't all been the result of random coincidences. Merry narrowed her eyes, trying to remember the chain of events. How often had she been manipulated? Had it been Theo's idea to go wild swimming or hers? She couldn't remember precisely but it was obvious Theo had been leading her in the right direction. Hadn't he been the one to reveal Jared's love of cows? That Edina wore tiaras? Wasn't he the one who'd mentioned Kenzy's affection for lavender oil and Duncan's broken torch? A sob rose in her throat. This wasn't just dishonesty – the whole partners in crime, superhero and sidekick joke had been a lie. Theo was no different from her brothers, hovering over her, trying to help because they didn't trust her to do anything for herself. All her assumptions about the vet being like Dan – giving her the room to finally break free from the chains she'd allowed herself to live inside – were wrong. All along he'd become part of the problem. A tear slipped down her cheek and she clasped the Post-it notes to her chest, rising when she heard footsteps in the hallway. When Theo saw her face, he stopped.

'What's happened?' he asked, closing the space between

them. 'Is Chewy okay?' He spotted the rabbit on the ground and then his attention caught on the colourful squares in her hand. 'Oh.' His sigh was more of a groan. 'I can explain,' he said gruffly.

'Can you?' Merry asked, trying to side-step him. 'I'm not interested. I want to go home.'

Theo shook his head and stepped ahead, blocking her way. 'I need to tell you what happened.' He swiped a hand across his forehead before clutching the top of his nose. 'Please.'

'You lied,' Merry bit back. 'You've been helping me solve the Secret Santa clues. How did you even know about them? Did Ava tell you?' she whispered. Had her aunt not trusted her to do the job either? The thought cut deep into her bones.

'It has nothing to do with your aunt. I guessed,' Theo said rapidly. 'Chewy ate your notes, then all the gifts arrived and Tavish talked about Secret Santa when I was in the pub and he was wearing his Christmas jumper. He told me he suspected your aunt.' He swallowed. 'Once I remembered the red sack I found in your post box and the presents, all the pieces fell together. I wasn't trying to take over,' he insisted. 'I knew it was important to you to do things on your own. Especially after you told me why you'd come to Christmas Village, but...' His shoulders sagged. 'I wanted to help.'

'You didn't trust me,' Merry said sadly as a tear fell down her cheek.

Theo reached out a fingertip to wipe it away but she stepped out of his reach. She couldn't bear the idea of him touching her. 'That's not true.' He shrugged, looking hurt. 'I believed in you. I know I went the wrong way about helping but I wasn't trying to interfere, I just...' He rolled his eyes to the ceiling. 'Jake's right. I want to help. Maybe I do want to save everyone because it's programmed into my DNA. I can't help myself. But I wasn't trying to take anything from you, I didn't intend to take over. I thought it would be easy – a few clues here and there, just pointing you in the right direction.' He winced. 'I care about you…'

'If you cared, you'd have, I don't know…' Merry tossed her hands in the air, her stomach reeling.

'What?' Theo asked. 'Told you I knew, that I'd somehow guessed about Secret Santa? Your brothers have made you suspicious of everyone's motives. Would you have believed that I just wanted to help, or would you have accused me of trying to take over, of trying to control you?'

Merry frowned. Would she? She shook her head.

'I didn't want to tell you, but once I guessed and I saw how many presents you had to match, I wanted to make sure you didn't fail. Please, Merry.' He held out a hand and she thought about taking it. She felt stripped bare – but was she overreacting? Theo hadn't tried to take over; he'd just helped her work things out for herself. He hadn't interfered, told her what to think, or made her feel incapable.

'I don't know…' Her thoughts and emotions were jumbled.

'Will you sit down and talk to me, please?' he pleaded. Merry was about to say yes but the doorbell rang and Theo froze. 'I'm not expecting anyone.' He twisted to look towards the door as Dot scrambled out of the kitchen into the hallway. The bell rang again, and this time the caller left their finger resting on the button so it continued to buzz. 'I have to get that; it might be someone from the surgery. It's obviously urgent.' Theo sighed. 'Would you wait there please so we can talk about this more?' He held up a palm, looking so unhappy Merry found herself nodding. She could talk to Theo, give him a chance to explain. Tell him how she felt. Her eyes strayed back to the Post-it notes as she began to calculate all the clues she'd solved herself. Perhaps she could forgive him, if he was honest with her now…

'Merry!' someone bellowed from the hallway and Merry spun round, shocked because she recognised that voice.

'Noah?' she asked, disbelieving, as her brother came charging ahead of Theo into the kitchen. 'Why are you here?' she squeaked. Her brother looked good and despite her surprise, she was pleased to see him. She gave Noah a hug and he wrapped her in his arms, squeezing her tight before stepping away.

'What are you wearing?' he asked, his brow knitting as he took in her bare legs and the oversized T-shirt before his eyes narrowed and shot to Theo.

'I drove here last night because Chewy, Aunt Ava's rabbit, got electrocuted. It wasn't safe for me to drive home so I stayed.' Merry tugged at the T-shirt, trying to stretch it over her knees. 'Theo lent me something to wear.' She stopped and cocked her head as something began to gnaw at the corners of her brain. 'Why *you* here?' she asked, frowning. 'I asked you not to come to Christmas Village.'

Noah's dark eyebrows met as he surveyed Theo's kitchen. He looked tired and his thick black sweater was rumpled, suggesting he'd been driving for a long time. 'I saw the weather forecast,' he grumbled, shooting Theo a glare. 'The storm. I got your message, but when I tried to call back,' he heaved out a long breath, 'I got your voicemail. I thought I'd better come up, make sure you were safe. I've been driving all night.'

'I'm fine,' Merry said. 'This isn't what we agreed.' She stilled suddenly. 'How did you know I was at Theo's?' Her voice cracked. Noah had never met the vet.

Her brother gave Theo an unreadable look. Noah was a handsome man, but many had described him as foreboding – for the first time Merry understood why. 'I checked family-sharing on my phone when I was driving up. I saw this address.' He sounded surly. 'I didn't realise it belonged to *your* vet.' His voice was ice. 'I know I asked you to keep an eye on my sister, but I didn't mean for you to get *this* close,' he said furiously.

Everything inside Merry stopped – her heart, her pulse,

even her blood seemed to slow to a crawl. She watched Theo's face, saw the shadow of guilt as he turned to look at her. 'You what?' she whispered, struggling to stay upright. She moved backwards so she was closer to a wall and placed a palm on it for support. 'You really have been spying on me?'

'No!' Theo stepped forwards. He might have reached her if Noah hadn't got in his way. 'That's not how it was.' Theo was taller than her brother and she could see his face over Noah's shoulder. Could see the guilt in his eyes. 'I didn't tell him anything about what you've done,' he continued. His eyes widened as if he was hoping she could see into his brain and divine the truth. 'I agreed to talk to him because otherwise all three of your brothers would have come to Scotland – and I understood how much you didn't want that.'

'You didn't tell me anything?' Noah growled, pushing the vet backwards, away from Merry. Then he stopped and jerked around. 'Did you say you drove here?' His cheeks paled. 'Down that helter-skelter of a hill, in the middle of last night's storm?'

Merry levelled her chin and her brother's jaw dropped. 'And I was fine.' She narrowed her eyes, disgusted with both of them. 'I've been wild swimming too, did Theo tell you that?'

'I didn't tell him anything,' Theo repeated quietly.

Noah's jaw crunched and he frowned at the vet, his expression murderous. 'So it seems.' His voice was calm, too calm. 'But I'm sure he'll be filling me in on all your activities now... if he wants to live.' He let the words fall between them as he took in Merry's half-dressed state again. 'Once we get a proper chance to talk.'

'Oh, you'll get that now,' she bit out, marching up to face him. Noah was over a foot taller but she stared him down. 'What I do with my life is none of your business,' she snapped, prodding a fingertip against his chest. 'This ends now. I'm in Christmas Village to move on, to make my own life. I know you're scared, I know all of this,' she spun her hands around, 'and your desire to keep me safe come from a good place, but it's suffocating.' Merry's voice cracked and she could see the moment her brother understood, because his shoulders slackened and all the tension left his face.

'I'm sorry.' His eyes clouded. 'All we've ever tried to do was look out for you.'

'I know.' Merry patted his shoulder, keeping her voice light. 'But I'm twenty-five and it's time you let me look out for myself. I'm going back to Chestnut Cottage now.'

'I'll come,' Noah said quickly.

'Oh no.' Merry shook her head, frowning. 'You can stay here. With him.' She pointed at Theo, who'd been watching the exchange. 'You have lots to talk about, remember?'

Noah stepped aside and watched as Merry stalked past Theo without looking at him. She ran up to his bedroom and heard the soft pad of his feet after her. She knew he was watching when she leaned down to gather her clothes from the floor, quickly pulling on her underwear, jumper and jeans with her back to him before she turned and placed her hands on her hips. He opened his mouth but she held up a hand. 'No! Whatever you're going to say, please don't. I don't want to hear it.'

'I'm going to say it anyway,' Theo said hoarsely. 'I didn't tell your brothers anything.'

'I've no idea what to believe. I do know you lied to me,' she shot back, feeling the prickle of tears at the corners of her eyes. But she wouldn't give Theo the satisfaction of seeing them – had no intention of sharing her grief. 'You were supposed to be like Dan,' she whispered and saw him flinch. 'You helped me learn to be brave and push my boundaries. You were supposed to be someone I could rely on. The first person I've ever helped save.'

Theo looked shaken. 'That's not how it works,' he said. 'I understand about wanting to save someone, I get that because I've done it my whole life, but it doesn't have to be a one-way street. I learned that with you. It's where I've gone wrong my whole life.' He took a step forwards and she shook her head. 'I've been over-protective, I know.' Theo cleared his throat. 'I accept what I did was wrong, I wasn't honest. But Merry, I didn't tell your brothers anything... I only told them I'd keep an eye on you to stop them coming up.'

'You've been saving me by stealth,' she snapped. 'I'm not sure if that's worse than Noah coming to check up on me.' She blinked away tears. 'At least he was honest about it.'

Theo stared at Merry as she shoved on her socks before pushing past him. She felt an overwhelming need to touch him, but she couldn't do it. She'd never forgive him for lying. And for doing all the same suffocating things her brothers had always done.

'I did the wrong thing for the right reasons, Merry,' Theo said softly as she reached the doorway. She paused before looking around.

'Your brother was right,' she murmured. 'You are a German Shepherd in human form – I really don't think you can help yourself. I told you when we met, I already have three brothers looking out for me, Theo. I don't want or need any more.' With that, she turned and ran down the stairs as a sob climbed up her throat.

A few minutes later, holding Simba's carrier, Rowan's empty casserole dish and with Chewy under one arm, Merry swept out of Holly Lodge. Her whole body churned with emotion as she headed for the Jeep, ignoring the snow swirling like glitter around it. She didn't turn when she heard a man's voice shout from the doorway; instead, she climbed into the car and quickly reversed as a desperate sob escaped her at last.

20

'I'm going to fold.' Jared puffed out a breath as he lay his cards face down on the orange Formica table in the centre of Tavish Doherty's kitchen. The room was situated in the flat above The Corner Shop. It was minimally furnished and military neat – with shiny white cabinets and grey countertops that were so glossy you could see yourself wink in them. Someone had spent time hanging festive decorations – a multitude of colourful cut-outs in the shapes of Santa Claus, reindeer and Christmas trees which had been spaced evenly across the pristine paintwork.

Beside Tavish, Noah blew his cheeks out like mini globes before laying his cards face-down too. Sam sighed loudly and his cards joined the others on the table. Theo took a moment to glance around at the eclectic bunch of men before studying his poker hand and realising he could make up a respectable four of a kind.

'I'm in,' he said, looking at what remained of the golden chocolate coins that Sam had divided equally between the players when they'd first sat down. He positioned one beside the growing mound in the middle of the table.

'I'll see you,' Tavish said, pushing a coin in too before setting out his cards and displaying a royal flush, making the rest of the players groan. Tavish grinned before taking his winnings and adding them to his large pile. 'Unlucky at cards, but lucky in love, eh?' he asked before his eyes shot to the other four men and his face dropped.

'Not exactly,' Theo murmured. He hadn't seen Merry for two days. She'd rejected all his calls and even when he'd turned up at Chestnut Cottage along with Noah, ready to beg her for forgiveness again, she'd refused to open the door. He had no idea of how to put things right, no sense of how to make her understand. He puffed out a breath as Dot nudged his leg, demanding attention.

'Aye, well.' Sam let out a long sigh. 'That's true for some of us. But you're the only one who seems to be lucky in both at the moment, Da.' His eyes moved to Jared and Noah. 'Perhaps I'm wrong about the two of you. But it's why I set up this boys' night.' His blue eyes skimmed the table. 'I wanted to take my mind off my disastrous love life, but I think we'll all need another evening to get over our woeful card-playing soon. Hopefully next time Jack and Logan will be able to make it too – they're both with the loves of their lives so their good luck might rub off.' He swallowed, looking genuinely upset. 'Who fancies a beer? And while I'm getting them, feel free to give me tips on poker strategy or relationships – either will do.'

'I'll have a beer,' Noah said and Theo nodded too. Jared's sprained ankle was much improved and he'd already offered to drive them home.

'Ach, well, I'm not sure I've got any advice to give you, lad. I can't play cards and I've made a mess of things with the one interesting woman I've met in years – and I still don't understand what I'm doing wrong.' The older vet scratched his chin before sipping from a tall glass of fruit juice. 'I did exactly what you advised.' His blue eyes shot to Theo. 'But Kirsteen's *still* not talking to me.' His lips pinched, filled with reproach. 'If anything, the lass is more annoyed with me now.'

'What did you tell him to do?' Sam asked as he finished serving the drinks and gathered everyone's cards before shuffling.

'He told me to make her a meal,' Jared interrupted before Theo could reply. 'Kirsteen offered to cook a casserole one evening and I told her I was planning on watching one of my favourite documentaries.' He winced. 'The lad showed me the error of my ways and said I should make her dinner.'

'I think I said you should *take* her to dinner,' Theo corrected. 'What exactly did you do?'

The older man frowned. 'I made my favourite chicken curry and left it on her desk at the surgery as a surprise.' His eyes widened. 'Ach.' He dipped his chin as a blush swept across his cheeks. 'I think I might now see where I went wrong.'

Sam tipped his head back and belly-laughed. 'You left her a meal to eat alone.' He stopped chuckling when Tavish patted a playful palm against his shoulder.

'You're not doing much better,' he pointed out.

'Aye, sorry.' All remnants of Sam's good humour dissolved. 'Da's right. Don't listen to me. I've managed to alienate the love of my life and there's little chance of her ever forgiving me.' He started to dole out the cards, shaking his head.

'What did *you* do?' Jared asked Sam, picking up each card as it was dealt before smiling at them. His partner had clearly never heard of a poker face.

Sam's shoulders sagged. 'Hannah and I were childhood sweethearts. Everyone thought we'd marry eventually – even me.'

'Aye,' Tavish said softly, his eyes hooded.

'But... I don't know. One day I was working in the shop with Da and I realised my whole life was planned out ahead of me, day after day.' Sam swallowed. 'It terrified me.'

'The lad wasn't ready for life as a shopkeeper,' Tavish said, looking unhappy.

'It wasn't that.' Sam shook his head. 'I loved working here, still do. I just wasn't ready for that kind of certainty. I was only eighteen. I didn't want to wake up one morning and resent what I had. It was too precious...' Sam sighed. 'I always wanted to be like you,' he said to Tavish. 'So I joined the army and just... went.' He looked embarrassed.

'Aye, well that's...' Tavish cleared his throat, looking a little overwhelmed.

'You didn't tell her?' Noah asked, pulling an *'ohhhh bad move'* face.

'Nae.' Sam winced. 'I was too afraid that if I did I wouldn't be able to go – or perhaps I was just too much of a coward.' He shrugged. 'Leaving was the right thing to do because I got the adventure I craved and grew up – but I never forgot Hannah. I think I thought she'd still be here waiting, and that was selfish. Not telling her was where I made my mistake. Perhaps if I had, she'd have waited or come too. At least now she'd trust me.' His mouth screwed up. 'Instead, she thinks I'm a faithless eejit.'

'Right.' Noah's attention fixed on Theo. 'Honesty can be a deal-breaker.'

'Says the man who asked me to spy on his sister,' Theo said under his breath.

Noah must have heard because he shot him a thoughtful look. 'You might have a point,' he said softly.

'Hannah is determined not to give me another chance,' Sam continued. 'I can't say I blame her. Her ex-husband left her and Ace – and I left too – so she has an issue with trust. But I need to work out how to prove I'm not going anywhere this time; that she can rely on me no matter what. It's just...'

'You don't know how,' Jared finished, watching as Sam turned over the first card on the table. The vet's eyes lit up and Theo wondered if it was even worth continuing to play his hand. 'I'm not sure you'll want to listen to any of my advice because the only thing I'm good at is fixing animals,' Jared said.

'He's not much better.' Noah snorted, pointing at Theo.

'Merry isn't talking to you, either,' Theo noted. 'Looks like none of us know what we're doing when it comes to the people we care for the most.'

The group fell silent. 'Ach, you eejits all need some sense knocking into you,' Tavish grumbled, shaking his head. 'You,' he jabbed a finger at Jared, 'need to ask Kirsteen out on a proper date. It's not rocket science. You,' he glared at his son, 'need to prove to Hannah that you're not going to leave Christmas Village again – she has to know you're not going to let her down, or that wee lad.'

'How do I do that?' Sam protested. 'She's barely talking to me.'

'I have an idea, but it's something you've got to figure out for yourself.' Tavish frowned at his cards.

'I'm afraid there's not much hope for *you*,' Noah said scornfully, looking at Theo. 'Merry doesn't want to talk to you. Even if she does, she's going to be back with me, Ollie and Liam as soon as Aunt Ava comes home.'

'Well, if you give up that easily,' Tavish said to Theo, looking disappointed, 'I'd say you don't deserve the lass.'

Theo blew out a long breath as he stared at his cards. He was going to lose the game and he was going to lose Merry too. Despite his early intentions to hold back and not get involved he'd managed to fall for her. Then he'd messed up and he had no idea how to put things right...

Holly Lodge was quiet when Jared finally dropped Theo and Noah off after the poker night ended. Tavish had won the full complement of chocolate coins, but he'd dished out a handful to each of the men before seeing them off – and Theo had already eaten two.

'Want another beer?' he asked Noah as he strode into the kitchen ahead of Dot, who immediately jumped up onto the bench by the window and curled into a misshapen ball.

'Yep.' Noah wandered up to take in the view. 'It's pretty here,' he said quietly. 'I can see why you like it. Must get lonely, though.'

'When I bought the place I didn't imagine living here alone,' Theo said honestly, handing Merry's brother a bottle he'd uncapped. He didn't know what he'd imagined – a life with a woman who was nothing like Miranda, someone who didn't want or need anything from him. But now that fantasy seemed so empty and cold. If you didn't give to or care for someone, where did that leave you? 'What about you, what are your plans for the future?' he asked, taking a seat at the table so he could twist and stare out of the window. It was a beautiful view – one of the things that had most drawn him to the house – but he'd not spent much time enjoying it. Theo might have watched the sunrise with Merry in this exact spot the other day but instead, he'd thoroughly screwed up.

Noah cleared his throat and swigged some beer. Despite Merry's brother living here for the last two days because she wouldn't let him stay with her, they'd barely talked about anything beyond who wanted coffee and when they were going to drive up to Chestnut Cottage. Co-existing as strangers had seemed easier, but after the poker game tonight, hearing everyone opening up, Theo had a sudden urge to find out more about him.

'I don't know.' Noah shrugged. 'I'm a policeman and what I do fulfils me so I'm not planning a change of career.' He pulled a golden coin from his pocket and unwrapped it, popping the chocolate into his mouth. Theo waited while he considered the question and swallowed. 'I had a girlfriend until Merry's acci-

dent. After that...' He shut his eyes and Theo saw raw pain
cross his face.

'It must have been difficult,' he said. 'My parents died in a
fire when I was nineteen and I looked after my brother for a few
years.'

Noah opened his eyes again and gave Theo an assessing
look. 'Right. So maybe you do get it. Making sure my sister is
safe and happy is...' He shrugged. 'It's everything.'

Theo took another sip from the beer as he measured his
next words. He was walking a tightrope, but being around Noah
and Merry had given him new insights into his own behaviour –
something he'd never properly examined before – and he didn't
like what he saw. 'I used to be so afraid something would
happen to Jake or that he'd be unhappy. I spent my life trying to
fix everything that went wrong in his. It became a habit,
perhaps more about what *I* needed and less about what was
right for him.'

Noah raised a dark eyebrow – whether he'd figured out the
glaring subtext wasn't clear. 'What happened?'

Theo huffed out a breath. 'As soon as my brother was old
enough he bought himself a round-the-world ticket and I
haven't seen him for two years. He's currently surfing in
Australia surrounded by sharks.' He winced. 'The man-eating
variety, apparently. Sometimes I think he tells me just because
he knows it drives me crazy.'

'Right.' Noah gulped. 'Bummer.'

'Yep, well, I've only just decided that maybe Jake did the
right thing, getting away. I wasn't happy because I couldn't keep
an eye on him, but...' Theo sighed. 'The thing is, I think the
main reason he wanted to travel was to get away from me.' It
was the first time Theo had admitted it and he felt the weight of
the words grow heavy in his chest. 'I was so busy trying to save
him, I suffocated him instead.' He'd done the same with

Miranda, although she'd been happy enough to take advantage of that.

Noah placed his bottle on the table and puffed out a breath. 'You think that's what my brothers and I are doing with Merry?' His voice was tense.

'I'm saying I recognise the signs,' Theo said softly. 'And I understand how you feel. But I'm also saying perhaps it's time to let go? Allow your sister to make her own mistakes, stop trying to fix everything. It doesn't mean you have to stop caring, just... take a step back. I've spent the last two weeks with her and I can tell you she's more capable than you think. She's looked after your aunt's animals by herself, and lived alone in that huge, creaky house.'

Noah made a huffing sound and tapped his fingers onto the table. 'Are you saying all this because you want to date her and you want my permission? Because you're not going to get it. I'm not that evolved.'

Theo snorted. 'I don't need it. If Merry wants to see me again, if we're going to embark on a long-distance romance then that's up to her – but it's not looking very likely at the moment.' He shut his eyes as pain grated his chest. 'I'm saying it because it's true. I'm not sure if your sister is ever going to speak to me again, let alone spend time with me. She trusted me and I let her down.'

Noah regarded him seriously. His eyes were the same brown as Merry's and just as suspicious. 'You didn't tell us anything though, did you?' he asked, softly.

Theo shook his head. 'Nope,' he agreed. 'In the interests of transparency, I took her out driving and wild swimming and I'd do it again.'

Noah's lips thinned. 'I still can't believe she drove down that hill in a storm, especially after the accident.' He winced.

Theo chuckled. 'You wouldn't have caught me doing it – she really is quite incredible.' His chest puffed like a firework had just exploded under his ribs. 'I think you'd probably see that if you let her be herself.'

'How?' Noah asked.

'Talk to her,' Theo said softly. 'Don't lecture or tell, let her show you how far she's come. Merry doesn't need saving, she's done a damn good job of doing it herself.'

Her brother shook his head. 'I'll have to speak to Liam and Ollie.' He sighed. 'This isn't just up to me but...' He swallowed. 'Perhaps, in a small way,' he pinched his thumb and index finger together, leaving a sliver of space, 'you could be right. At least, you might be.' He shook his head again and stared back out of the window, looking unhappy. 'It's hard to let go...'

'But sometimes we have to,' Theo said, wondering if he'd ever be strong enough to let Merry go too, knowing already he never truly would.

21

The chickens hadn't laid again and Merry had run out of medicine. She wiped snow from the bottom of her boots as she walked to the kitchen in Chestnut Cottage so she could open her laptop. She still wasn't ready to speak to Theo and couldn't risk calling the surgery to ask for Jared in case the younger vet turned up instead. She typed 'Egg Drop Syndrome' into the search box and quickly scanned the screen – she could fix the problem herself. She didn't need *him*.

> *Egg Drop Syndrome is typified by the creation of soft-shelled and shell-less eggs by apparently healthy chickens.*

'What!' Merry's vital organs felt like they'd just been submerged in a wave machine. 'Theo told me Egg Drop Syndrome was to do with the hens not laying at all. He lied about that, too!' Her cheeks flamed and she shook her head at Chewy, who'd wandered over to join her by the kitchen table. 'Was anything he told me true?' The rabbit wriggled and Merry decided to interpret the movement as a 'no'. 'You're right; he doesn't know the meaning of the word,' she snapped. 'Oh

Chewy, I wish you could talk.' Suddenly feeling lonely and overwhelmed, she pulled up a chair so she could sink into it and rested her chin on her hand. Her eyes caught on the remaining Secret Santa gifts and she dragged them away. There were still three stragglers to match with the correct villagers and wrap. A set of colourful bangles and a couple of necklaces. Just three people Theo hadn't managed to point her towards – probably because she'd found him out. She hadn't left the house for days and couldn't face going into Christmas Village. But she'd have to eventually: she wasn't going to let her aunt down.

Her eyes filled as she remembered being at Holly Lodge and finding out Theo had been lying to her. The disappointment had lanced through her, cutting to the bone. She wasn't sure if she was angrier with him for furtively helping with Secret Santa or because he'd been spying on her for her brothers. In collusion with Noah, Ollie and Liam who, despite her repeated requests, were still trying to protect and control her from afar. Would they ever let her live her own life? Her lips pinched – they had no choice. Being in Christmas Village had taught her she was more capable than she'd ever imagined. She'd refused to see Noah or to take any of her brothers' calls and had switched off her mobile and unplugged the canary-yellow phone when it rang over and over. She'd have to deal with them eventually, but not yet.

'This is ridiculous. I'll give it another few days and see if the chickens start laying again,' she said to the rabbit and closed down the browser on her laptop, studying the blank screen. She hadn't written for days. Every time she'd tried, her head had filled with Theo and she'd had to slam the lid shut when her eyes had filled. But she'd have to finish her novel sometime. Sighing, Merry pulled up the manuscript and scrolled to where she'd left off. It had been just before Chewy had electrocuted himself and the lights had gone out during the storm. Mere hours before she'd been in bed making love with Theo – but she wasn't going to think about that again.

Merry let out a long sigh as she scanned the last few paragraphs of the scene she'd been writing. Carmel had been about to rescue Dan and was using one of her hairclips to pick the lock...

'You need to leave,' Dan said and Carmel could hear fear in his voice.

'I'm here to rescue you. We need to finish our adventure together – as a team.' Carmel watched Dan's indigo-blue eyes dilate, then bit back a moan when she saw a surge of protectiveness wash through them.

'I won't be able to concentrate if I think you're in danger,' Dan pleaded.

Carmel recoiled. 'What do you mean?' What was going on?

'Go and find a place to hide. Then stay there and keep yourself safe.' Dan tugged the clip from Carmel's fingers, ignoring her gasp of protest. 'I'll get myself out of this mess – and then we can make it to Tinsel Mountain together.' His face softened. 'I can't risk you getting hurt...'

'Dammit!' Merry's fingers flew up from the laptop as if the keyboard had suddenly burst into flames. What was going on in her novel? What had happened to Dan? Why was the gentle hero who'd been so supportive of Carmel up until this moment suddenly morphing into an over-protective fool? She gulped. She was used to her characters taking over, used to surprises when she wrote. Merry might be the one typing the words but these fictional people were in her head, coming more alive with every word. Unfortunately, they sometimes had their own ideas about how they were going to behave. But she hadn't been

prepared for this – hadn't been prepared for Dan to turn into...
Theo.

Disgusted, she went back and deleted the words she'd just
typed, pausing so she could consider what to put in instead.
The Dan in her head would soothe, he'd be proud of Carmel,
patiently sit back and let himself be rescued – wouldn't he? She
frowned, suddenly confused – would a man like Dan really be
so passive? Would Carmel even want that from him?

There was a knock at the front door and for a beat, Merry
thought about not answering. It could be Noah and Theo, but it
might also be Belle who'd promised to pop in to drop off a
Christmas cake. She tracked slowly to the door.

'Merry?' Noah shouted. 'Ouch,' he yelled and she could
hear loud gobbles and warbles coming from the porch. 'Look,
can you let me in?' He hammered loudly on the door again.
'There's a massive bird out here and it's just— ouch! You'd
better open up or it's going to eat me alive.'

'Henry,' Merry murmured, reluctantly swinging the door
open and taking a step back so her brother could fall inside. He
didn't greet her; instead, he quickly turned and slammed the
door.

'What the hell was that?' he snapped, his eyes wide.

'Aunt Ava's turkey, Henry.' She frowned. 'He hates men. I
thought Theo would have mentioned it. Isn't he here too?' She
didn't want to see the vet, but couldn't help feeling disappointed that he hadn't bothered to come. Was he afraid to face
her, or did he simply not care? The thought made her stomach
hurt.

'I wanted to talk to you on my own.' Noah frowned. 'I'm
guessing not telling me anything was Theo's revenge for me
manipulating him into spying on you,' he said darkly. Then he
sighed as he gazed down at her.

Her brother was tall with dark hair and he'd always towered
over her, making her feel fragile and inept – but for the second

time in days, Merry stood her ground and held his eye. Things had changed – being in Christmas Village had changed her – and she wasn't going to go back to the fearful hermit she'd allowed herself to become. 'Why are you here?' She took a step forwards, lifting her chin.

Noah shoved his hands into his pockets as he glanced down the hallway and spotted Simba and Chewy scrutinizing him from the end. 'I've got some things to say.' His voice was raspy and he cleared his throat. 'If that's okay?'

'Sure,' Merry said, surprised her brother had asked. 'I'll make coffee.' She wandered into the kitchen and put the kettle on without turning around. She heard Noah pull out one of the chairs at the table before slumping down. He remained silent as she made the drinks – a gingerbread latte for herself and an instant espresso for him. Then she pulled out the chair opposite and slipped into it before taking a long sip of her coffee.

'Are you writing?' Noah said, pointing to her laptop.

'Why?' Merry asked sweetly. 'Are you here to tell me I'm not capable of that, too?'

'No.' Her brother pinched the bridge of his nose, looking unhappy. 'I guess I deserved that.' His chest heaved. 'I came to say I'm sorry.'

'Why?' Merry leaned forwards. She wasn't sure whether to be suspicious of Noah's motives or to jump up from the table and perform a celebratory pirouette. She watched his face, waiting for him to continue.

He sipped his coffee, looking uncomfortable. 'I talked to Theo. He...' He sighed and put the mug back on the table. 'He gave me a new perspective on the way I've been behaving.' He scrubbed a hand through his hair. 'The way Ollie, Liam and I have treated you since the accident.' He winced. 'Perhaps even before that.'

'What new perspective?' What could Theo have said –

surely he'd spent the last few days swapping tips with her brother on rescuing feeble damsels in distress?

'You're a grown woman.' His eyes met hers. 'It's time you get to live the life you want without...' His shoulders sagged. 'Without everyone trying to stop you because they're so afraid you might get hurt.'

'Is this a trick?' she asked.

Noah shook his head, looking weary. 'I was so terrified after your accident.' His chest seemed to deflate to half its original size. 'It's difficult to explain but I'll try. All the time you were in the hospital, in the coma, I sat by your bedside feeling like I should have done something to protect you. Should have found a way to stop you from being hurt.'

'It wasn't your fault,' Merry said softly. 'You weren't even there.'

'I know.' Noah cleared his throat. 'But when Dad died while you were still in the coma, I felt like our family was disappearing. I wanted to protect you, to keep you safe – and Liam and Ollie felt the same. You're our little sister, the only one we have.' His lips twisted. 'The more I thought about you being injured or hurt, the more I wanted to shelter you and keep you safe.'

Merry closed her eyes. 'I'm a grown woman. It's not your job.'

'I know that too. I've also realised I want you to be happy and you're not going to feel that way if we're constantly breathing down your neck, stopping you from doing the things you love.' Noah blew out a long breath. 'I can't say I'll ever be totally comfortable with the idea of you driving.' He turned his head to look at the laptop. 'And I hate the thought of anyone criticising what you write, making you question your talent. But what you do isn't up to me, Liam or Ollie. It's not anyone's business but your own.'

Merry frowned. 'Wait, wind back. Theo helped you to see

this?' She folded her arms. 'Is that the same Theo who's been spying on me?'

'I think we've established your vet didn't tell me a thing.' Noah leaned his arms onto the table so he could stare into her eyes. 'Theo lied when he told us he'd keep an eye on you. He only did it to keep the three of us from coming to Chestnut Cottage. I didn't really give him much choice.' He flushed. 'I called a few times and he told me what I wanted to hear, so I'd say his intentions were honest.'

'You still came,' Merry said darkly. 'He must have given you a reason to drive up.' She wasn't ready to give up on her anger yet, but she could feel a warm buzz in her stomach, a shimmer of hope.

'I came because of the storm. I couldn't stand the idea of you being in the middle of nowhere alone. I suppose I didn't trust Theo to watch you. I thought you'd be scared,' he muttered.

'I wasn't,' she said.

'I know.' Noah looked bewildered.

'Theo lied to me so many times, made up stupid reasons to come here to see me.' Merry pulled a face, thinking about when he'd told her the chickens had Egg Drop Syndrome – he'd even brought fake medicine to make it sound real.

'Lying isn't right, but I suspect he was just trying to find ways of doing the right thing. As I said, I'm not sure I gave him much choice.' Noah skimmed a hand across the table until it was inches from hers. 'I hope you'll forgive me for that.'

Merry stared at him.

'I'd like to agree a truce,' Noah continued. 'I want you to live your life the way you want and I'll do my best – we'll *all* do our best – not to interfere.' He shut his eyes. 'But if you could please refrain from driving down something resembling a black ski run in the eye of a hurricane I'd really appreciate it.' His voice shook.

Merry cleared her throat. 'I'll do my best,' she said, placing her palm over his. 'Am I dreaming? Because if I am, I really don't want to wake up.' She raised the corner of her mouth.

Noah chuckled. 'You're lucid,' he said. 'I meant every word. Your vet made some good points.' His eyebrow lifted. 'That doesn't mean I approve of him, especially considering he just let me walk into a turkey ambush, but...' He paused, his mouth twisting like he didn't want to say the words. 'He seems genuine and he cares about you...'

Merry swallowed. 'Does he?'

Noah nodded. 'Now I suppose you have to decide how you feel about him.'

'I really don't know...' Merry blew out a long breath, wondering if that was true.

22

'So class, for our final lesson with Ms McKenzie, you're going to take it in turns to share your Christmas stories with her so she can give you her feedback and read out her favourite three – and then we'll pin them all to the wall,' Belle announced to her Primary Three class. She pointed to the empty display area at the back of the classroom which had already been decorated with an impressive quantity of silver tinsel.

Ace put his hand in the air and stood. 'Before you start listening to our writing, please could you read out the next chapter of your book?' He directed the question to Merry – and Belle and the rest of the class turned to stare at her expectantly.

'I'm sorry but I haven't written anything new since last week.' She shuffled the papers she'd brought, feeling embarrassed. In truth, she hadn't typed a word since Noah's visit three days before – just after she'd deleted the last disastrous attempt. Merry was still confused, still unsure of what she was going to do about Theo. Her brothers had finally agreed to let her live her own life and so she wasn't sure if she immediately wanted to accept another hero into her life. She didn't want to be rescued or controlled, she was sick of it. Confusion reigned and every time she sat at her laptop, the words refused to come. Dan was still locked in a cell and Carmel was poised to rescue him. But neither seemed able to agree on what was going to happen next. Both characters were intent on rescuing the other and both were too stubborn to back down. Was this a case of art imitating life? If so, how could she move on?

'Do you need some help?' Alison asked seriously. 'Ms Albany taught us how to brainstorm ideas in our English lesson last month.'

'Aye, my mam always tells us two heads are better than one,' Lennie said, nudging his twin Bonnie, who gave Merry an identical smile.

Merry frowned and perched on the edge of Belle's desk, folding her arms. She'd tried to talk her dilemma through with Chewy yesterday afternoon but the rabbit had been absolutely no help. 'Okay,' she said – there was no harm in discussing the options. It could be a good creative exercise for the children, too.

'Tell us about the scene you want to write,' Belle asked, picking up a black marker from her desk.

'Well, Dan is trapped in a dungeon and Carmel wants to rescue him. She has a hairclip she wants to use to unpick the padlock,' Merry explained and the teacher wrote 'Dan is trapped in a dungeon' on the board and followed it up with a line drawing of a stick figure stuck behind bars. Then she drew another stick figure with a skirt holding an enormous hair grip.

'Did the baddies catch Dan?' Adam asked, his eyes widening as the rest of the class let out a collective groan.

'Yeah.' Merry winced. 'I'm afraid the Jeep broke down and they caught up with him at the edge of the jungle, but Carmel managed to escape with the jewel.'

'Why hasn't Carmel rescued Dan yet?' Mazey looked surprised. 'Is she injured?'

'No.' Merry shook her head. 'She was going to.' She folded her arms. 'But, it's complicated—'

'Does she need help?' Belle asked, gently. 'Is that why she hasn't been able to rescue him?'

'Aye,' Lennie said seriously. 'When I do my chores at home, Bonnie does them with me because that way we do a better job. We just decorated our Christmas tree and it only took an hour – but when Da does it by himself it usually takes three.' He snickered.

'Mam says everything's better when you work as a team,' his sister said.

'Your mam's right,' Belle agreed, writing 'teamwork' on the board.

'I'm not sure how that would work.' Merry frowned. Especially since neither of her characters seemed inclined to co-operate at the moment. 'Dan wants to rescue himself but Carmel's already waiting outside the cell.'

'Could Santa break Dan out instead?' the boy with freckles and red hair asked, putting up his hand.

'I don't think Father Christmas has a part in Ms McKenzie's novel, but that's a great idea, Angus – perhaps you could use it in a story one day?' Belle suggested, earning herself a nod from the young man.

'Maybe Santa's elves could set off some fireworks?' Magnus asked eagerly.

'I'm pretty sure there aren't any elves in Ms McKenzie's story either.' Belle chuckled and Merry had to fight a smile. The children's enthusiasm for her book was so refreshing – listening to their ideas and watching their beaming faces was such a boon after the last few days.

She had no idea what she'd do when she returned to Hertfordshire, but perhaps teaching writing skills to children was something she should consider? Merry knew she'd never have had the courage before coming to Christmas Village, but things had changed.

'I love all your ideas,' Merry said. 'You've got such amazing imaginations. But the only characters I was planning on including in this scene were Carmel and Dan – aside from the men who've been following them. They'll probably chase them after they escape.'

'Carmel could create a diversion,' Mazey suggested, her eyes firing. 'Then if she gives Dan the hairclip, he could use it to escape.'

Belle looked excited. 'Good idea! That way they'd be working as a team.'

'Then they'd both be heroes,' Doug gushed and the rest of the class started to cheer.

'That could work,' Merry said, thinking her characters might be okay with it. Working together was fitting – and this way Dan would be able to rescue himself and Carmel would be able to help without putting herself in danger. Was there a lesson in there somewhere for her and Theo too?

'It's been so wonderful having you in our lessons. I wish you were staying in Christmas Village for longer so you could visit us again. You'd make an amazing teacher.' Belle gave Merry a hug as they walked towards the school reception area half an hour later as the children filed past, heading for the playground in time for their break.

'I've loved it.' Merry clutched a large red envelope containing a card the children had made and signed to thank her for her help in their classes. She'd spent the last hour listening to their stories, overwhelmed by how amazing their ideas were. Belle had promised to pin their handwritten work onto the huge board at the back of their classroom and Merry had told the children she'd visit before they broke up to see the display. She'd miss going to the school – being around the kids had given her a much-needed buzz and they'd even helped her work out how to finish her story. Which was more than any of the people on the writing website she used to frequent had done.

'I didn't realise you were here!' Hannah said as Belle and Merry walked into the school reception area which doubled as a small library. The younger woman was sitting in front of a tall wooden booth cluttered with piles of leaflets, a tissue box and a small Christmas tree that hosted so many baubles Merry wondered how it managed to stay upright. Hannah skipped over so she could give Merry a hug. 'I've just finished running the library and thought I'd wait for Ace. How did the lesson go? My boy was so excited about sharing his story.'

'Merry was brilliant.' Belle beamed.

'Your son's ideas are excellent – he's got real talent,' Merry gushed. 'I could see him being a writer one day.'

Hannah grinned. 'Ach. He has such an incredible imagination, but you've really inspired him. He's been writing most evenings.' Her smile suddenly dropped as she spotted something over Merry's shoulder. 'What are you doing here?' Hannah demanded, stepping around the two women before marching towards the entrance of the school where Sam Doherty was standing, holding two shopping bags.

'I came to see you. I know you run the library on Wednesday afternoons,' the young man said nervously, putting the carriers on the ground. He'd dressed up in a smart suit and coat and was clenching and unclenching his hands.

'Have you come to say goodbye?' Hannah asked sweetly, stepping closer so she could stare into his eyes. 'I knew you'd leave in the end, although this visit was short even for you. I suppose I should be grateful you came to tell me you're going, this time round.' There was an ache in her voice and Sam must have heard it too because he gave her a sad smile.

'I'm sorry about the way I left before and I'm sorry you don't feel you can trust me,' he said softly. 'But I meant what I said – I'm not going anywhere without you again.' When Hannah didn't respond, Sam took another step towards her.

'If that's not your packing, what's in those?' She pointed to the bags angrily.

'I've been trying to think of a way to prove I'm going to stay,' Sam said.

'You can't!' Hannah snapped, her eyes glistening.

Merry swallowed and glanced at Belle. The teacher was watching the couple too, nibbling her bottom lip, obviously affected by their distress.

Sam frowned. 'I saved money when I was working in the army. I knew I'd want to put down roots someday and I also knew there was only one place in the world I'd want them to grow.'

'So you've brought seeds?' Hannah asked, sarcastically. 'Because I know how easy it is to plant something, Sam – it's the watering, feeding and nurturing, hanging around to watch them grow that really counts.' She shook her head. 'I've been taken in by two men in my life, let myself love them and believe they'd stick.' She huffed. 'Bags don't mean commitment. Bags are the things you pack when you're going to leave.' She began to turn away, but Sam took her hand and gently spun her around.

Then he reached into one of the carriers and pulled out a tin. 'This was the first meal we ever shared. I was thirteen and I went to your house for dinner. Your mam served baked beans with toast and told me you loved them.' Sam handed the baked beans to Hannah, and Merry watched her frown at the can. 'I eat them whenever I'm homesick – or whenever I want to feel close to you.' Sam bent and pulled a handful of carrots from the bag too. 'These are your favourite vegetables – your da used to grow them in his allotment especially for you and in the autumn you used to help him pick them on Sunday afternoons.' He pushed the bundle into Hannah's other hand and she gazed at them, looking confused. Then he grabbed a bar of chocolate from the other carrier.

'You like milk chocolate in the evenings just before you go to bed,' he said softly, picking up another bar and adding it to the growing pile cradled in Hannah's arms. 'But you prefer dark with a cup of tea just after you get up. I used to sneak you some into school.'

'I can't believe you remember all this.' Hannah cleared her throat. 'What's it supposed to mean?'

'That I never forgot you,' Sam said softly. 'I'm trying to show you I never will.'

'A handful of shopping doesn't prove you're not going to leave again though, does it?' she asked, although her voice sounded less angry. Merry thought she could hear something new in it now – perhaps it was hope?

'Maybe these will.' Sam dug into the bag and drew out a set of keys and handed them to Hannah. 'I bought into The Corner Shop,' he said softly. 'Da's been wanting to semi-retire for a while and he's been searching for the right partner.' He shoved his hands into his pockets and gazed at her. 'I've decided it's going to be me. I've spent every penny I have – I want you to know I'm all in.' He swallowed. 'I understand it might take you a while to trust me, but I want you to know I'm here to stay and I'm prepared to wait until you're ready. That there's nowhere else I'd rather be.'

'I don't know what to say...' Hannah said faintly.

Sam shrugged. 'Just say you'll give me a chance.'

Hannah stared at him with her mouth open.

'I'm sorry it took me so long to come back to Christmas Village; I'm even sorrier I didn't get in touch.'

'Why didn't you call?' Hannah asked, clutching the shopping to her chest. 'I never understood.'

He lifted a shoulder. 'At first I knew if I did, I wouldn't be able to stay away. Later, I heard you got married and I didn't think it would be fair. Then I lost track of you. Or maybe it was just easier to try to forget because I knew I'd lost you.' He let out a long breath. 'Then Da told me a few months ago that you'd returned to Christmas Village. I knew then it was time for me to come home too. I was thinking of re-enlisting but it changed everything. It's why I came back now.'

Hannah stared at him, then she looked down at the shopping in her arms before taking a step away. 'I'm going to need to think about this.' Her voice was strained again.

'I understand.' Sam cleared his throat. 'I've been gone a long time.'

'A lot of things have changed,' she said gently.

Sam's shoulders sank. 'Do you mean it's too late?'

Hannah stared at him, then she slowly shook her head. 'Maybe not, but for future reference,' she leaned forwards and Sam's eyes widened, 'my favourite vegetables are Brussels sprouts.'

23

Merry sat at the kitchen table in Chestnut Cottage the following day and tentatively opened her laptop before studying the screen for a few moments. After her disastrous attempt to write about Dan's rescue, she wasn't sure she was brave enough to try again. What would happen if her hero behaved in the same way? What if he continued to refuse Carmel's help? She sucked in a breath. There was only one way to find out.

'Don't let me down, Dan,' she pleaded, diving back into the scene in the dungeon where she'd last left off. Dan was locked in a cell and Carmel was still hoping to rescue him by unpicking the lock. Relief flooded Merry's limbs as her fingers few across the keyboard and the story unfolded in her head, the words tumbling out and filling the screen just as she'd imagined them.

Something important had changed since the last time she'd attempted to write. Her vet had returned. The thoughtful man who knew when to help and when to step back. Merry grinned as Carmel gave Dan the hairclip and then ran off to create a diversion, allowing him to unpick the lock and escape…

Dan was waiting by the horses when Carmel emerged from the end of the cave. He was holding the reins and as soon as he spotted her, he grinned. Then he scooped her into his arms and framed her face so he could give her a long, deep kiss. 'Ready?' he asked huskily, sweeping a hand towards the horses – then he watched as she swung herself into the saddle. As soon as Dan was on his horse too they set off, riding into the sunset, heading towards Tinsel Mountain and the end of their adventure.

Merry sat back in her seat and smiled at the laptop. Dan and Carmel had escaped from the clutches of the men who were trying to steal the diamond, and they'd worked together. They were both heroes, neither trying to hold the other back. Could the same approach be applied to her relationship with Theo? He still hadn't called or come to find her – maybe he was worried about how she'd react, or he didn't want to crowd her? So perhaps it was time for her to take the initiative and find him.

Merry closed the lid of her laptop and grabbed a coat and Simba's cat carrier from the closet at the bottom of the stairs. She knew what she needed to do – show Theo she was a match for him. That she'd changed since she'd come to Christmas Village – that he didn't need to rescue her. She'd show him they could work together and be the ultimate team.

Christmas Village high street was busy when Merry finally parked her Aunt Ava's Jeep at the bottom of the road, away from the shopfronts, villagers and traffic. She'd driven around for almost an hour and a half, checking the narrow lanes in the area in the hope she'd catch sight of the one-eyed cat. But she hadn't seen even a hint of it. Now she'd search where she and Theo had seen the cat before in the hope it might appear – although she didn't hold out much hope. The stray had all but disappeared.

She grabbed the carrier and wandered along the pavement, searching underneath benches and bins, before heading into

The Corner Shop, pausing in the doorway and remembering when Theo had brought her here for the first time. He'd obviously known Tavish might be wearing his Christmas jumper and he'd let her walk ahead, probably hoping she'd realise the shopkeeper should receive the Secret Santa hat and gloves. In retrospect, Theo had been working with her, not taking over. He'd let Merry work things out for herself.

'You okay, lass?' Tavish appeared from the back room and stood at the counter, his eyes dropping to the carrier. 'Have you lost one of Ava's pets?'

Merry shook her head. 'I wondered if you'd seen the one-eyed cat recently? I thought I'd try to find it for Theo.'

Tavish shook his head. 'Nae, I've had a few of my customers looking out, but no sign yet.' He pursed his lips. 'Sam ordered some new-fangled cat treats for the shop.' He wandered from behind the counter and headed for the shelves, shuffling behind some tins before holding up a small yellow pack. 'You could try them?' he offered, twisting his hands so he could read the text printed on the back. 'Says every cat will love them or your money back.' He handed her the bag and smiled when she dug into her handbag, searching for her purse. 'On the house.' He waved the offer away. 'It's the least I can do. I hear you've been inspiring all the kiddies in Belle's class. Seems like we might have a few more authors in our midst. I'm guessing that will be good for business when they're all famous.'

'Thank you,' Merry said, feeling her heart fill. She'd miss the lessons; being around the children had made her feel like she fitted, somehow. She'd enjoyed the way they'd reacted to Dan and Carmel, loved how they'd all developed as writers in their own right as a result of her work. The children had helped her see she could be just like her heroine – confident and strong. But more than that, they'd shown her that being independent didn't mean doing everything for yourself.

She turned and headed out of the shop, towards the large fir tree where the Christmas carol concert would take place and the Secret Santa gifts would be handed out. She paused as she approached the clearing, feeling suddenly sad. Was she ready to leave Christmas Village? It had been years since she'd felt so in control of her destiny and life, years since she'd felt brave enough to try anything new. Taking a deep breath, Merry put the carrier on the floor and opened the packet of cat treats. 'Woah,' she complained, shoving the sachet away from her nose. They stank, but perhaps the pungent aroma would attract the stray, because nothing else had.

She ambled around the clearing, poking her head underneath the nearby shrubs, making kissy sounds. She couldn't see any obvious prints, even as she spread her search wider – where was the animal? After twenty minutes, Merry returned to the clearing and sat on one of the small circular wooden blocks so she could wait. She picked up the packet of treats every now and again to shake it, hoping the one-eyed cat might miraculously appear.

As Merry sat, she gazed at the baubles on the tree and her mind wandered as she imagined Christmas morning, thinking about the villagers who'd receive her Aunt Ava's gifts. The Secret Santa sack was almost full and Merry mentally ticked off all the items she'd matched with a local. There was the tiara for Edina; Rowan's chef's hat; the cute cow picture which had clearly been chosen for Jared; Kenzy was a perfect lavender bath oil match; Tavish would love his coordinating hat and gloves; Belle would probably give all her cake boxes away before the new year; the torch was Duncan's; the knitting patterns belonged to Rachel; Moira and Julie were destined to receive their swimming hats just in time for a festive swim; Logan was obviously the owner of the tool wrist band; Jack's gift was the snow shovel; Clyde was a perfect match with the microwaveable slippers. Then there was Isla's sewing kit, Bram's silver tankard, Robina's glasses chain, Matt's plectrum, and now it was just the bangles and two necklaces to allocate – although Merry was pretty sure she'd guessed who should receive the latter. Theo didn't have a gift, probably because he hadn't lived in Christmas Village for long enough for her Aunt Ava to consider him worthy. Merry wondered about buying him something. But what would she get?

Half an hour later, Merry's toes felt like frozen blocks. She wrapped her arms around herself as she picked up the treats and put them into her pocket, grabbing the carrier so she could make her way back to the car. Perhaps she'd try again later this afternoon? She'd bring a tin of Simba's food next time, maybe a fluffy blanket? Surely no creature on earth could resist one of those.

As Merry approached the Jeep, she squinted when she saw something spread-eagled across its bonnet. As she drew closer, she softened her footsteps and slowed as she recognised the black and white cat and realised it was asleep. She'd driven around for so long searching for him, the metal bonnet must have warmed up. The cat suddenly woke, yawned then looked up and blinked its one good eye as Merry drew closer. Before it thought about dashing away, Merry pulled the packet of treats from her pocket and laid them carefully on the heated metal. Then she reached out and tentatively stroked the cat's head, frowning at the closed eye which looked puffy and swollen.

'You really need to see a vet,' she said softly as it began to purr and creep closer to the treats, obviously hungry. 'Lucky for you, I know just the right one. He can be a little controlling,' she murmured as she carefully placed Simba's carrier onto the bonnet close to the cat and laid a trail of treats leading into the crate. 'But once you get to know him, you'll realise his heart is in exactly the right place.' Merry moved backwards a step and waited as the one-eyed cat sniffed the delicacies again, before nibbling along the trail, taking one tiny step at a time until it was all the way inside. Then Merry slowly shut the door and locked it. 'Now it's time for both of us to find Theo,' she said. 'I've a feeling I need him in my life as much as you do.'

24

The surgery was quiet even though it was early afternoon and Theo sat in his office contemplating his mobile before picking it up and dialling Jake. It would be stupid o'clock in Australia now and the first time he'd ever called his brother to ask for help but... He sighed.

'Theo?' Jake barked in between jaw-cracking yawns. 'I've just gone to bed – all my limbs are intact, I've eaten my vegetables and the last time I checked my bank account I was just about solvent. You really don't need to check up on me.'

Theo sighed and shut his eyes. 'I've been seeing this woman...'

He heard a sharp intake of breath and then a soft chuckle. 'The one who wears yellow?'

'Mmmm.' Theo thought about Merry.

'I thought you didn't like yellow?' Jake asked, sounding amused.

'I do now,' Theo grumbled. 'I tried to help her with something but... she thinks I've been spying on her for her brothers and—' He paused as his cheeks heated. He wasn't used to Jake seeing him as vulnerable, wasn't used to admitting he was wrong. 'It's a long story, which you probably don't need to hear about now, but... the thing is, I need your advice...'

Jake was silent for a beat, then Theo heard the rustle of blankets and soon after, footsteps on a wooden floor. 'I need to put some coffee on. I have to digest some caffeine because I must be dreaming. My big brother would never ask me for help.' He yawned again and Theo heard the sound of a tap running.

'Perhaps it's time I did,' he said gruffly. 'I'm not sure how much you'll be able to assist, though. I need to change and I'm not sure I can. You once told me I was a German Shepherd in human form—'

'I'm not going to apologise for that – or take it back,' Jack retorted and Theo heard the sound of a mug clattering on a metal counter.

'I'm not saying you should – I'm agreeing with you.' Theo sighed. He was too set in his ways to change now. Wasn't even sure he wanted to.

'Which would be a first,' Jake said. 'What have you done to make things up to this... What's her name?'

'Merry.' Theo cleared his throat. 'I told her brother he had to back off,' he said, wincing. 'He took it pretty well, probably better than I would in his position.'

Jake must have finished making the coffee because Theo heard him pull out a chair. 'But you've talked to Merry, right? Explained why you did what you did, made sure she understands you're not a complete idiot?'

Theo frowned. 'Not exactly. I don't know what to say: *I'm sorry I tried to secretly help you; I wish I hadn't lied about talking to your brothers; I'm not sure I can stop myself from helping again; I don't know if I can change, but I'll try?*'

'Maybe she doesn't want you to change,' Jake said softly. 'Have you considered that?'

'Well...'

'Because you have a lot of wonderful qualities – although I'll deny ever having said that.' He took a noisy sip of coffee.

'Yep, so many wonderful qualities that you couldn't wait to move to the other side of the world,' Theo said. 'I know my faults, Jake, it's why I came to Christmas Village, to try to move on from them. I came to find a woman who didn't need me, but it seems that's not what I really want.' He sighed. 'I'm over-protective, suffocating, controlling...' He gritted his teeth, feeling annoyed. Even Dot whined from the corner of the room as if she could read his thoughts.

'I'll bet those are all words from Miranda's vocabulary,' Jake guessed. 'You're also loyal, thoughtful and you'd fight to the death for the people you care about. Theo, I didn't come to Australia to get away from you – I came to grow up, maybe even to learn to be a little more like my big brother. But without you in my life I wonder if I'd ever have had the courage.' He sighed. 'Everyone needs a Theo – everyone needs to know that when the chips are down they have somewhere to turn, someone who's got their back, who'd do anything to make sure they're happy and safe – or achieve what they need to.'

Theo's jaw dropped.

'If your yellow-obsessed lady doesn't get that, she's really not worthy.'

'Well, I...' Theo's mouth ran out of words.

'I don't think you need to change. You just have to understand not everyone wants to be saved *all* of the time. You also have to be prepared to take help from others when it's offered. Even though it's not in your nature. Your kindness is why you're a vet and it's why I'm glad you're my big brother.' He let out a slow breath.

'Well, I...' Theo echoed.

'So now we've cleared that up...'

He heard the clatter of Jake's mug as it connected with the table.

'I'm going back to bed. Call me again when you've talked to this Merry. I'm hoping she's got a brain on her shoulders and a good set of ears – I'm hoping she'll meet you halfway.' With that, his brother hung up.

Theo stared at the mobile for a few minutes before putting it on the table. Then he tapped the keyboard on his computer, checking through Google until he found the website he'd been looking for. It took him a few minutes to order what he needed. But he hoped Merry would understand what he was trying to say.

The reception area of the surgery was quiet when Theo wandered out of his office a few minutes later. He knew Jared had visited the doctor this morning and the older vet was probably now injury-free, which meant he'd take over the out-of-surgery visits from now on.

Kirsteen came out of the stockroom carrying a ream of paper, heading for the reception desk, her pretty, long skirts rustling. She glanced at Theo as he leaned against the doorframe of his consulting room.

'It's quiet.' Theo scoured the empty space.

'Aye, for at least another ten minutes – enjoy the calm before the storm because you've an afternoon of back-to-back appointments.' She shot him a curious look. 'Everything okay? Because I'm here to talk if you need an ear.'

Theo cleared his throat. 'I'm all talked out – but thank you,' he added. It felt good to be cared for, nice not to be the only person doing it. Perhaps his decision to move here had been a smart one, after all?

The doors at the entrance to the surgery suddenly swished open and Jared came marching inside. He barely looked at Theo; instead, he walked up to the front desk and frowned at Kirsteen as she gazed at her computer, ignoring him.

'I have a question,' he said quietly.

'For whom?' the receptionist asked without looking up, but

Theo saw bright triangles of red spread across the tips of her cheeks. 'Because if you're looking for cows, you'll have more luck at the farm next door. Perhaps you could join them for lunch?'

Jared frowned. 'I've booked a table for tonight in a restaurant on the road to Morridon.' He squeezed his hands by his sides. 'And...' He puffed out a breath, looking desperately towards where Theo was standing, but Theo merely gestured at him to continue.

'What?' Kirsteen asked impatiently.

Jared swallowed. 'I wondered if you'd like to go,' he asked rapidly.

The older woman looked up and pursed her lips, then she folded her arms on the top of her desk. 'Alone?' She sounded suspicious. 'Because I'm really not interested.'

'No, lass,' Jared said, sighing. 'With me.'

Kirsteen raised an eyebrow. 'Because?'

The vet threw up his arms. 'I don't know.'

Theo was about to step forwards, but stopped himself from intervening. He watched the receptionist's jaw flex, then saw the older vet deflate.

'I'm not good with people,' he said quietly. 'That's why I like cows; they're easy to understand and they don't need much. Just food, the odd head stroke and in some cases, milking. I don't have to put myself out there and worry that I don't measure up.' He shut his eyes for a beat. 'For some reason, cows like me and that makes it easy to like them too.' He sighed.

Kirsteen made a huffing sound.

'But... I've realised sometimes easy and safe isn't best. Sometimes it would be nice,' Jared swallowed, 'to spend time with someone who occasionally – or maybe often – talks back.' He waited for Kirsteen to digest his words.

'I talk back,' she said after a long pause. 'But you might not always like what I have to say.'

'Aye, well, I think I might enjoy the odd sparring match. I think I might be ready to put myself out there when it comes to you,' Jared murmured, shoving his hands into his pockets. 'It can get lonely spending all your time alone, no matter how many cow documentaries you've saved to watch.'

Kirsteen's cheeks flushed. 'Boring as well,' she said softly. 'I'll go on that date with you, Jared Dunbar.' Her eyes flashed. 'You scrub up well and I know you've a good head on those shoulders, even if you don't always use it. But...' She leaned further forwards on the desk and speared him with a look that might have floored a lesser man. 'The subject of oxen, bulls, calves, cattle or bovine entities of any kind is off limits.'

Jared belly-laughed. 'I can promise you that. I'm hoping we can just talk about you...' With that, he spun on his heel and headed towards his office, his gait spritely as Kirsteen gazed after him with a warm smile decorating her face.

Kirsteen poked her head into Theo's examination room an hour and twenty minutes later. The rush of clients had been legendary and had included a myriad collection of poorly pets including a dog with an upset stomach, a restless goat and an insomniac hamster.

'I wondered if I could squeeze in an emergency appointment?' she whispered, peering over her shoulder to make sure no one in the waiting room could hear. 'I know you're back-to-back, so it'll mean no downtime, but...' She pulled a mug of coffee from behind her skirt and placed it on his table. 'I've a feeling you'll want to see this one.' She winked.

'Why?' Theo asked, picking up the hot drink. His head hurt and he needed a break, maybe some time to figure out how he was going to approach Merry, but they both knew he'd never say no to a sick animal. He sighed. 'Send them in.' Theo pushed a pile of papers to the edge of his desk and rose as Kirsteen opened the door and scooted out, rattling her bangles as Merry walked into his office holding an animal carrier.

'Who's hurt?' he asked, drinking her in, feeling every cell of his anatomy perk up and then settle for the first time in days. He strode forwards as Merry carefully placed the carrier onto the examination table. 'Is it Chewy or Simba?'

'They're both fine. This is a peace offering,' Merry said, opening the door of the carrier and looking a little flustered.

Theo swallowed. 'I thought...' He sighed, leaning down so he could peer into the cage. 'It's the one-eyed cat,' he gasped. Then he carefully drew the animal onto the table so he could examine its face and check both eyes. Despite being a stray, the cat was calmer than he'd expected and even began to purr. As he'd suspected, one of the eyes was infected which was why it was puffy and almost completely shut.

'You really are a natural at saving things,' Merry said softly.

Theo cleared his throat. 'I'm not sure if that's always a good thing.' He turned back to the cat when Merry didn't respond. 'He needs cleaning up and a dose of strong antibiotics. But it looks like you found him just in time. Thank you.' He looked into her eyes and felt his chest inflate when Merry gazed back at him. She didn't look angry now and for the first time since she'd walked out on him he began to feel hope.

'He?' Merry asked, reaching out so she could stroke the cat too, letting their little fingers caress as their hands moved. Was it an accident, or had she meant them to touch?

Theo nodded, feeling confused. 'Where did you find him?'

Merry shrugged. 'By the Christmas tree on the high street.'

He frowned. 'I've been searching around there for days.' It had been a good distraction when he hadn't been able to sleep.

'I suppose that's why the best teams come in twos,' Merry said, swallowing. 'Noah said you didn't tell him anything about me.' She looked down at their hands which were still touching.

'I didn't,' Theo said. 'But I know talking to him at all was wrong.'

'I've been thinking about how you let me care for the animals myself, how you encouraged me to drive and swim, and helped me solve all the Secret Santa clues without letting on that you knew,' she murmured.

Theo sighed. 'I'm sorry.' He closed his eyes.

'Maybe you shouldn't be.' Merry put her palm over his and squeezed and he opened them again. 'You remind me of Dan,' she said, gazing at him, her eyes wide. 'He lets Carmel be who she needs to be but sometimes she needs his help – although...' She pulled a face. 'It took her a while to come around to the idea, too.'

'What do you mean?' Theo felt his heartbeat pick up as hope bloomed.

She blew out a breath. 'I've realised it's okay to have someone on your side helping. Not when they're trying to hold you back or crowd you, but when they're all about making sure you succeed. It's about being part of a team.' She looked around. 'Being in Christmas Village helped me to see that. Being around you.'

Theo cleared his throat. 'So... what, you're saying it's okay if I want to help you?'

Merry frowned. 'I'm saying it's all right if we want to help each other. I'm SuperMerry, I can do what I want, but perhaps I can do a lot more with you – and maybe you can too.' Her mouth twisted. 'It's why I found the one-eyed cat: I wanted us to save him together. I know we live miles from each other, but I want to see if we can give this thing between us a chance.'

Theo felt something inside his chest click. He leaned down so he could trace his lips over hers just as Kirsteen knocked on the door and wandered in, her bracelets jangling again. 'Sorry!' she yelped. 'I was coming to see if you needed anything. Um...

obviously not.' Her eyes shone as she looked between Merry and Theo. 'I'll just...' She backed out and shut the door.

Merry looked into Theo's eyes. 'Was she wearing bangles?'

He grinned down at her. 'Yep.'

She beamed. 'That was the final present I needed to match. I think I've guessed who the necklaces are for. Secret Santa might just be finished.' She shook her head. 'I didn't think I'd do it. I mean, I knew I'd try, but when I realised my aunt's notes were shredded I don't think I really believed...'

Theo pressed a gentle finger against her lips. 'I get the feeling you could do anything you set your mind to, Merry McKenzie.' He swallowed. 'With or without anyone's help.'

Merry grinned. 'Maybe. But as a wise boy once said, two heads are better than one. So, tonight I think I'd like your help.'

'Anything,' Theo said softly.

'Perhaps you could come by Chestnut Cottage to help me wrap the rest of the presents and feed the animals? I'd like my sidekick on hand just in case of any emergencies.'

When Theo grinned, Merry went up onto her tiptoes and brushed her lips against his.

25

Merry finished wrapping and labelling the gift she'd chosen for Theo and hid it carefully inside the large red sack. Then she placed a large cardboard box filled with the remaining unwrapped Secret Santa presents and wrapping paper onto the kitchen table ready for when the vet arrived. She sipped some of her gingerbread latte then checked her watch as Chewy scampered across the floor.

'Theo won't be long,' she murmured. 'He was going to drop Noah at the Christmas Pud Inn to meet with Sam and come straight over. I think he wants to make sure my big brother is occupied.' Merry grinned as she glanced around. She'd lit a fire earlier and it crackled, throwing light and heat into the room. The Christmas tree twinkled beside it and the whole place glittered and glowed. Just a few weeks ago she'd have hated being stuck here alone, but now it felt like home.

A floorboard squeaked above Merry's head and she glared at the ceiling. 'I'm going to have to check that out. I can't leave it any longer.' She swallowed, then headed to one of the kitchen drawers to pick out a spatula, before trotting up the stairs. She heard Chewy scurrying behind, but knew the rabbit wouldn't make it past the bottom step. It was probably for the best; she had to do this by herself. Merry crept slowly across the landing, holding the spatula in front of her like a weapon as she headed for the airing cupboard. She'd kept the door firmly shut during her stay, but knew the time had finally come to face her fears. 'Think Carmel,' she ordered herself, wishing Theo was there but knowing she didn't really need him. Two heads were definitely better than one, but sometimes, one was all you needed – some things you had to face yourself. Putting her hand on the circular knob, she took one final breath, then almost jumped out of her skin when the doorbell rang. 'Theo!' Relieved, Merry retraced her steps and dashed downstairs to the front door. 'Hannah?' she gasped as it swung open.

'I'm sorry, I have to talk to someone. Ace is with my mam and I thought I'd come and see you.' The young woman pulled off her blue bobble hat and grasped it between her fingers. 'I can't sleep.'

'Come in,' Merry said, standing to one side and glancing into the driveway. Snow was falling again and there was no sign of Theo. 'Has something happened?'

Hannah frowned. 'Nothing new, but I don't know what to do about Sam,' she said hoarsely, following Merry down the hallway towards the kitchen as she shrugged off her coat. 'This is pretty,' she gasped as she walked up to the fire and leaned down to stroke Simba's head. While she wasn't looking, Merry quickly closed the lid on the box of Secret Santa gifts and set it onto the floor out of the way before pushing the red sack into the shadows.

'Ace wants to get a cat, I was thinking of adopting one in the new year.'

'I'm sure Theo could help with that,' Merry promised, feeling bereft as she wondered where she'd be living in January. The thought of being back in Hertfordshire with her brothers didn't sit right. She'd moved on, gained her independence; she didn't want to live her old life now. 'Gingerbread latte?'

'Please.' Hannah walked across the room to hover by the table while Merry busied herself refilling her mug and making one more. 'I just need an objective opinion. Everyone else has lived in Christmas Village for so long they won't be able to give me one.' She sighed.

Merry put their mugs on the table and indicated that Hannah should sit. 'I can't say I'm an expert or anything.'

'You write romance novels – which means you know all about happy endings.' Hannah blinked. 'I'd like to finally get one of those.' She leaned her elbows on the table. 'You know Sam and my history, what's been going on between us.' She flushed. 'You've had a front-row seat for most of it.'

'You want to know what I think?' Merry asked softly, feeling a tingle of something in her chest. It felt good to be needed, for her opinion to count, and it had been years since she'd felt qualified to offer one.

Hannah exhaled. 'Can I trust what Sam says? Is this going to work out?' she asked, pulling a face.

Merry sipped some of her coffee, thinking about the handsome, wiry man and how he'd looked at Hannah whenever they'd been together. 'He came back to Christmas Village because he knew you were here...'

'That's what he told me,' Hannah said quietly.

'Then he bought into The Corner Shop to prove he's going to stay,' she continued.

'I suppose he did,' Hannah murmured. 'He's been working there every day and Edina confirmed that Tavish is planning to semi-retire. When he does, Sam will take over the running of it full time.'

'If you think about the shopping he got, he obviously knows you inside out. If I were writing this – if it were my romance novel – I'd say he's doing everything he can to show he loves you and he's not planning on going anywhere again. There are no guarantees, but those are all elements of a successful romantic story.'

Hannah stared at her for a beat before she swallowed. 'I guess you're right. According to Ace, the only thing missing would be the car chase...'

'I'm pretty sure if you asked, Sam would deliver one of those too,' Merry joked. 'Sometimes we've just got to go with our gut.' Her mind drifted to Theo again. 'People make mistakes: what counts is what they do next.'

Hannah gazed at her. 'My son is right, you really are very talented,' she said, flushing. 'I hope you don't leave Christmas Village anytime soon.' She polished off the rest of her coffee. 'Thank you. You've given me a lot to think about.' As Hannah rose, the canary-yellow phone began to ring. 'You get that,' she said, waving at the wall. 'I'll see myself out.'

'Merry!' The voice at the other end of the line sounded tinny and far away. Merry heard the front door close quietly as she gripped the receiver to her ear.

'Aunt Ava. I thought you couldn't call me?' she asked, confused. 'Are you okay?'

'Fine, lass. A few of us were travelling to town for supplies. It's a four-hour drive but they have Wi-Fi and a phone signal here. I thought I'd take a chance and see if you were home. How are you?' her aunt sang.

Merry scoured the kitchen. 'Good, great. All the animals are well too.' She'd tell her aunt about Chewy getting electro-cuted some other time. 'Although, Cluck, Eggitha and Hennifer haven't been laying.'

'Don't worry about that. The girls often take the day off – didn't you see that in my notes?' Ava sounded confused.

'I must have missed it.' Merry didn't want to tell her aunt about the lost notes now. 'What's it like out there?'

'Hot but brilliant. The reason I'm calling is that I want to know if you'd be happy to animal-sit for me again? You don't have to say yes straight away,' she rushed when Merry opened her mouth. 'But I wanted to give you time to think. We can talk when I come home in January, but I've been asked to help out at another animal sanctuary – this time for a whole year!' she squeaked in obvious delight. 'Don't feel you have to, lass, I can find somebody else, but if you want—'

'I'd love to,' Merry interrupted. It would give her and Theo a chance to be together – to see if things between them would work.

'That's a relief, because I'll be gone from the middle of January until next Christmas so I'll need you to take over Secret Santa again too.' Her aunt paused and Merry heard someone talking in the background.

'I can do that.' Merry grinned. After the ordeal of losing the list and having to work out which gift matched up with whom, she was an expert.

'Sorry love, I've got to go soon: there's a queue for the phone,' her aunt said. 'Before I do, I know there are still a few days left, but did you get all the presents wrapped?'

'Almost.' Merry smiled again, glancing across the kitchen to where she could see the box on the floor by the table. 'I'll be finishing them up tonight.'

'Fantastic! I can't wait to see you when I return, we've got so much to catch up on. Happy Christmas, see you soon!' With that, the line went dead.

Merry replaced the receiver and skipped across the kitchen so she could clear up the coffee mugs and place the box of Secret Santa gifts back on the table. She heard a creak upstairs and headed towards the hallway, grabbing the spatula she'd left on a bookshelf on her way. 'I'm going to do it this time, Chewy,' she said as she climbed the stairs. 'If I'll be living here for another year, I can't be scared of every small sound. It won't be a Yeti, the cupboard's too small.' Merry shut her eyes and placed a tentative hand on the knob. Then she twisted it and let the door swing open, waving the spatula as she opened her eyes.

Then Merry dropped to her knees in relief when she spotted a tiny mouse scamper towards the back of the cupboard. 'Definitely not a Yeti,' Merry said, then she began to laugh.

'It's just these last few things,' Merry explained half an hour later as she led Theo into the kitchen, to the table where the presents were laid out beside a roll of colourful wrapping paper, labels and sticky tape. He was wearing jeans and a green sweatshirt and looked good enough to eat.

'Sorry I'm late. Your brother got talking with Sam – he wanted some advice on what to do about Hannah, and I didn't have the heart to refuse. Not sure why he thought I'd know what I was talking about.' He shoved his hands into his pockets as he gazed at her. 'You're wearing yellow,' he said softly and Merry glanced down at her jumper.

'It's my favourite colour,' she faltered.

'I think it might be mine too,' Theo said huskily, walking up to her and pulling her into his arms. 'Do we have to do the wrapping right away?' He nibbled the edge of her ear then dropped his mouth to her collarbone and Merry's knees began to buckle.

'Um, we've still got a few days,' she rasped, wriggling as Theo's hands moved to the bottom of her jumper. 'I thought you liked yellow,' she whispered as he began to tug it up.

'I like you better,' he whispered before pulling it all the way off.

26

It was snowing again on Christmas morning and the whole of the village stood beside the small clearing at the end of the high street while Tavish Doherty dipped up and down, searching through the thick bushes. Lights twinkled on the huge fir tree in the centre and Merry looked up and stuck out her tongue so she could catch a snowflake on the tip. She gazed up at the sky which seemed to sparkle and glow down at them.

'I found it!' Tavish yelled suddenly, squeezing his large body from between two bulging evergreens as he tugged a heavy red velvet sack into the clearing where the villagers were all waiting. Merry recognised it immediately and smiled up at Theo who winked.

'Good find!' Jack shouted from the other side of the clearing as Belle hooked an arm through his, looking excited. Around them, the rest of the villagers cheered too and some of the children hopped up and down on fresh pillowy snow.

'Who wants to give out the presents?' the shopkeeper asked as his eyes scoured the sea of delighted faces. It was Christmas morning and the group had assembled ten minutes earlier, ready to sing carols before waiting for the Secret Santa gifts to be found and distributed.

'I'll do it!' Sam offered, striding forwards so he could take the sack from his dad. On the opposite side of the tree, Merry saw Hannah flush as the younger man sought her attention and winked. It was clear even after their conversation a few days before that Hannah still hadn't decided what to do about him.

Merry felt her cheeks flush as Theo squeezed her hand, then leaned down to kiss the edge of her face. Her heart was in her throat as she wondered if she'd managed to get all the gift recipients right. In a few minutes she'd know. Know if she'd fulfilled her Aunt Ava's wishes and done her Secret Santa family proud. It had been such an incredible few weeks, totally life-changing. She'd arrived afraid of everything, determined to change her life and she'd achieved it. Not only that, she'd finally finished her book and found her perfect man.

'Good luck,' Theo murmured, pressing his lips to her ear. Beside him, Noah made a huffing sound. Her brother had stayed the night before at Chestnut Cottage and the three of them had risen early this morning and wandered into the village with Dot after feeding Aunt Ava's pets. Even Henry had shuffled into the garden to eat a handful of cranberries from Theo's palm, although the turkey had directed a series of threatening yelps and squawks at Noah when he'd tried to join in. Her vet really did have a magic touch.

'I should say good luck to you too,' Merry whispered, pressing her mouth to Theo's, ignoring her brother's teasing groans. Theo had helped her to wrap all of the outstanding Secret Santa presents and then heaved the heavy sack onto the porch at the back of her aunt's house the morning before.

'So, the first gift is for Jared Dunbar,' Sam said loudly, drawing the square package from the top and looking around the crowd. The vet was standing beside Kirsteen and she patted his arm gently as she guided him to the front. They all watched as Jared slowly unwrapped his gift, before chuckling at the cow picture and waving it above his head.

'It's bonnie, Secret Santa, whoever you are, and I thank you,' he barked into the gathering. 'But it's not as bonnie as my Kirsteen,' he added, twisting around to kiss the surprised receptionist on the mouth. She squealed and wrapped her arms around his shoulders as the rest of the villagers roared in delight.

Sam cleared his throat, waiting for the excitement to die down. 'Well, I hope the rest of the presents get that kind of reception.' He laughed, pulling out what Merry guessed was a wrapped tiara. The younger man twisted it in his palm so he could read the label. 'This one's for Edina Lachlan,' he shouted, grinning when the older woman let out a loud cheer and the crowd parted to let her through to the front.

They all watched as Edina unwrapped the pretty red and green paper to reveal a stunning imitation sapphire tiara. 'Ach, it's just perfect!' she declared, whipping off the ruby tiara she was wearing before placing the new one on her head. 'What do you think, Tavish?' she asked the older man.

'Aye, it looks good,' he said, blushing as he wound an arm around her shoulder and Sam dug back into the bag.

'This one's for Jack Hamilton-Kirk.' Sam offered the gift as the younger man let go of Belle and trotted up to claim it. He unwrapped it slowly and chuckled before winking at Logan.

'I suppose I won't be needing your help next time I get stuck in the snow,' Jack joked.

'You won't get stuck at all if you buy yourself a decent car,' Logan countered and everybody roared.

Belle's present came next and she opened it to reveal the flat-packed boxes.

'That can only be good news for us!' Clyde shouted. 'Because it means more of Belle's bonnie cakes!' The whole village cheered.

Ten minutes later, most of the gifts had been handed out and unwrapped and Merry knew she'd got them all right. There were just a few more for Sam to deliver and she hoped they'd be just as perfect. She watched as he pulled out two tiny presents and read the labels. 'These are for Hannah McDowell and...' He frowned, looking surprised. 'Me.' Sam swallowed as Hannah wandered up to join him, holding tightly onto Ace's hand.

'What is it, Mam?' the boy asked, looking excited as Hannah unpeeled her gloves from her fingers and gazed down at it. 'It looks the same as yours,' she said to Sam, pushing a strand of curly hair from her cheek.

'Shall we open them at the same time?' Sam asked. 'That way, we both get a surprise.'

'Aye,' Hannah said and they each slowly unpeeled the paper from their gifts. Merry knew what they'd reveal. She'd guessed the couple were the intended recipients and when she saw their faces light up, she knew she'd been right. 'They're broken hearts,' Hannah said, her voice filled with wonder.

'But when you put them together,' Sam gulped, 'they become whole.'

'Put them together then,' Tavish demanded and the crowd waited as Hannah held up her silver charm and Sam pressed his half of the heart to hers.

'Together,' Hannah whispered, glancing at Merry.

'Together, always,' Sam echoed, his lips curving as Ace began to bounce on his heels. Then they watched as Hannah turned to Sam and slowly nodded before lifting her mouth to his.

Everyone began to cheer and clap again and Tavish stepped in front of the couple to give them some privacy as he dug into the sack. Merry waited, chewing her bottom lip, knowing he was about to take out the gift she'd organised and wrapped for Theo. She just hoped he understood what it meant...

'This one is for Merry McKenzie,' Tavish yelled and Merry jumped before glancing at Theo.

'But I don't understand,' she gasped, wondering if she'd somehow made a mistake on the label. Theo gazed at her and winked as the older man handed her the parcel and Merry stared at it.

'Open it, then!' a voice shouted and when she looked up she saw Liam standing beside Ollie. 'We drove up this morning,' Ollie explained when she opened her mouth to ask.

'Noah told us there's plenty of room at Chestnut Cottage and we didn't want to miss out on Christmas Day with our little sister,' Liam said, beaming. Merry felt her insides lift as she gazed at her brothers. They were here and they were smiling and none of them were running towards her trying to save her – or swaddle her in bubble wrap or cotton wool.

'Open it!' Ollie called and Merry began to rip at the paper, then she chuckled when she saw what it contained.

'SuperMerry,' she said softly as she unfolded the bright yellow T-shirt with navy letters printed across the front and Theo leaned down to whisper in her ear.

'Because you are and will always be that to me,' he said. 'I'm sorry I ever made you feel like you couldn't be or do whatever you wanted...'

Merry shook her head as a bubble of happiness exploded in her throat and she watched Tavish dig into the sack again. 'This is the final Secret Santa present,' the older man boomed. 'And it's for our new vet.' He handed the square package to Theo.

'What?' Theo said as he stared at the present Merry had sneaked into the sack.

'Open it! Open it!' the crowd chanted.

'Aye, I want to sing Christmas carols,' Ace piped up.

'And I want to get back to Evergreen Castle – Belle's made mince pies!' Edina yelled as everyone began to applaud.

Merry watched as Theo opened his gift, saw his mouth

curve. 'Great minds...' he whispered, unfolding the yellow T-shirt she'd had made for him which read, 'The Best Heroes Come in Twos'. Theo turned to her and swept her into his arms. 'They really do,' he muttered into her ear before kissing her firmly on the mouth, setting off a huge firework display in her chest.

Merry clung on as Theo lifted her off her toes, thinking about Carmel and Dan and the last few weeks which had changed her life. She knew she'd be staying in Christmas Village and had no idea what would come next – but for the first time in years she knew she could do anything she wanted. She wasn't afraid any more. She was ready for her next chapter – and hopefully she'd write it with Theo by her side...

A LETTER FROM DONNA

I want to say a big thank you for choosing to read *Snowflakes and Secrets in the Scottish Highlands*. If you enjoyed it, and want to keep up-to-date with all my latest releases, just sign up at the following link. Your email address will never be shared and you can unsubscribe at any time.

www.bookouture.com/donna-ashcroft

I adore Secret Santa – the idea that someone might choose something for me anonymously conjures all the excited feelings of Christmas. That's why I loved the idea of a village Secret Santa – a tradition that goes back generations where nobody suspects who the mystery purveyor of gifts is. What, I wondered, might happen if someone else was suddenly responsible for delivering those gifts? What if that person had no idea which presents were intended for which recipient? Which is, of course, exactly the position Merry McKenzie finds herself in. Throw in gorgeous vet Theo Ellis-Lee, who guesses Merry's dilemma and has to help her without giving away either that he knows, or that he's assisting her, and you've got a fun and festive romp – filled with a menagerie of animals and the quirky characters from Christmas Village.

But there's a more serious thread here too. Merry is looking to reclaim her life and break free from her three over-protective brothers – to recover emotionally from a car accident and subsequent coma which has eroded her confidence. While Theo is determined to suppress his natural instinct to help and rescue everyone he comes into contact with. On the surface these two are the perfect couple, but they both have a lot to learn about themselves in order to recognise that.

I hope you enjoyed this light-hearted and festive story as much as I loved writing it. If you did, it would be wonderful if you could please leave a short review. Not only do I want to know what you thought, it might encourage a new reader to pick up my book for the first time.

I really love hearing from my readers – so please say hi on my Facebook page, through Twitter, TikTok, on Instagram or my beautiful website.

Thanks,

Donna Ashcroft

www.donna-writes.co.uk

facebook.com/DonnaAshcroftAuthor

twitter.com/Donnashc

instagram.com/donnaashcroftauthor

tiktok.com/@donnashc

ACKNOWLEDGEMENTS

I recently found a scrapbook I made when I was twelve. In it were a lot of hilarious notes about my brothers being annoying (they were, back then), but I'd also written that I wanted to be an author. Fast forward a lot of years and my ambitions were finally realised. But writing isn't a one-person goal – it takes a whole team of people and Natasha Harding (my editor) is one of the reasons I got published. She believed in me and has continued to believe in me throughout my ten books as she's helped to mould me into a better writer. I remember her saying my writing gave her tingles and every time I'm having a crisis of confidence I remember those words – and that she still believes in me now. This book (and all the others) wouldn't exist without that faith. Thank you, Natasha – I've been waiting to dedicate a Christmas book to you because I know how much you love everything festive!

On a day-to-day basis, I'm fortunate to have a lot of other people who have faith in me. My writing buddy, Jules Wake, is always on hand to give me sympathy, Prosecco or a kick up the bum whenever I'm sagging. This book hit a very sticky patch part way through and I was fortunate enough to have some excellent book-doctoring help from the lovely Jules Wake, Sarah Bennett and Bella Osborne during a writing break. I'm also blessed with the faith of my partner Chris who is always on hand to deliver tea or wine (depending on the time of day) and my children, Erren and Charlie. Finally, my oldest friends

Jackie Campbell and Julie Anderson who I've known since I started writing and who always believed I'd make it in the end.

Thanks also to Matt Wake (Jules Wake's son) who once told her to put a car chase in her romance novel – which is why my heroine's book includes one! I'm also indebted to Anita Chapman for all the amazing social media help and to Elizabeth Finn for the wonderful writing breaks. To my lovely niece Ava Roberts who Aunt Ava is named for (and who is also a lover of animals). I've been fortunate to be inspired by friends and family with ideas for Secret Santa gifts. My mum and daughter, Erren, are very fond of jangly bangles! Paul Campbell has an affinity with cows (and his daughter Kirstie painted him a beautiful cow picture for his birthday). My OH Chris is a skilled DIY'er so the tool bracelet was inspired by him. Julie Anderson is a keen wild swimmer (as is my brother Peter) so the hats were inspired by them. Jackie Campbell, like me, loves anything that helps her sleep so the lavender bath oil was inspired by her.

As always, thanks to the fabulous team at Bookouture including Natasha Harding, Lizzie Brien, Kim Nash, Noelle Holten, Jess Readett, Alexandra Holmes, Sarah Hardy, Peta Nightingale, Richard King and Saidah Graham. Also to Caroline Hogg, Rachel Rowlands and Jennie Ayres for their work on this book. Thanks also to the other Bookouture authors for your amazing support and to Carla Kovach for the Motivation Station!

To wonderful friends, bloggers, NetGalley users and readers who support me by buying and reading my books, letting me know they've enjoyed them, reviewing, blogging and cheering me on. Thank you! In particular to Cindy L Spear, Karen Spicer King, Ian Wilfred, Alison Phillips, Anne Winckworth, Jan Dunham, Meena Kumari and Helen Neaves-Wilde.

Thanks as always to my family – Dad (for the card and Prosecco you deliver to me on every publication day), Mum,

John, Peter, Christelle, Lucie, Mathis, Joseph, Lynda, Louis, Auntie Rita, Auntie Gillian, Tanya, James, Rosie, Ava, Philip, Sonia, Stephanie and Muriel.

Finally, to the readers who have been there with me throughout my journey – I wouldn't be here without you xx

Made in the USA
Las Vegas, NV
20 November 2022

59639883R00148